Farewell My Country

A.J. Harris

ISBN   978-0-9847825-3-6 (hardback)
        978-0-9847825-1-2 (paperback)
        978-0-9847825-2-9 (ebook)

Published by Murder Mystery Press, www.murdermysterypress.com

Murder Mystery Press
Santa Barbara, California

Author: A.J. Harris, M.D.
Book Shepherd: Mark E. Anderson, www.aquazebra.com
Editor: Geoff Aggeler
Cover photographer: Mark E. Anderson, www.aquazebra.com
Author photo: Mark Davidson, www.markdavidsonphotography.com
Remaining photos courtesy of Michael O. Harris and Jonathan Harris
Cover/interior design: Mark E. Anderson, www.aquazebra.com

AQUA ZEBRA™

Library of Congress Control Number: 2013947826

Printed in the United States of America

Special Acknowledgement

*To my wonderful wife, Yetta, who encouraged the concept,
the research, and who maintained all levels of correspondence to
bring this book to fruition.*

Acknowledgments

This book has been enriched from the data gathered by the tireless research efforts of Dr. Kevin A. Yelvington of the Department of Anthropology, University of South Florida. His determination in uncovering details about the exploits of Dr. Jack S. Harris has had him traveling from the east to the west coast, to England and Costa Rica. He has searched files from the F.B.I., O.S.S., State Department, and the archives of the Ralph J. Bunche papers collection, at the Charles E. Young Research Library at the University of California at Los Angeles. In addition he has found many letters written between Dr. Harris and Dr. Melville Herskovits at the Northwestern University Archives, Africana Manuscripts. Correspondence with Ruth Benedict was researched from her papers at Vassar College.

Dr. Yelvington interviewed Dr. Harris at his home in Costa Rica several years prior to his death. The interview, "A Life In And Out of Anthropology," appeared in the Critique of Anthropology, Vol. 28 No. 4. He also interviewed Dr. Harris's sons, Michael and Jonathan, and this author, his brother, many times.

The book might best be classified as a biographical novel, like Norman Mailer's Executioner's Song. While it adheres faithfully to what is known concerning Dr. Harris's experiences, there are segments imaginatively recreating what could not be documented. The imaginative weaving of incidents is, however, in harmony with what is known and events related to the author by friends and relatives.

Some of the names have been changed to protect families; others have not because their personalities and activities have been well-publicized. The author has sought to represent actual persons as accurately as his information would permit. Invaluable sources he possessed were countless letters written by Dr. Harris as he corresponded with persons who shaped his career. In addition, Dr. Harris published numerous articles and was himself the subject of articles by people who recognized his importance both in the field of anthropology and in his non-academic areas of endeavor. One author described him as one of America's foremost anthropologists who became one of Latin America's most successful entrepreneurs.

The following are people to whom the author is grateful for having given their expertise to the manuscript: Dr. Geoff Aggeler, Dr. Helen Gordon, Joan Marks, Muriel Schloss, Dr. Robert Baum, Lee Buckmaster, Rita Weinberg, Joan Anawalt, Harry Dutt, Lois Allison, Jo Anne Yinger, Laura Smith, Ted Delotta, Yetta Harris, Nina Markos, Brad Oliver, Jean Denning, Sylvia Selfman, Elia Gentry, Richard Vasquez, Robert L. Crogan and the late Dr. Joyce Wade-Maltais.

To my editor, Dr. Geoff Aggeler, I'm deeply indebted for his many criticisms and suggestions. My gratitude also goes to Mark Anderson, my book shepherd, who arranged the form, appearance and chapters into a neat and tidy volume.

Dedication

This book is dedicated to the memory of Dr. Jack S. Harris who devoted much of his remarkable life to the care and protection of the disadvantaged. He remains a hero because of his challenge to the forces of evil who sought to discredit him.

Prologue

One of the darkest decades in the political history of the United States followed World War II when Washington became subject to the machinations of demagogues exploiting fears about an erstwhile ally, Soviet Russia. In 1946 Churchill had given his Iron Curtain speech, in effect launching the Cold War, and members of Congress seizing an opportunity for their own political advancement, warned of the imminent Communist takeover of the United States Government.

Strongly reminiscent of the witch hunts in seventeenth century Salem, their investigations generated a state of paranoia and an appetite for vengeance upon the perceived enemies of the State. So-called Communists were ferreted out of the State Department and the United Nations and paraded before the public by an obliging news media craving the sensational.

American citizens denied protection under the Constitution and civil laws were condemned by several committees. Senator Joseph McCarthy of Wisconsin headed one of those committees, The Senate Permanent Subcommittee on Investigations. Another committee, the Senate Internal Security Subcommittee, was headed by Senator Patrick McCarran of Nevada.

Trapped in a wide net cast by these congressional Communist witch hunters, an intrepid champion for freedom and the welfare of the oppressed, Dr. Jack S. Harris, was vilified as a Communist and a traitor to his country. His heroic wartime service in the O.S.S. and his outstanding record as a senior member of the U.N. Secretariat were disregarded.

Now, almost sixty years later, he is hailed by scholars on both sides of the Atlantic as a staunch defender of truth, freedom and democracy. The world was a better place because of him.

This is his story.

CHAPTER 1

Monday, October 18, 1953 New York County Courthouse

Dr. Jack Sargent Harris, with the stride of a military man, walked into the smoke-filled senate chamber crowded with reporters and photographers whose light bulbs flashed at him. Undisturbed by the tumult, he walked toward the front of the chamber and sat next to his attorney, Leonard Boudin. Both men sat solemnly as the speaker seated on a raised platform with seven others, struck a gavel to bring the hearing to order.

Senator Patrick McCarran of Nevada cleared his throat, leaned into a microphone and pointed his stubby finger at the accused. "All right, Dr. Harris, you know why you've been called to this hearing. You have been accused of being a Communist, a traitor to your country. You can make matters much better for yourself by giving me the names of five people you know who are or were Communists. That's all you have to do. Give me five names. After that you can get back to whatever you do at the United Nations. If you don't give me those names, I promise you, you'll lose your job at the U.N., and you'll never teach in any American university again." Leaning closer to the microphone, he said, "Do I make myself clear? You'll be blacklisted, branded a Communist, a traitor to your country. You have forty-eight hours to decide."

Looking at his watch, McCarran said, "We'll recess for lunch and return in one hour. When we reconvene,

Professor," he emphasized the title derisively, "I expect *you* as a patriotic citizen to cooperate fully and give us any information you have regarding Communist affiliation." Jack regarded the chairman with unconcealed malice, but McCarran remained unfazed and continued, "Let me remind you, Professor, you won't be doing yourself any favor by invoking the Fifth Amendment."

Jack's attorney, Leonard Boudin, stood. "Mr. Chairman, I object. Dr. Harris has every right …"

McCarran interrupted. "Let me remind you, Mr. Boudin, this is *not* a court room, and this is *not* a trial. We're not using conventional legal procedures here. This is only a hearing," his voice struck a note of finality. His searing stare, his beaked nose and white hair gathered behind his ears like tufted feathers gave him the appearance of a bird of prey. He stood and his chair moved backward pushing one of the twelve cameramen standing behind the members of the Senate Internal Security Subcommittee.

McCarran had been described by members of the liberal press as a seething mad dog, a subversive, a destroyer of the Bill of Rights and Constitutional guarantees.

Presidents Truman and Eisenhower agreed on few matters, but regarding McCarran, they found common ground: both detested the bully, publicity-seeking Senator from Nevada. He held the improbable posts of Chairman of the Judiciary Committee and Chairman of the committee controlling budgets for the State and Justice Departments. He boasted to his cronies that he had more power than the president for whom he harbored the utmost contempt. When Adlai Stevenson challenged Eisenhower for the presidency, he said they were two dummies misled by Kikes and Commies.

As both men left the chamber, Jack said to his attorney, "I can't eat, I'm too upset. Those bastards are out to skewer me. You go ahead; I'll call Shirley. I know she's worried and eager to hear from me. I'll meet you back here in an hour." Reporters and cameramen swarmed around Jack, their flashing cameras and cloying questions agitated him further. At a phone booth, he slammed the accordion door and turned his back to them. He reached into his pocket for a handful of change to feed the phone, then dialed. He relayed the proceedings to his wife, Shirley.

"*What did you tell McCarran?*"

"I told him to go fuck himself."

"*Did you really?*"

"Not in so many words, but he understood me, all right. The sonofabitch asked if I was loyal to my country. Can you believe the gall of that sonofabitch? I would have yelled at him, but my attorney touched my arm and shook his head. I said, 'Of course I'm loyal to my country, and you have no right to question my loyalty.' That stopped the bastard. He knew better than to pursue that line of questioning. I had to remind him that I risked my life for my country more than once. My record had been well documented, and he damn well knew it. He cut me off—didn't want to hear about my work with the OSS. He kept harping on the same goddamned stupid question, 'Are you now or have you ever been a member of the Communist Party?' I kept invoking the Fifth Amendment until I thought the sonofabitch would explode."

Jack pushed his way through the group of newsmen after leaving the phone booth, then headed outside for a cigarette. He tried to ignore one reporter from the *New York Times* who persisted in badgering him.

"Sir, do you consider yourself a traitor? Do you?"

Jack flicked his cigarette into the gutter, hiked his shoulders and with a grimace approached the reporter who retreated toward the safety of the courthouse. He repeated, "Sorry, sir, sorry."

After the lunch break, Jack and his attorney returned to the hearing room before the committee members reentered. He leaned towards Boudin. "Leonard, tell me what you know about this guy McCarran."

Boudin smiled wanly. "He's a contentious old goat who represents the worst in judicial judgment. His views are an abomination and in direct contradiction to lawful procedures. He's flagrantly disregarded Constitutional guarantees and has trampled civil code. His idea of good law is comparable to pre-Civil War Southern States' judgments on Negro infractions...maybe worse."

Jack's brow knitted. "How can he make illegal judgments, that is, disregard Constitutional Law?"

"Because those who could stop him, won't. They're too fearful. He and his cronies have created a climate of dreadful apprehension. They're aided and abetted by headline seeking newsmen. People are generally fed-up with Congress—a government that seems to do nothing for them. When members of the State Department or the U.N. are accused of being Communists, John Q. Public sees that as an 'aha moment'.

"McCarran basically is an old-fashioned western judge of the rope-hanging type. A one-man vigilante who is bound to drive the east coast liberal eggheads out of our government and our government out of the U.N. He's a gunslinger who came up the hard way, but now that he's on top, he doesn't want any changes in his landscape."

"What's his obsession with Communists? Have any been discovered in the government?"

"Not a damn one of any consequence. One or two held minor positions, clerical and the like and have admitted to being card-carrying members at one time. They've been paraded around by the committee as examples of traitors in government."

Boudin continued, "McCarran is despised for many reasons. He established a law that effectively stops immigration at Ellis Island because of his paranoia about subversives coming into this country.

"He was not only an anti-communist ideologue but

actively proposed a bill to send billions to Nationalist China, Chiang Kai-shek's forces. The problem with that was those funds found a circular way back to McCarran.

"There were many more unsavory sweetheart deals, and of course, there's his very special relationship with the Las Vegas and Reno casino owners. He managed to exclude them from paying federal taxes.

"Simply put, he wants the U.S. out of the U.N., and he will doggedly prosecute any U.S. citizen in that group if he thinks they are liberal and have an interest in international affairs." He paused to look at Jack. "And, of course, that means you."

The committee members took their seats. The chamber grew quiet. McCarran waited until the last cameraman signaled his readiness, then he called out, "Let the hearings come to order." McCarran hunched over the microphone and stared at Jack again. "Sir, your name was submitted as one who attended a meeting of Communists." Shuffling papers on his desk, he said in a patronizing tone, "Now surely you remember that meeting? It was held for the members of local Communist cell block..."

A glimmer of recall occurred to Jack, an event six years ago when he listened to someone haranguing about the virtues of the great Russian government. After several minutes he left that meeting and wondered how he got suckered into going there in the first place; he recalled Skip Nelson asking him to hear a dynamic speaker. Knowing Skip, he should have been wary since Skip had openly expressed leftist sympathies. But who in the hell had revealed his brief presence at that meeting held so long ago to this gang of inquisitors? Then he thought: that's a stupid question. Those meetings were infiltrated with informers wearing wiretaps and hidden Minox cameras. He knew about that kind of spying. That's what he had been trained to do in the O.S.S.

Chapter 2

Entering his new two-story home at 5 Cherry Lane, Kings Point, Long Island, Jack tossed his suit jacket on the living room club chair, loosened his tie and slumped onto the sofa. Shirley handed him the Scotch and water she had prepared in anticipation of his arrival. She sat on the sofa beside him, hands clasped in her lap and waited until he sipped his drink. She asked a question she had thought about for some time. "Darling, do you recall at any time in the distant past joining the Communist party?"

Already filled with loathing from his ordeal with the committee, he snapped, "Of course not! This whole goddamned charade, all this bullshit with McCarran, McCarthy, Roy Cohn and the rest of those whores posturing and preaching before the cameras has been one pain in the ass, and now *you* ask me if I was a Communist?"

"I'm sorry, Dear, I just had to hear it from you."

Apologetic for his outburst, he said, "Those creatures aren't looking for the truth. They're not protecting any freedoms. They're trying to condemn people—as many as they can. They want the world to think they're some kind of saviors. I'll tell you what they really are: they're grandstanding sonsofbitches without a conscience—totally amoral and arrogant. Do you think they care that two people have committed suicide because their lives were ruined by these jackals?"

Shirley took his hand, looked deep into his eyes and

asked, "Darling, what do you intend to do? If you don't give them their pound of flesh, you can probably say goodbye to your academic career. No university will jeopardize its funding or its reputation by having a so-called communist on its staff. If you were to name five people you could retain your position at the United Nations." She asked, "Do you know five people who were or are Communists?"

"Five? Hell, I could name twenty-five who expressed appreciation for what the Russians did during the war. That didn't make them Communists. The Russians were our allies. Remember? Wait a minute. You're not suggesting that I name..."

"Oh, of course not! I want to be sure we're thinking alike, that's all. I couldn't live with someone who'd do something as despicable as that."

"Christ, you know me better than that. We may lose everything, but we can't ruin other peoples' lives just to protect what we have." He reached for a cigarette, lit it and took a long drag. "Don't worry. We'll live through this. We've faced shitty times before. If necessary, we'll start over."

Shirley started to sob softly and her snuffling interrupted her conversation. She also knew that he was resilient, and even if those publicity-seeking witch-hunters succeeded in their rotten project, he would never allow himself to be beaten down. It was all so damned unfair. She knew how he enjoyed his position at the U.N., seeking food for the starving, bringing water and medical supplies to the needy, and how he loved teaching. Was it all going to be snatched away? When she thought how he suffered and almost lost his life in Africa with the O.S.S....those long months of illness and those painful treatments at the marine hospital...those awful tropical diseases.

Jack placed his arm around her shoulders and kissed the top of her head. "I've got another day or two with those bastards; then we'll make our plans. My attorney says that any unfavorable ruling will be challenged; we'll sue." He smiled weakly. "In case you've forgotten, I'm descended from a long line of ancient noblemen who faced problems a hell of a lot more serious."

Despite his bravado, Jack did worry about the immediate future for his wife and his four-year old son, Michael. He thought of those twenty years of academic endeavor wrested from his soul. Never teaching again, never doing field research, never counseling with so-called primitive peoples was too painful to contemplate. How did this unimaginable horror occur and why? A mere eight years had passed since the end of a war that might have ended in the collapse of the entire civilized world, and again the howling dogs of calumny were seeking to destroy innocent victims.

Later that evening, lying next to Shirley, unable to doze off, he tried to divert his thoughts from the troubles he faced by reviewing his life and how he had become who he was.

CHAPTER 3

Chicago, winter 1929

When does a boy cross a threshold and become a man? For Jack it was at age seventeen. He was remarkably gifted in mind and body. Six feet tall and with an athlete's physique, he carried himself with grace, and when he spoke his pleasing baritone drew people to him. Like his father, he was fair complexioned, blond and blue eyed, unlike his two older siblings, who had their mother's olive coloration, brown eyes and dark hair. In spite of being undeniably handsome, Jack was devoid of conceit and would have dismissed any suggestion that he had godlike attributes as, "Bullshit."

Jack lived at home with his parents and five siblings on Chicago's Westside. Home was a forty-six year old two-story building: a grocery store on the first floor with a two bedroom flat plus a kitchen behind it. The second floor consisted of a living room, three bedrooms, a kitchen and one bathroom with a twenty-five gallon water heater standing in a corner of the kitchen. His father, who was called Pa, purchased the building in 1925 with a thirty-year mortgage. Monthly payments were made easily until the crushing depression that started with the stock market failure in October 1929.

The neighborhood was a community of mostly white Protestants with a few Catholics and Jews and a Chinese family operating a hand laundry on Harrison Street.

His mother and father were Romanian immigrants

who observed kosher dietary laws and respected the high holy days. With his father's insistence, he began Hebrew studies, like his older brother. That would have culminated in a Bar Mitzvah at age 13. After several months in Cheder, a school for religious studies, Jack refused to attend. The Hebrew teacher, he insisted, was a bearded tyrant who taught him little and disciplined too much with a yardstick.

Jack's public school chums included the sons of second or third generation Irish, Italian, German and Polish immigrants, but he didn't hang around with them. He didn't participate in team sports; they required too much practice time, but he did enjoy swimming and weight lifting on his own. Time after school was largely taken up with homework and various jobs.

During the bleakest of economic times, when work was scarce, Jack was never without employment. As a teenager, he declared that he would never work in a grocery store, not his father's or anyone else's. For him, that kind of work was too confining, too menial. He found work after school and on weekends in a downtown floral shop where he prepared and delivered bouquets and potted plants. He saved his weekly salary and tips for college tuition.

During his high school years he had admired several of his male teachers. While he knew they didn't make a lot of money, they had something that money couldn't buy. They had class. It showed in their dress, their manner of speaking, and in their impeccable grooming. Like most young fellows about to become men, Jack looked for male role models, and these gentlemen seemed worthy of emulation. Their profession was an honorable one that he might want to follow.

Following high school graduation, he worked at McGraw-Hill Publishing Company as an office boy and was almost immediately promoted to the position of assistant to the production manager. With the deepening depression and cutbacks in employment, he was told that he could remain employed, but only as an office boy with a cut in salary. The demotion was too degrading and he quit. He was confident he could find a better job and soon did.

In 1925 as a chubby thirteen year old, he entered John Marshall High School on Chicago's west side. Over the next four years as he progressed toward manhood, he worked to perfect the natural attributes with which he had been liberally endowed. He planned his own diet and maintained a routine of exercises, including daily swimming at the school pool and lifting weights. By the age of seventeen he had transformed himself into an Adonis-like figure, and all the young girls on the cusp of glorious womanhood were noticing. Though not conceited, he couldn't help being gratified by their attention and asserting his prerogative of savoring the delights they offered.

One gal, Martha Tobin, a student in his American History class, sidled up to him one day. "Jack, you would make the perfect handsome hero in our next school play. How about trying out for the part?"

"I don't know the first thing about acting."

With her fluttering doe-like eyes Martha enticed him to join the drama club. She was the prettiest filly he had ever seen, and absolutely irresistible; her voice was sweet and melodic, her movements silky and seductive; her smile magnificent. They played their romantic roles convincingly in the play. One afternoon, he cornered her backstage between acts and kissed her boldly on the lips. He didn't know how she'd respond but was delighted when she returned the favor. In a whirlwind courtship that brought greater intimacy, he was determined to have her completely and forever.

Many years later while reminiscing with an old friend, Jack said, "Shortly before our high school graduation, Martha and I talked about getting married. After all, I was about to turn eighteen and she was only slightly younger. We figured with both of us working, we could find a cheap rental, and she didn't eat much. I discovered Martha didn't have much in the way of domestic skills; she couldn't even boil an egg, but I could make a mean omelet and fix baloney sandwiches. Anyway, the two of us knowing absolutely nothing about adult responsibilities decided we could manage. Our love was all that mattered."

He continued, "One glorious spring morning, Martha and I played hooky from class and boarded a streetcar to the Chicago Courthouse downtown. The anticipation of our secret created an excitement like I'd never known. We ran up the broad stairs of that formidable old grayish-brown building. Martha held my hand and smiled bravely; I knew she was nervous. I had my own wavering thoughts, but I never would have told her so.

"We queued up to obtain the marriage license for two dollars. Both of us signed our names to a certificate, and with that, the clerk congratulated us, then waved the next couple forward.

"We kissed and I called her by her new name; she giggled, then smiled that perfectly lovely smile, and we hugged. When we started walking towards the Palmer House hand-in-hand, she complained about her feet hurting in the borrowed high-heeled shoes she wore for the occasion. I was hoping not to spend cab fare and was relieved when she dug into her purse and pulled out a dollar bill and change and suggested that we split the tab.

"I called Ma from a pay phone in the hotel lobby to tell her I would be sleeping over at a friend's for the night and not to wait up for me."

Jack leaned back, closed his eyes and in reverie murmured, "The next twelve or so hours were the most magnificent I'd ever known. We loved, we laughed, we explored each another; we spoke of our plans excitedly: we'd work, take night classes, have children..." He tapered off; a troubled thought had invaded his memory.

The following morning he called home. "Hello, Ma? Remember that pretty girl I introduced you to, Martha Tobin? Well, you've got your first daughter-in-law... Hello, Ma, are you there?"

Jack pulled the receiver away from his ear as Pa's tirade heated the phone line. "You think I'm already dead?" He shouted. "How could you do this without telling me?" Jack had violated the ancient rule of seeking paternal permission. Pa continued, "Listen, I don't care what you tell me, Mr. Big Shot, you're *not* married, so get that idea out of your head! You're nothing but a boy, a little *pisser*. You think getting married makes you a man?" Pa didn't wait for an answer. "I'm having lawyer Solomon annul this nonsense." With that, he banged down the receiver. Jack knew their matrimonial experience had ended but not before he and Martha enjoyed another round of connubial bliss in the hotel room paid for until noon.

True to his word, Pa arranged an annulment. Jack and Martha went home to live with their parents. It had been a blissful interlude, a memory to be cherished.

Chapter 4

Summer 1930

With the global economy severely blighted, opportunities for employment were becoming almost non-existent. At eighteen Jack was becoming desperate. The stagnant economy was making life in the city unbearably oppressive. He had long dreamt of getting away, sailing to far off ports of call; finally he decided that's exactly what he would do. When he told Ma and Pa that he had to leave, they were anxious for him but understood that he, like countless other young men across the country, had to leave home to find work. He didn't tell them that he planned to go to sea.

He gathered a few toilet articles, some socks and underwear, two shirts and a pair of trousers and put them into a fiber/cardboard suitcase. Before leaving, for God only knew where, he kissed Ma on the forehead then shook Pa's hand and told them he would be gone for a while and would call or mail a letter to let them know where he was. Their aching, concerned expressions made him leave hurriedly, besides he did not want to try explaining that which he really could not.

He walked three blocks to the Jackson Boulevard bus, which headed five miles east to the Union Railroad Station on Canal Street. He purchased a one-way ticket to board the New York Central, then counted his remaining savings, twenty-four dollars and ninety-five cents. He placed four five-dollar bills in his sock and the singles and change in his pants pocket along with four Hershey bars. This was all he needed to get started.

At the Union Station he sat on a wooden bench, his suitcase beside him and waited for departure time. For the first time a troubling thought occurred: *maybe I won't be able to find a job on a ship. What will I do then? No point in worrying now, something's bound to come up.*

He boarded the train and found his seat in the middle of the car. This was a sitting only car, no sleeping accommodations. The seats were covered in a kind of diamond patterned green velour and had a mawkish smell from spray—all of which was quite acceptable and more pleasant than the only other railroad travel he knew: a dirty, drafty box car that bounced and vibrated when he and his friends hopped cars to ride to Michigan City, Indiana for an afternoon at the beach.

The partially opened window in the summer heat, allowed the soot from the engine to cling to his clothes and skin, causing him to feel unclean. After two days of travel with intermittent sleeping in the sitting position and feeding on the candy which he doled out sparingly, he felt achy but with an underlying excitement. He was traveling through places he had only read about: Indiana, Ohio, Pennsylvania...A map obtained free from the local Phillips 66 gas station lay spread on his lap to indicate his route from Chicago to New York City. On the empty seat beside him lay his open book: *Seamanship for the Beginner.*

Arriving in New York, Jack gawked at skyscrapers so tall they seemed to pierce the clouds. He had seen tall buildings in Chicago like the Tribune Tower and the Wrigley Building, but they were as nothing compared to these. And the traffic—lines of autos, taxis, blaring horns, unsmiling people pushing, shoving—the city had a beat, a throbbing, pulsating rhythm that fascinated him. There was more vitality here than he could have ever imagined. And he liked it.

After walking a number of city blocks, and making inquiries of passers-by, he entered the office of the Maritime Service for the Ports of New York and New Jersey where he hoped to find a freighter that could use the services of an eager novice. A number of men sat around on worn chairs, some smoked, some chewed tobacco; all stared at him as he walked into the room. Their glum expressions offered no encouragement. Jack suspected that they were unemployed. He approached a caged window where a woman looked at him with a melancholy expression as she anticipated his request. "I'm sorry," she said, "but there are no calls for ships hands. Times being as bad as they are... well, you understand." Jack's shoulders slumped. She continued, "You do have a valid seaman's certificate, don't you?"

Jack shook his head. "No."

"You'll need one, young man, to get any work, if any becomes available."

Dejected, Jack turned to walk away when a grizzled old man on a nearby chair summoned him with his crooked finger. He whispered, "Give me a fin, son, I'll getcha a certificate in a half hour. You wait here."

Skeptical but desperate, Jack took his shoe off, dipped into his sock and handed the man a folded, flattened five dollar bill. The old guy limped away and Jack wondered if he might have been scammed. To quell his anxiety, he walked around the room looking at the framed pictures of sleek passenger vessels and imagined himself in a double-breasted navy blazer with brass buttons and a white beaked hat. He would be an assistant to the captain or maybe a first mate. It was hard to maintain such fanciful notions when he took notice of the walls with faded, peeling green paint, cigarette ashtrays filled with butts, and the pervasive stink of stale tobacco buried in the fabric of worn chairs and discolored curtains.

He looked at his watch repeatedly. Thirty minutes passed. He stared out the window hoping to see the old man. An hour passed and every minute caused gut-wrenching despair. Convinced that the old man absconded with his money, Jack prepared to leave when he saw the limping old man waving. As he approached Jack, the old man pulled him aside and handed him the certificate, then apologized for being late. "I had to stop for a mug o'java." His breath suggested otherwise.

Relieved and more confident, Jack walked along the loading docks hoping to find a ship to sign on to. His empty stomach growled as he made inquiries at two ships lading cargo. The dockworkers shook their heads when he inquired about work.

Walking along the dock with a little less confidence, he stopped to watch a crane lifting a large wooden container nearing the ship's deck. A suspension line snapped, and the dangling cargo, slipping and jerking in midair was about to come crashing down. A sailor working on the dock below was unaware of his peril. Tossing his suitcase aside, Jack made a flying tackle to shove the sailor out of the way. Both fell clear of the container just as it crashed, exploding into fragments and splinters to expose the steel machine parts it contained. They had just cheated death.

The ship's captain who had been watching from the deck hurried down the gangplank. He ran to assist the sailor who stood up shaken and confused. The captain placed his arm around the sailor's shoulders. "You all right, Jess?"

Unsteady and bewildered, he nodded. "Aye, aye, Sir."

The captain, a portly man in a dark turtleneck sweater and a hat with a visor, shook Jack's hand. "Son, you saved Jess's life. You okay? That was one hell of a tackle. Can I buy you a drink?"

"I wouldn't mind, but to tell the truth, Sir, I need to use a toilet, and then if you can scare up a sandwich, I'd be grateful."

The captain laughed and patted Jack on the back. "Fair enough, young fella. Climb aboard." They ascended the gangplank, Jack held onto the cable rail since he too felt a bit wobbly. "Jess'll show you the head; then the three of us'll go to the galley. I'll have the cook scare up some vittles."

His affable manner put Jack at ease while he devoured a steak sandwich with scrambled eggs and fries washed down with a bottle of German beer. With America deprived of easy access to alcoholic beverages for the past decade because of prohibition, the beer was a welcome treat.

Captain Arnold Holstrum, a man in his early fifties, sat next to Jack. "We're grateful for what you did down there, son, saving Jess from sure death." He studied Jack who was absorbed in eating. "What brought you down here to the docks?"

Jack kept chewing as he answered, "I was hoping to find a berth on a freighter..."

The captain shook his head before answering. "Sorry, son, there's no job on this ship and no money to..."

"Beggin' your pardon, Cap'n," Jess interrupted, "Malvern from the fire room ain't reported back. If I know him, he's four sheets to the wind and shacking up with a whore somewhere. He could be gone for days, just like he done before. Best we plan on shippin' out without him. Replacing him now might be a good idea."

The captain frowned and scratched the back of his head. "Damn!" He looked at Jack. "You wanna look after the boilers? You'll apprentice our fireman down there."

Jack nodded quickly. "I'll do anything, Sir. I'm no engineer, but I can learn fast."

"That's fine, we'll teach you. Jess'll show you to your berth in the fo'c'sle. By the way, what's your name?"

Jack pulled out his certificate, glanced at it, then blurted out, "Russell—Russell Sumner, Sir."

The captain turned to Jess. "Take Sumner here to Malvern's locker and let him wear his clothes." The captain looked at Jack and said, "He looks to be about his size."

Jack was about to become a seaman. In addition to controlling the furnaces, Jack learned every scut task: cleaning the head, degreasing the galley stoves, polishing pots and pans, swabbing the deck, and the never-ending job of derusting and painting. He tore into each task with the zeal of a novice eager to please the captain and the first mate.

At every port landing he made copious notes of the changing scenes and their inhabitants. His daily log of observations grew rapidly.

CHAPTER 5

When his ship, the *Zarembo*, landed at the Gold Coast in West Africa, Jack eagerly surveyed the port city, although he was more curious about the natives. He hired an old taxicab to take him to a nearby village. His fascination with the natives there kept him too long. Seeing that it was about time for his ship to leave, he had the taxi hurry him back to the port, but he didn't make it in time and watched in panic as the ship steamed off. He ran to the company agent who told him, "There's nothing I can do now. You'll have to stay until the next freighter arrives."

"When in the hell would that be?"

"In two or three days. I'd advise you to find a room at the company hotel here at the port."

That night he returned to the village to watch the natives who were wearing exotic wooden masks dance in an area lit by torches. Deeply stirred by the intoxicating rhythms, the haunting beat of the drums that pierced the stillness of the night, Jack watched as the masks came to life with the movements of the dancers. This enchanting world captivated him.

He was sitting with his legs crossed when one of the native women stopped before him, pulled him up and playfully urged him to start dancing. Imitating her moves, Jack bent his hips and knees, kept his back straight, extended his arms forward and hopped. His head and neck moved forward and back much like a rooster pecking. The natives stopped to watch and roared with laughter as this white stranger attempted to join them in their festivities.

He managed to secure a berth on another ship, and when it docked on the Cape Coast he was able to visit the Elmine, a fabled slave-built castle. It was a handsome but forbidding fortress with a dark, cruel history involving the trading of slaves. He learned of the slave trade from several of the natives who spoke pidgin English. He was told how every major European country bartered for slaves with clothing, silk, rum, spices, pots, pans and other items. He learned how the Europeans had been plundering Africa of its natural resources and devaluing its currency. In the short time he spent with the natives he became aware of the inequities of the trading and more than that of man's inhumanity to man. Many of the slave traders were Arabs, but some were natives who kidnapped members of neighboring tribes and traded them for European goods. He was emotionally shaken by what he saw and learned. He was appalled by the actual sight of the castle's holding pens where slaves were shackled to the walls and to the floors.

While the Europeans had stopped buying slaves over two hundred years ago, they were still exploiting Africa and draining the continent of its wealth. Jack yearned to do something to remedy the palpable injustices and vowed to return someday.

What he saw and experienced was more exciting than anything he could ever have imagined, so many fascinating people in strange lands. He recorded a great deal in long but infrequent letters home.

Over the next two and a half years, aboard a freighter, Jack experienced every kind of weather condition: storms, squalls and deluges that nearly capsized the ship. He served in every capacity even as helmsman taking the ship through the Southern Hemisphere and the Panama Canal. He had sailed to many of the European seaports as well as to Central and North American ports.

In early 1933, his ship tied up for extended repairs and maintenance at a New York harbor. Jack thought the interlude would provide enough time for a trip home and a much-needed visit with family and friends, especially Martha with whom he was eager to resume his relationship.

When he bade the skipper and crew goodbye, he learned no sailings were scheduled for the near future. Commerce on the high seas had slowed to reflect the depths of the worldwide depression.

Like the prodigal son returning, he was feted at home and succumbed to Ma's treats for everything he loved to eat. The rooms behind the store were permeated with the fragrances of his favorite foods: chicken soup, roasted meats, vegetables, puddings, challah, pies and cakes. Ma delighted in Jack's eating orgy. She savored those moments alone with Jack, but she found that he had changed: he had developed a taste for liquor, along with a chain-smoking habit. And though he was always a gentleman and watched his language around her and his sisters, he cussed freely, like the proverbial sailor, in conversation with Pa and his brothers.

Much of his time was taken with visits to Martha and two old friends, but after several days the old ennui returned, and he expressed a longing for freedom from the confines of home life.

CHAPTER 6

In an effort to counter the economic debacle of the early 1930s, President Franklin Roosevelt established the Civilian Conservation Corps. Two and a half million men and eight thousand women between the ages of eighteen and twenty-five enlisted for thirty dollars a month. Twenty-five of those dollars were automatically sent to parents or guardians.

Full-page newspaper ads for the Corps were compelling, and once again Jack left home to enlist at Fort Sheridan, Illinois. Along with several hundred others he was assigned to details of road building and clearing wooded areas for recreational purposes. Initially, outdoor life was exhilarating, and he enjoyed the strenuous labor for several months, but barracks life soon become intolerable.

Many of the young fellows were bigots who would hold forth and feed each other's mindless hatred of Blacks, Jews, Catholics and the foreign-born. Jack had always been disgusted by expressions of racial and religious intolerance.

At this time, Anti-Semitism and Anti-Negro sentiment were being fed by the incendiary radio haranguing of Father Charles E. Coughlin, Gerald L. K. Smith and others of their ilk. When these demagogues were on the air, the young bigots in Jack's barracks would turn up the volume, ignoring Jack's protests and subjecting him to loathsome tirades.

Regimented life consisted of rising at 5:30 am, formation for chow at 6:00, then mounting a canvas-topped truck for work detail at 7:00. The routine grew thin, and Jack longed once again for greater freedom. He felt the need to get away from the stultifying company of his corps mates and the repetitive drudgery of road construction. There remained lands to be explored; countries with strange names and their people who beckoned.

He would need to return to the east coast to find a berth on a tramp steamer. That would mean leaving Martha and his family, whom he had been able to visit while he was at Fort Sheridan. But he was desperate to get away from this stifling environment. With his seaman's certificate and his sea-faring experiences, finding work should be easier. After completing a work schedule one afternoon, he dressed in his civilian clothes, gathered his mess gear, dress uniform and fatigues to return them to the supply depot. His worn cardboard suitcase with faux leather straps and handle accommodated his few belongings easily.

Seated behind a desk in a barracks converted to head-quarters for the unit, a paunchy clerk handed Jack a release form. The clerk's uncanny resemblance to a boar pig with a fleshy turned-up snout revealing large nostrils, squinty eyes, and fleshy jowls earned him the nickname "Porky"— not to his face, of course. He was disliked because of his attitude, which could be described charitably as "chicken-shit." The clerk regarded Jack dismissively, even contemp-tuously; a cigarette dangled from his thick lips, while his pale flabby face attested to a sedentary existence. He looked at Jack's application form and made a mental note of his religion, which read, *Hebrew*. Jack leaned over the desk to sign the release form.

The clerk looked up. "This life too hard for ya, Jew Boy?" He leered at Jack.

"What was that?" Jack stared at him.

"You hard of hearing, too?" Porky smirked and winked at the young girl seated at a nearby desk.

Jack's jaw muscles alternately tightened and relaxed,

but he told himself to ignore the sonofabitch. Taking Jack's silence as a sign of weakness, Porky continued, "Your race was never big on honest work, was it?"

Jack straightened his shoulders, and then tilted his head toward the door. "How about stepping outside and repeating that?"

Porky looked at the female clerk who lowered her head slightly, raised her eyebrows and nodded, signifying that she thought he had to meet Jack's challenge.

"All right, Jew Boy, let's go outside and settle this." Porky threw his pencil on the desk, a cigarette still dangled from his lips as he sauntered toward the exit. He opened the door then slammed it just as Jack approached it. Jack kicked it open and walked closely behind Porky as he walked towards the rear of the barracks where the gasoline pumps were located. The asphalt around the pumps had a number of oil slicks. As Jack turned to set his suitcase down, Porky attempted to kick him in the buttocks. Out of the corner of his eye, Jack saw the clerk's raised foot and hopped aside. The foot on which Porky stood, slipped on an oil slick, and he fell forcefully on his rump. An audible snap from his ankle that had turned grotesquely inward signaled a probable fracture. Porky squealed in pain, then placed his hands behind him in an effort to stand, but he slipped on the oily surface again.

Jack got behind him and pulled him from under his shoulders to get him out of the oil spill. "Don't move. I'll have the clerk call the medics."

When Jack returned, Porky still regarded him with contempt. Jack leaned into his face and Porky pulled back. "Listen, you sonofabitch, this might be your lucky day, because if you didn't fall on your fat ass I would have beat the shit out of you. In fact I might yet." Jack made a show of rolling up his sleeves.

"No, no, please don't!" the fat clerk pleaded.

"Apologize for what you said in there."

Porky pouted but said nothing until Jack grabbed his shirt and pulled him forward.

"I'm sorry, I'm sorry." He whimpered. "Don't hit me." Porky lowered his head, tears welled, and mucous dribbled over his lips from his pig-like snout.

When he heard the wailing siren of the ambulance, Jack picked up his suitcase and left.

The half-mile walk to the highway gave Jack time to ruminate about what he was going to do. *Further schooling was out of the question in this depression. Years of study would be necessary for training that would prepare me for a living. But that was the dilemma. What kind of living? Doing what? Becoming a medical doctor? That would be my fondest dream come true. But another eight to ten years of training? Forget it. I don't have the money and that's all there is to that. Writing I did reasonably well in high school. Short stories, essays, anything in English Lit. ... but that was high school, dreamy kid stuff. How many times do I need to remind myself? There was simply no money for tuition.* He thought about books that had inspired him: *Two Years Before The Mast, Call of the Wild, Captains Courageous...* exciting adventure books like that he would enjoy writing.

Hitchhiking, Jack watched a number of vehicles whisk by until the air brakes of a huge Mack truck brought it to a screeching halt. A cloud of dust from the shoulder of the highway covered him. The burly driver leaned toward the open passenger window and shouted, "Hop in. Toss the suitcase behind the seat. Where d'ya say you're headed?" He put the truck into a low gear and pulled into traffic. "New York? That's a long way off. I'm going as far as Akron. You can pick up another ride there." He had to shout above the noise of the engine and the grinding of the gears. "What ya gonna do in New York?" The herky-jerky motion of the transmission needed his constant attention, and the noise of the engine made his words barely audible. "Got family or friends there?"

Jack shook his head, and then yelled over the engine

noise, "No."

"It's a hell of a city if you haven't got connections. Lotta guys looking for a handout there. But what the hell, one soup line is as lousy as another, I guess." He glanced at Jack. "Know what I'd do if I were you, kid?" He didn't wait for a reply. "I'd hop an ocean freighter, yes sir, see the world. Why not? You're young. You've got the rest of your life to be saddled to some shitty job, sitting on your ass in an office shuffling papers or working on an assembly line putting widgets together, then going home to a nagging wife and a passel of snot-nosed kids. Don't settle for that—at least, not yet.

"Take it from an old fool who's been around the horn a few times. The best education you can give your-self is to travel. Yes sir, see the world. Meet people who look different, dress funny and talk so's you can't under-stand 'em. Eventually, you'll be able to communicate, and you'll find you've got more in common than you think." He elbowed Jack and smiled. "And getting a good lay is wonderful, anywhere in the world."

Jack listened to the homely philosophy and wondered how this truck driver came to spout such wisdom. "You talk like you've been around."

"Spent six years in the Merchant Marines—best years of my life. Got the clap a couple times, but hell that was no big deal."

Jack was not about to tell him that he already had two and a half years on the sea. He wanted to hear this man's impressions of life on the water. "Why did you quit sailing?"

"Simple. I got leave when we docked in Houston one day, twenty-four years ago; took a train to Davenport, Iowa to see my folks after being at sea for over a year. When I got home, I saw Melva—pretty as a picture, she was. We got to talking; I invited her out, and we had a drink or two; one thing led to another and she got pregnant. Then we got married. That's the way it was done back then. I told her I was going back to the sea, and she gave me an ultimatum. 'The sea or me,' she said. And here I am—simple as that."

The trucker dominated the conversation revealing his desperate need for a listener. "When you got the chance—and mind you, it might be your only chance—take it and run with it. See the world; fill your head with the sights, sounds and smells of faraway places. You can get your share of liquor and pussy, but remember that's not the best part of it. Talking to the people, knowing what they want, what they're willing to fight for and how they scratch to make a living—that's what this whole world's all about. Right? You gotta see for yourself how so many poor devils work their asses off for pennies a day while their bosses pull in the big bucks. If you know how the world works, you'll be better informed than those kids coming out of college today. People will listen and respect what you've got to say."

"You talk like a man with a social conscience."

"Listen fella, I seen it all and what's more I know it's true and it ain't right. If I was educated I'd let the world know how I feel." Putting the truck into lower gear to ascend a slight incline, the trucker continued, "I missed my chance to do something about it. Don't make the mistake I did."

CHAPTER 7

Jack's pulse quickened every time he saw the big ships at dockside...like leviathans resting before their next great ocean-going voyages. He watched as the diminishing waves slapped against the barnacle-laden piers, and he welcomed the clean pervasive smell of creosote from the harbor timbers. He moved cautiously among the crane operators and stevedores handling cargo. This was the world where he belonged, where real men made real things happen. Here he found excitement and contentment.

His assigned freighter, the *Danish Prince,* built before WWI was loading wooden crates with stenciled names like John Deere and Fordson tractors plus bales of cotton and pallets of canned beef and pork products.

With his duffle bag slung over his shoulder, he trudged up the gangplank to the deck where he met the first mate. Both men moved quickly to avoid a crate as it was lowered near them.

"Much of this stuff gets unloaded at Helsinki and Leningrad," the first mate said while giving Jack's seamanship certificate a cursory glance. "Okay, Russell Sumner—what do you want to be called? Russell or Sumner?"

"Russ, will be fine."

"Okay, Russ, you can see we've got cargo up to the gunnels, and we're entertaining twelve round-headed Dutchmen, men and women, who'll make port at Amsterdam. With them aboard the grub'll be pretty good.

All we ask is that you stay out of their way and don't cuss or spit when they're around. Be polite, don't get too personal, and for Chris'sake, keep your pecker in your pants." He looked over his shoulder. "After a while, some of those hefty broads might get horny but pay them no mind. They're headed for whorehouses in Amsterdam, where their work is legal. We catch you fucking one of them, we'll beach you, and your shipping days'll be over, at least, on this bucket."

While the first mate was admonishing Jack about illicit activity, one of the Dutch women strolled towards them. She held a cigarette and interrupted their conversation to ask for a light. Jack reached for his lighter and brought it to the tip of her cigarette dangling between her moist and reddened lips. She reached out, looked into his eyes, and then held his wrist as he lit the cigarette. She released his wrist slowly and dragged her fingers across the back of his hand. "Thank you, you darling man," she said in a smoky voice.

Jack nodded. His eyes were riveted to the low cut of her blouse and the chasm-like cleavage formed by melon-sized breasts.

When she turned to walk off, both men watched her snug-fitting skirt and her derriere shift from side to side in a well-rehearsed gait. The men said nothing until she was out of hearing range. Tilting his head toward her, the first mate said, "She's just the kind of broad I was talking about. She can give you a hard-on in five seconds flat and fuck you while standing or give you a hand or blow job." He snapped his fingers. "Just like that!"

"That won't happen—not to me." Jack's dismissive response irritated the first mate.

"Listen, mister, I've heard that song before. Like I said: you get caught screwing around, it'll be your ass. I ain't kidding. Gals have sued the freight line claiming they were raped. A fifty-two year old broad said she got pregnant from one of our crew."

"Did she deliver?" Jack's tongue-in-cheek question

sailed over the first mate's head.

"How the hell would I know? That's not important. What is important is that you stay away from them."

"Fifty-two year old broads are definitely off my list."

On the second night out Jack drew the third watch, which meant patrolling the deck from 2400 to 0800 hours. His duty included checking cargo, security, fires, leaks and every improbable catastrophic occurrence the first mate could imagine. This cool evening the ship hummed smoothly through the calm dark blue waters at ten to fifteen knots.

Jack turned up the collar on his pea coat and pulled his wool-stocking hat over his ears. Completing his first round at 12:45 a.m., he moved between two crates to lean against the ship's rail. He pulled out a Pall Mall, lit it and took a deep drag, then exhaled slowly. One foot rested on a parallel bar below the rail. The serenity of the ocean and the sky, magical in dimension, had to inspire poets, composers and dreamers. He studied the firmament with its myriad glittering stars and constellations. This was the beauty, the enchantment of ocean sailing, where only the whooshing sounds of the waves striking the hull and the muffled hum of the ship's engines could be heard. Beyond the stern a long wake of white water seemed to stretch for miles.

He inhaled the salt air with its indefinable smell. This evening it had a distinctive perfumed fragrance. Strange that he had never been aware of it before, and it seemed to be getting stronger. As he leaned forward to look toward the bow, he felt a feathery sensation ascending his inner thigh. He looked down then whirled around. The Dutch gal, the one who asked him to light her cigarette earlier, stood in a nubby bathrobe and smiled. She put her finger to her lips. "Sh-sh." The moon provided enough light for Jack to see her robe parting to reveal her nudity—enormous breasts, wide hips and a dark pubic shield.

This broad is looking to get laid right here, but I'm not about to get thrown off this bucket just for a quickie.

She put her arms around his neck and pressed her body against his. "Would you like a little Dutch treat, you handsome devil?"

Jack pulled her arms off his neck then turned away and began walking aft. "Come back, love!" She pleaded. He kept on walking, and she shouted at his retreating back: "Coward! Bet you can't satisfy a real woman!"

At a safe distance, Jack turned to see a large man, probably the pimp who would be managing her in Amsterdam pulling the reluctant woman toward the passenger compartments. A torrent of Dutch and English invectives ensued. Jack understood some of the words and phrases: "whore...prostitute...fairy-man...sissy." The shouting continued after they reached their cabin, and several other cabin lights went on.

The following morning the first mate approached Jack. "Anything unusual to report, Russ?"

"No, nothing—nothing at all."

Jasper, an agile bewhiskered older sailor with a mischievous glint, sidled up to Jack and with ill-fitting dentures that clacked when he spoke, said, "I've got a stash of Johnny Walker Black Label, a crate I snatched from inventory at Glasgow." His nose and cheeks revealed the chronic tippler's pinkish glow with spider web-like vessels and a breath that exuded recently ingested Scotch.

"After we unload in Leningrad, we'll have ourselves a little party." Jasper looked around and leaned closer. "There's a tavern where we can get some pretty good vittles, listen to some Russkies plunkin' balalaikas; afterwards we can shack up with a couple broads." He elbowed Jack's ribs. "That way, you'll really get to know the people inside and out. Get my meaning?" He laughed and slapped Jack on the back.

Doubtful about participating in this kind of cultural exchange, Jack submitted that he would probably be too tired at the end of the day, and besides, the ship would be sailing at daybreak, and he didn't want to miss it.

Jasper leaned backward with dramatic disapproval then came forward to stare into Jack's eyes. "Listen, mate, you need to get off this tub long enough to stretch your legs and give your cock a workout. If you don't, that bugger can wither away and fall off like a dried-up banana, and those balls'll shrink to pea-size and maybe turn green." He nodded and laughed again. "You don't want that to happen, no sir. Heh, heh." His dentures clacked and the lower plate slipped slightly forward.

Jack opened one eye slowly to meet the painful daylight. Scrunching up his face and smacking his tongue against a dry palate, he tasted the offensive remains of Scotch and Vodka and whatever mish-mash he had eaten the night before. He lay fully clothed on a narrow, sagging bed with a blanket-thin mattress that offered no relief to an aching back. Groaning, he sat at the edge of the bed to cradle his throbbing head. Slowly he attempted to stand but suffered momentary vertigo and leaned against the wall until his equilibrium returned. He surveyed the room and was repulsed by the worn and slovenly furnishings: an ancient dresser with stains from liquor bottles, drinking glasses and cigarette burns, a cane-backed chair with holes and a floor lamp with a soiled and tilted shade.

Reaching into his back pocket for his wallet and passport, he panicked—they were gone. He patted his front pockets repeatedly; they weren't there either. He pulled the dirty mattress off and looked under the bed. Yanking open the dresser drawers and feeling around; he found nothing—*not a goddamned thing.*

Banging his fist on top of the dresser, he cursed. *What in the hell am I doing in this God-forsaken place? I don't speak the language, I don't have any ID, and I don't have money. Shit! I never should have listened to that crazy Jasper.* He looked at his wristwatch. Whoever had taken his wallet and passport didn't think his dollar Ingersoll was worth snatching. 10:05. *Goddamnit! My ship left four hours ago.* Pushing aside a bed sheet used as a curtain, he saw rows of apartment buildings across the street from his second floor window. The neighborhood was old with small shops below and rentals above.

Slowly he opened the room door, and then stepped into a long dimly lit hallway with a shaft of light at the far end. He walked softly until he reached the down stairwell. Outside, he looked in both directions and wondered where he was and how he got to this place. In a foggy recollection of events from the night before, he remembered drinking a boatload of Vodka and Scotch with Jasper and being approached by two broads with overloaded make-up who cozied up to him. Images of plunking balalaikas, guys doing a kazachki in pantaloons, boots and Cossack hats came to him.

A streetcar rumbled by; he watched it turn at the next block onto a busy street and decided to walk there. The name on the corner of a commercial building read, *Nevskiy Prospekt.* He could not even ask questions of any passersby. His total Russian vocabulary consisted of "Da" and "Nyet." The dour people walked by and ignored him while his stomach growled and his need for a cup of coffee and a cigarette grew intense. But first, he had to find a maritime office or the U.S. Embassy, if either one existed there.

A display in a department store window revealed clothing of uninspired styling hanging on faceless mannequins. In the reflection of one window, he watched as a black sedan seemed to slow and keep pace with his walking. A premonition gripped him as he turned to look at the vehicle. When it moved forward, he walked with less anxiety until it stopped curbside some fifty yards in front of him. He slowed his pace and watched anxiously as two burly men in black suits jumped out; their fedoras pulled down and their gait quickened as they ran to press in on him. The one on the right grumbled in Russian as Jack was shoved into the open rear door of a 1929 black Hudson sedan.

"Hey! What the hell's going on here?" Jack resisted but was muscled into the backseat.

The driver looked over his shoulder at Jack crowded between the two black suits. The one on his right answered the driver who asked, "Americansky?"

"Da."

"Where are you taking me?"

Both men turned to look at him but said nothing, then looked away. None of them said a word in English. The captor to his right reached up and pulled down the side window shade; the one to his left did the same.

Why are they drawing the shades? To beat me? I'd jump out, but I don't know that I could take on these gorillas. Who the hell are these guys? Secret police? Resigned to his abduction, he pushed back into the seat and spread his thighs slightly to look down at the gray mohair upholstery. He was sitting on an irregular ring of discoloration. *Was this someone's dried piss or vomit or a bloodstain? And that smell? Jesus, was it them or me? I haven't washed in two days or changed my clothes or brushed my teeth, and I know my breath is foul.*

The Hudson picked up speed, which meant they were beyond heavy traffic. Jack made another attempt at communication. "Guys, where are we going?" Looking to his right, he got no response from the Slavic-faced captor. Turning to his left he saw the face of a Mongolian-mix whose sneer could only mean trouble.

Darkness enveloped the car as it dipped and stopped

in some kind of enclosure. His eyes had not yet adjusted to the darkness when the black suit to his right opened the door and motioned Jack to follow while the other pushed him from behind. Since he was not shackled, blindfolded or looking down the barrel of a semi-automatic, he felt a small measure of reassurance. *What the hell's going to happen now? People disappear without a trace in Stalin's country. I have no ID, no passport, no money, nothing to tie me to a known entity. If some sonofabitch wants me dead, what was there to stop him? Maybe I could talk to someone who speaks English? How about high school Latin? Latin? Fat chance.*

Jack and his two captors left the car with its driver and walked about thirty feet toward a double door. One of the captors opened the door that revealed a stunning broad crimson-carpeted stairwell with polished brass handrails and ornamental wall sconces. One of the men pointed to the second floor as they passed the first. Down an expansive corridor with doors on either side, the trio walked to the end of a long hall to a closed door with gold letters in Cyrillic. A guard in front of the door gave a rifle salute as the trio approached.

The captor to the right said a few words in Russian to the guard who opened the door. Jack and the men on either side moved in and stopped before a man in a military uniform seated at an ornate desk of some King Louis design with ormolu embellishments. The black suits made some cursory comments after being questioned by the official who then dismissed them. The official pointed to a chair on the other side of his desk for Jack.

Sitting uneasily, Jack looked around the spacious office with its elegant furnishings from early French or Italian periods. Vases, urns and figurines of old Sevres, Dresden and Capo di Monte added touches of bourgeoisie privilege. The Persian rug covering most of the parquet flooring showed wear in the foot paths while the faded red velvet drapes hung on either side of the tall arched windows.

Cracks and chipping marred the gilt appliqués of the furnishings and picture frames. An enormous chandelier hanging from the mid-ceiling dripped with tiers of crystals in progressively smaller circles.

The man behind the desk rested his chin on tented fingers as he studied Jack. In his mid to late forties, the man wore a brown military tunic buttoned to the neck; his dark thick hair was trimmed in the brush manner of the Supreme Secretary, Josef Stalin, whose picture hung on the wall behind him.

In a heavily accented voice sounding like a pronouncement from the mountaintop, he said in easily understood English, "You are thinking all this luxury does not belong in a proletariat state?"

Surprised by the official, who seemed amazingly perceptive, Jack had a feeling of guarded relief but said nothing.

"This building, young comrade was built 130 years ago as the Smolnyy Institute for young noblewomen whose families lavished many rubles on them. Their parents hoped to have their daughters trained for positions of importance in the Tsarina's court. You noticed those converted horse stables downstairs. Young women were trained to ride horses to accompany the Tsarina and her royal children. Unfortunately for them there is no longer a need for them to be trained."

Remaining diffident, Jack listened without comment.

The secretary continued, "Do you think those indulgent parents ever dreamed that one day a fiery little man by the name of Lenin would be sitting in this very chair and directing the Bolshevik Revolution of October 1917? The same revolution that did away with their precious Tsar, his Tsarina and all their well-fed offspring?" With that he gave a deep-throated laugh, pushed back his chair then stood. "Comrade, my name is Sergei Kirov. I am the secretary of the Leningrad Communist Party."

Jack stood and offered his hand tentatively, not quite sure

of protocol; he stammered, "My-my name is Russell Sum..."

"Sumner," Kirov finished the statement. "I know, young man, I know. You're a sailor from a Dutch cargo vessel." He pointed to the chair. "Now, sit down again. We shall talk, and I will advise you of a thing or two."

Jack, astonished by the man's apparent clairvoyance, sat down slowly. Kirov continued, "Ordinarily, my security agents handle these cases, but I was curious to see, first hand, what a spy looks like from the great western power. Recently, your government has sent men as well as women as undercover agents to spy upon us, not here but to Moscow. Your congressional members do not favor our Bolshevik regime. They wanted the White Russians to succeed. That would have been better for them but unfortunate for us. One day, we will be a mighty force, and we will challenge your government for world domination."

Jack assaulted by Kirov's polemics had his own thoughts. *If this guy thinks I'm a spy, I'm as good as dead. How in the hell did he know my name? Are they going to feed me before they put me in chains and lead me to a dungeon with rats to bite my ass while I'm sitting on a slop can? I'd better start talking fast before this guy calls the black suits back to drive me to some medieval castle or tie me up and throw me in the Neva River.*

Waiting for a break in Kirov's lecture, Jack hurried to say, "Sir, surely you can't believe I'm a spy. I don't speak or understand a word of Russian. I was at a tavern last night..."

"Yes, yes, I know," Kirov interrupted. "You foolishly allowed a prostitute to take you to an apartment where she stripped you of your wallet and your dignity." The secretary opened the top drawer of his desk, removed a wallet and passport and slid them across the desk. "Those women are our first level intelligence agents. They did not think you were worthy of better accommodations. I apologize for their bad manners." He laughed again.

"Russell Sumner, or whatever your name is, I know you are not a spy. You are too young and too naïve. Your seaman's certificate says you are forty-five years of age, so obviously this was not issued to you. It is counterfeit or belongs to someone else. This name, Russell Sumner, does not come up in our files of suspicious persons."

Jack smiled tentatively and asked, "Sir, does this mean I'm free to go?"

Kirov leaned back in his chair, his fingers intertwined across his abdomen. "Yes and no."

Jack felt his heart pounding. *This has an ominous sound.*

"The next American vessel is not due to dock here for seventeen days. Tell me, where will you go, where will you eat and where will you sleep? We do not tolerate homeless people or street walkers." Before Jack could answer, the secretary said, "Let me offer the hospitality of the government of the USSR. We will send you to our lock-up. You can get meals and a cot for sleep until you ship out. When you get back to your country, you can tell everyone you were the guest of a hospitable Communist leader."

Feeling unsettled and queasy, sweat appeared on his brow.

Kirov noticed his discomfort. "What do you fear, comrade?"

Jack hesitated momentarily. "Truth is sir, I'm afraid that once I get locked up, I might never get out."

"Why do you say that?" Kirov asked.

"I read an English interpretation of a Pravda report that said you and Secretary General Stalin may not be on friendly terms. Suppose something should happen and Mr. Stalin no longer honors your agreement about letting me out..."

Kirov laughed aloud. "Don't worry, Mr. Russell Sumner, or whatever your name is, nothing is going to happen to me, and your safety is assured. The Secretary General and I occasionally have differences of opinion, but we respect those differences like gentlemen. We don't kill each other. Besides, Stalin regards me as his son. "

Kirov pushed a toggle switch on a black box on his desk and barked an order in Russian. An armed escort appeared to accompany Jack to the lock-up. Feeling a mix of relief and apprehension, Jack started to leave the secretary's office, then he stopped and turned around. "Sir, forgive my boldness, and I mean no disrespect, but if yours is a benevolent country, why do our newspapers report that thousands of anti-Bolsheviks were rounded-up and gunned down?" As soon as he said that, Jack thought that had to be the most stupid thing he could have asked. *Maybe now they'll just take me to the firing squad.*

Kirov, amused by Jack's impertinence, weighed his words before answering. "Comrade, do not believe what you read in your capitalist newspapers. Telling lies to the uninformed serves your government better than telling the truth. One day, you'll understand that better than you do now."

Chapter 8

The old Kresty prison, a foreboding five story structure consisting of two buildings in a cross shape, occupied an entire city block. Its solemn reddish-brown brick walls bespoke the sadness of those who languished and perished there. On the prison compound, rising above its walls, was the scalloped white-capped apse of the Alexander Nevsky cathedral that rose in defiance of the godless activities within the prison.

Stepping out of the USSR staff car, Jack gazed at the enormous edifice that was to serve as his home for the next two and a half weeks. Gripped by uncertainty, he felt an urge to tell the guard who accompanied him that he had changed his mind and would prefer not to accept Secretary Kirov's generous offer. He took a step backward, but the guard prodded him gently toward the prison entrance.

Two veteran campaigners from WWI and the Russian Civil War bedecked with rows of medals and campaign ribbons manned the formidable entrance and intercepted Jack and his guard. One of them accompanied Jack to the admissions clerk. Reluctantly, Jack surrendered his wallet, his seaman's certificate, his passport and signed his name to a form with all Russian lettering. For all he knew, he could have signed his death warrant.

With his identification confiscated, he thought these people could put him in the slammer forever or even kill him; he started to argue with the clerk about his papers.

Again he feared the loss of identification. The clerk indicated that he understood no English, waved him off with a shrug then walked away. A prison guard stepped toward him and moved him up a steel stairway to the second floor. Their clanking steps could be heard throughout the cellblock. When the guard opened the steel door and Jack stepped into the cell, he looked at his three cellmates who in turn cast unfriendly glances at him. A single dim overhead light hanging from the ceiling revealed walls of dingy mustard-yellow flaking paint. Four cots, two above and two below occupied one wall. The room reeking of cigarette smoke, cleaning compounds and disinfectants failed to mask the underlying fetid odor of human waste from the single open toilet at the far wall.

One of the cellmates, a gaunt man with sallow cheeks pointed to an upper cot for Jack. Sitting on the non-resilient mattress, Jack eagerly accepted a cigarette and a box of matches from one cellmate then smiled appreciatively.

His linguistic efforts to communicate were futile, but some measure of understanding was reached with sign and body language. After a short while the men indicated eating time and Jack followed them after their cell door was opened. They walked in a long single file to an enormous mess hall where other prisoners had already begun the evening meal. Jack followed as his cellmates picked up metal trays with compartments. He moved down a line looking and smelling unfamiliar foods. Unsmiling robust women standing behind each food station held ladles at the ready. They wore babushkas and aprons covering their ample bosoms and delivered lumps of food with a clink as their ladles struck the trays. Jack chose a watery pale green soupy substance with unknown floating particles, salted dried fish, a pudding and two slices of coarse black bread.

With his tray he followed his cellmates to a long wooden table with bench seats on either side. He set his tray down and started eating from it before sitting. He hadn't eaten for two days and his stomach had been growling in protest. The prison chatter, a roaring din, bounced off the barren walls causing his tapioca-like pudding to jiggle.

After three days Jack thought about his so-called freedom in this prison. At breakfast while drinking ersatz coffee and eating a slice of black bread smeared with some oleaginous spread, he thought of the long unproductive hours; the vacuum created by this period of inactivity became more than he could tolerate. In desperation, he summoned a guard and made him understand his need to see the commandant. After several exasperating minutes of gesturing, he was taken to some official's office. He stood before a middle-aged man seated at a utilitarian desk in a room stark with two wooden chairs and a wall of file cabinets. Behind the desk was the ubiquitous portrait of the supreme secretary with his avuncular smile, Josef Stalin.

The unsmiling official with a brush-type mustache that dipped downward at both ends creating a scowl, said, "So you want to leave our luxurious accommodations?"

Although Jack was relieved to hear English spoken, he was well aware of the official's sarcasm and worried to a nervous sweat that this man might want him as a permanent guest. Studying Jack's papers, the official fingered his mustache. "You understand we are not conducting a hotel for tourists to come and go *weely-neely.*" Jack made no response other than to nod. "You are fortunate, comrade, to be on friendly terms with Secretary Kirov. Even so, you will not come back here unless you return under criminal charges or as an enemy of the state. Let me warn you, if you do not find shelter and food and walk around like the living dead, we will lock you up as a vagrant under *our* terms." With that warning he stamped a paper three times, signed it and directed Jack to another office to receive his personal effects.

Jack experienced an overwhelming sense of relief but with a niggling worry about his new status as a free agent.

After all, he still needed to find food and lodging for about two weeks. Walking along the embankment of the Neva on which the prison was located, he became excited when he saw the old destroyer, *Aurora*. He knew from his reading that the Revolution started officially when a salvo was fired from this ship on that memorable day of October 25th, 1917. It remained anchored as a permanent monument to attest to the beginning struggle and formation of the great Union of all the Soviet Socialist Republics.

As he drew closer, he saw a group of school-aged youngsters gathered along the river bank presumably looking at the ship, but as he approached, he discovered that they had been staring not at the ship but at a young black man who was taking photographs. When Jack neared, the children opened a path for him to approach the photographer.

"Beg your pardon, do you speak English?"

With an engaging smile, the black man brought his Kodak box camera down and turned to face Jack. "Yeah, as a matter of fact, it's my only language." He extended his hand to shake Jack's. "Hi, I'm Lee Maxwell, just visiting like the rest of us." He looked at the children and smiled. "I guess I'm an attraction to them also. Apparently, they don't see many people of color around here."

Jack introduced himself, and then asked, "Who are the *rest* you referred to?"

"Members of the American Students' Confederation. We're holding seminars at the Astoria Hotel." He went on to explain, "American college students from across the States are convening and getting lectures on the origin and development of certain civil philosophies that have influenced the basics for current forms of government." The young man stopped and took a deep breath. "Wow, did that come out of me? Anyway, it's fascinating stuff and might help me understand my own problems in my cultural milieu."

Jack, in awe of Lee Maxwell's enthusiasm and the ease with which he verbalized, responded with an obvious lack of understanding to what Maxwell was saying. Aware of Jack's confusion, Maxwell assured him that he too did not understand everything he heard at the lectures. "Some of the stuff is heavy. Do you have any concept of the meaning of Marxian Dialectical Materialism?" Jack looked askance and shook his head. Maxwell continued, "Did you know that Lenin was a scholar of Marx's and Engels' and Hegel's theories, and that they in turn stole ideas quite liberally from the ancient Greek philosophers like Epicurus and Democritus?" Maxwell continued without a response from Jack. "Marx was an expert on stoicism and Lucretius's theories too. The ancients had problems with governing also, and as you recall they lost their civilizations to warring hordes who terrorized and destroyed their cities along with their concepts of civilized government."

Maxwell noted Jack's increasing signs of interest and continued, "Look, why don't you join our group for a lecture this evening. I'll introduce you to the president of our confederation, Arthur Fehrstock. He's a nice guy who..."

Jack interrupted. "Art Fehrstock? Hell, I went to high school with him. He was one of my closest friends. Sure, I'd like to attend. You have no idea how eager I am to see him." He hesitated. "But, I've got only my soiled, smelly clothes, and I need a shower and a shave."

"Don't give it a second thought." In an exaggerated Russian accent, Maxwell said, "Comrade, your old clothes will be the dress code of the day."

CHAPTER 9

Art Fehrstock came rushing towards Jack and threw his arms around him. "Jack Herscovitz, you old bastard, what the hell have you been doing to turn the world on its ass?"

"To begin Art, I've changed my name. On board ship I'm called Russell Sumner, but I plan on changing my name legally from Herscovitz to Harris when I get back to the States. If that all sounds complicated, well it is."

Art took a step back to appraise his old friend. "Christ, you look like the wrath of God, but you're trimmer than any guy around here. Did you change your brand of Scotch, or are you getting laid more often?" Art spoke rapidly with a knack for insulting then complimenting in the same breath. His demeanor suggested the insulation of the wealthy scion sheltered from the economic woes of a world in depression. But he gave time and effort to causes he deemed essential: students' rights to obtain freedom from obligatory military training and the abolition of restrictions on educational opportunities imposed by politicians and ultra conservatives.

"Tell me all about yourself," Fehrstock said. "What have you done in the three years since we left Marshall High?" Before Jack could respond, Fehrstock continued, "I had high hopes for you. I saw you as a budding statesman, a scholar going for an advanced degree or a literary giant. You wrote so well. But, Christ, look at you! You're like filthy vermin who just crawled out of a sewer."

Jack smiled wanly. "Thanks, friend. You always had a delicate and novel way with words." They sat on a sofa in the hotel lobby. Art offered Jack a cigarette from his box of Dunham's, then snapped his fingers to get the attention of a bellhop and ordered two brandies.

Art could lead a rag-tag army carrying a banner demanding unionization for field and factory workers and never see the schism between his life style and that of the people whose causes he espoused. Of course, Art living the good life while supporting the downtrodden was not a rare phenomenon, and yet he had retained the crass characteristics of some well-to-do. Snapping his fingers and ordering two brandies without the customary *please* was a demeaning gesture that bothered Jack. To his way of thinking, well-bred people just didn't do that. They treated the less advantaged with decency and respect.

That dichotomy between the privileged and the menial did not surface on a conscious level with Art. Jack thought perhaps this fiery liberal operated with free reign because of his indulging parents who did not know or did not care about their son's activities.

An oversized six-foot teddy bear of a man, Art in his rumpled suit seemed to be in constant motion. His hands when not gesticulating were plunged into his pockets; his shoulders slumped and his head bent forward. His posture, suggesting an old football lineman out of physical shape belied the acute, if not sensitive, analytical mind of the political scholar. His tousled hair fell over the left side of his forehead necessitating frequent brushing strokes as he spoke. He was ready to enter into a discussion of all governmental forms: oligarchies, plutocracies, technocracies, monarchies... In his view the world was like a giant chessboard and the pieces like whole populations could be manipulated by autocratic rulers. "Some, most I'd say, are self-promoting despots seeking to enslave...others, very few, may be truly benevolent dictators, but they're hard to come by."

Bolstered by the brandy that lessened inhibition, Jack asked, "Art, do you favor Communism? Do you believe these Russians are better off than those living in a democratic society?"

Fehrstock answered without hesitation. "They're a hell of a lot better off than they were under Tsarist rule. Let me tell you why..."

Jack interrupted. "Art, you're the consummate politician. You don't answer a question; you give your own comments and redirect the conversation. I'll ask you point-blank, are you a Communist?"

Art seemed amazed at the question. "Jack, with my family's capitalist background..."

He didn't finish, letting Jack draw his own conclusion. He was about to resume the conversation but halted as an attractive young woman displaying considerable décolletage approached with a cigarette in a long holder; her other hand rested on her hip. She raised her brow in a questioning gesture to Art.

Art glanced at her briefly, shook his head and waved her off. "Not now, Nina." She frowned and ambled off muttering in Russian.

Jack's eyes followed her, and then turning to Art, said, "Some things never change in any form of government."

Art didn't respond to the remark. He turned to Jack and said, "All right my peripatetic friend, give me a rundown of your activities since you left high school."

Recounting his travels abroad, his adventures as a merchant seaman and the books he had read to enhance his understanding of the peoples he had met, Jack waited for Art's comments.

"That's all well and good, Kiddo, but you've got to stop this farting around. Get a university degree if you're going to make..."

Interrupting him, Jack said, "Art, forget it. There's no

way I can afford to go to school."

"So what the hell are you going to do?" Before Jack could respond, Art continued, "Sail around the world again and write a travel guide for rich bastards to tell them where they can get whiskey at the lowest prices and where they can get laid at fancy-shmancy brothels? They don't need your advice."

"If you're thinking I can go to Northwestern... well, I simply can't."

"Hold on, let me finish. My family contributes a bushel of dough to the university every year. I can get you a grant that will take care of half your expenses; the other half will come from jobs you'll do around the campus."

"What kind of jobs?"

Art threw his arm around in a wide arc. "Jobs, like lawn maintenance, janitorial work..." With a broad smile he said, "You can even become a gigolo. Let some old broad provide your room and board." Art painted with rapid and broad strokes; the details were often glossed over. "You'll do well and you'll love it, trust me. Now come up to my room. You can shower, shave, put on some of my clothes and throw your shitty dungarees in the trash. You'll feel a hell of a lot better and you can enter the world of the living. Jesus, enough of this crazy wanderlust."

Art Fehrstock would shepherd Jack for the next ten days as they made their way through museums with ethnological exhibits in Leningrad and Moscow. Accompanying Art to several lectures, Jack became increasingly fascinated by the subject matter enhanced by Art's unbridled enthusiasm.

"Kiddo, does all this exposure serve as an epiphany?"

"Yeah. Maybe. You know, returning to school is more appealing now. I might just be able to make it work."

At the end of their time together, Art left Jack with enough rubles to pay for lodgings and meals until a ship arrived, and he could join a crew to get back to the States.

Chapter 10

December 1934

Jack had observed architectural wonders in Europe, but he remained impressed with the venerable neo-gothic buildings on the Northwestern campus located on the shore of Lake Michigan. To him, the buildings represented a kind of stability and dignity he equated with an institution of higher learning. Walking on the campus on this brisk cold day provided a sense of well-being, pride and a kind of masculine imperative that pleased him especially when some co-eds would steal glances as he passed.

Waiting in a long queue to register for classes in the upcoming semester, Jack picked up a discarded edition of the *Chicago Tribune* dated, December 2, 1934. On the bottom of the first page an article told of the cold-blooded murder of the Russian secretary, Sergei Kirov. *He was the guy who had shown me kindness while I was detained in Leningrad last year. Kirov's murder had occurred in the very office where he and I had spoken. He seemed quite civil, even friendly and assured me of my safety when we met.* Jack imagined with horror the scene when Kirov seated at that magnificent old desk looked up unsuspectingly and saw an assassin taking aim. It was too painful to contemplate. In the opinion of the editor, Stalin had ordered the slaying of Kirov. According to Pravda, the official Communist party newspaper, the assassination was ordered to eradicate a confirmed enemy of the state. Jack knew that Stalin had simply purged another possible contender for his crown, one who was becoming too popular and whose views were too moderate. *What irony. Kirov said that he and Stalin might have had differences of opinion but they would never kill each other. He said Stalin regarded him as a son.* Jack was beginning to better understand the madness and paranoia that drove Stalin.

He was convinced that a government without a bona fide court system, one without a jury of one's peers could only be repressive and despotic. Suddenly he felt the overwhelming privilege of living as a free man in a free society.

Jack registered for classes in Creative Writing, Early American History, Art Appreciation and an introduction to Anthropology. Being older and more mature than his classmates, he did not participate, nor was he interested in the fanfare of college athletics, high jinks or social events. His days were filled with class work and three jobs: assistant bookkeeper at the Evanston Packard auto agency, correspondent for a candy trade journal, and a dishwasher at a sorority house where he took his meals. Not even the flirting girls could alter his schedule for study and work—at least not on weekdays. Truth is, he couldn't afford the luxury of time away from his jobs or the cost of two sodas at the campus Sweet Shoppe.

On occasion, more frequently than not, after washing dishes in the evening, he would secrete some leftover foods, perhaps a half chicken or a steak only partially eaten. He would wrap the morsels in napkins and conceal them under his shirt or jacket and take them to his appreciative roommates: a football player and a basketball player both of whom constantly complained of being hungry.

Class work proved to be a snap and required little study for him to pass with excellent grades. The subject that intrigued him was Anthropology—the study of the origin, the physical, social, and cultural development and behavior of man. The professor teaching the class was Dr. Melville J. Herskovits whose last name was more than similar to his own, Herscovitz, before he had changed it to Harris several years earlier. When he was asked, years later, if his professor knew of the similarity in their names, he answered, "No." When asked why? He said quite simply, "I didn't want to curry favor."

Dr. Melville Herskovits, a man in his early forties, had been in charge of the newly formed department of Anthropology. Of the two dozen or so students in the class, most had selected the subject to satisfy hours of requirement. Jack listened with rapt interest as the man at the lectern methodically stripped away a number of notions Jack harbored about the superiority of his own family's background. He listened with fascination as the instructor outlined the physical similarities of man everywhere in the world and about the cultural differences, which separated and identified them.

The professor spoke with an enthusiasm and knowledge that captivated Jack's imagination. A personal relationship soon emerged in which Jack, an exceptional student, occupied more of the teacher's time with questions and comments to the exclusion of others. Although respectful and diffident toward his professor, Jack did not readily accept all of his mentor's theoretical proposals and would engage him in controversy citing the work of other people in the field.

Dr. Herskovits, not usually tolerant of a student's opposition to his teaching methods, gently accepted and parried Jack's challenges. Jack's demeanor and scholarship impressed the professor favorably and allowed Jack to query. One day when Jack called for the evidence to corroborate a claim the professor had made about certain African tribes, he was told to consider doing his own field work in Africa, since little was known about some natives in defined areas.

The idea of doing original fieldwork fired Jack's

imagination, and he pursued more detailed information. He combed the shelves at the library but found little to satisfy him in the literature. Herskovits encouraged him to get a copy of Margaret Mead's book, *Coming of Age In Samoa*, which had been published first in 1928, a mere six years before. A Columbia University graduate, like his professor, Mead was the first American woman to do a so-called field study. With critical intent, Jack pored over her work and found flaws. Discussing Mead's work with Herskovits, Jack had the temerity to challenge her results since they were collected in only two months of fact-finding. He was also critical of the fact that she lived apart from the people she described. Professor Herskovits acknowledged the criticism and regarded Jack's perception as exceptionally keen.

His increasing interest in doing fieldwork led him to read about everything available on the culture of so-called primitive African peoples. Herskovits invited him to attend the advanced studies sessions with graduate students, a privileged opportunity granted to few. He participated eagerly and contributed to the discourse in this higher echelon of academia. Yet for all the interest and excitement this study group generated, something had been missing from fulfilling his quest for knowledge. Reading and discussing other peoples' thoughts of man's behavior based on a relative paucity of fieldwork did not sit well with him. Conclusive statements based on too few samples and interpretations of behavior compared with standards established for western cultures were anathema to him.

He knew that if one were to study a people, one had to live among them for months, possibly a year or more.

CHAPTER 11

At the end of the school year, June 1936, Jack had packed his meager belongings and decided on another bold move. He grew restless with a compulsion to get away, to see more and along the way earn more money. This hand-to-mouth existence had become a tiresome jousting with the treasurer at the student loan office who sent frequent notices of payments due. With his suitcase in hand, he hurried after Professor Herskovits who was walking along the campus walkway. "Professor, mind if I walk with you?"

"Not at all, I'd be delighted. Are you going home for the summer?"

"Only for a short time."

"I noticed that you didn't seem as eager to participate in class discussion in the past several days. Is there a problem?" He looked up at Jack who stood several inches taller than he.

"Your class is super, but to tell the truth, I feel as though I'm not moving as fast as I should be. It's as though I'm walking in a field of sticky gumbo and everything is whizzing by me. I just feel the need to get away."

Herskovits nodded. "Perhaps you need some time off. Quite frankly, I don't know how you do it. Holding down three jobs, taking a full curriculum..." They walked in silence for a few moments when the professor began again. "I hope you're not thinking of leaving the university for an extended time. I'd like to see you remain at the university

to complete your undergraduate work. It's been my observation that once a student leaves, he seldom returns. For
selfish reasons, I don't want that to happen to you. A good
student, I mean a very good student like you, comes along
infrequently. Your success in this field would reflect favorably upon the university and me."

Jack smiled. "Thanks for your vote of confidence."

"Why don't you take some time off; go somewhere
to relax?"

"I do on occasion."

"If you don't mind my asking, I'd like to know where
you go and what you do?"

"If you promise not to censure, I'll tell you."

"Jack, what you do is your affair, but I am curious."

"One of my roommates and I hop a freight train and go
down to New Orleans... a little jazz and some Cajun food."
He looked at his mentor out of the corner of his eye.

The professor smiled and shook his head. "Apparently
that little diversion doesn't satisfy your wanderlust or your
need for adventure for any significant time. You're a restless soul—a stormy petrel."

"Maybe. While I'm young and still crazy, I'd like to go
back to the sea. I'm never as happy as when I'm sailing.
There's a kind of joyful freedom on the ocean that's unlike
anything I've ever known—a bracing wind; sea foam
sprinkling in my face, the gentle rolling and pitching of
the ship that soothes the tormented soul—there's really
nothing like it."

"You're sounding poetic." Unable to conceal his disappointment, the professor continued, "The University obviously doesn't have as much sustaining power for you as the
open sea."

"That's not completely true." Jack had to defend his
position and yet be tactful. "I'm older by several years
than most of the kids in my classes. I don't mean to sound
superior, but I've had some real life experiences that are

beyond most of the kids' comprehension and even some of the instructors. Frankly, some of the didactic material bores me. I simply feel that I have to get away from this pampered environment. Of course, I'm not referring to you or your courses."

"That's comforting to know. If you sail to Nigeria I'll give you the names of several people who would be willing to show you around. One of my first works, *The American Negro: A Study in Racial Crossing* was printed in 1928 after my trip to Africa and was received quite well. It helped me get established in the academic community. My mentor at the time, Dr. Franz Boas, a wonderful gentleman, at Columbia, encouraged me to do that research, and for that I'll be eternally grateful. One day, before he retires, I'd like you to have the opportunity to study under him."

"I'd like that."

"Africa is a vast continent and its people must be studied." Herskovits went on, "Not that we anthropologists are necessarily problem solvers, but we can identify and expose some of the injustices that exist there. For instance, there is devastating economic exploitation. Are you aware that even as recently as fifty to sixty years ago some European nations sailed into Africa, totally uninvited, of course, and carved up pieces of that continent without the consent of the people? What's more, these interlopers, these invaders, had no idea of the significance of the land they had confiscated, and more importantly, they knew little about the people living on the land."

This conversation fascinated Jack who listened raptly.

Herskovits continued, "The British made their incursions as early as the fifteenth century, and their record for humane treatment was shabby. The fact that they abolished their slave trade long before the Americans or other Europeans, I suppose, earns them a modicum of praise. But exploitation of these people continues to this day in the oil fields, gold mines, diamond and platinum mines, just to name a few areas."

Jack remained thoughtful, then asked, "You mean there's no way to stop exploiting these people?"

Shaking his head, the professor said, "Would you suggest that an international police force under the aegis of an effete League of Nations would prohibit its own members from committing illegal acts? You know that would never happen." He looked at Jack and in a voice almost pleading said, "Jack, put your wanderlust behind you; come back and finish up here. I promise I'll help launch you upon the biggest and most exciting adventure of your life."

Jack shook his mentor's hand and said, "I'll remember that promise, and I sincerely hope to take advantage of it."

After they parted, Jack took one more look at the ivy-covered buildings then headed toward the bus stop wondering when or if he would ever return to this place. He was fond of Professor Herskovits and his classes in Anthropology, but the constriction of his after-class working schedule, the constant need for money and the lure of the open sea were forces he could not or would not resist.

Was he seeking excuses for not facing up to problems? Actually he enjoyed being a student, but the information came largely from books and lectures that were often dated and stilted. Looking into the future, he believed he could earn a B.A. degree, plod along for another year or two and get his Master's. After that, he'd apply for a high school teacher's certificate and teach a class in social studies. The salary would be good enough to allow him to raise a small family, put a down payment on a home and car, and then live the good conservative life. Ultimately, a retirement fund would see him through his last years. As he dwelled on those prospects, the less inviting they seemed. The thought of mundane orderliness, the dismal routine and the petty politics of a board of education became unacceptable—downright repulsive.

For now he wanted another taste of freedom away

from the classrooms where spoon-fed wealthy kids lived their sheltered existences on a campus harboring exclusive fraternities and sororities.

One wag observed: some men who finished school went into daddy's lucrative business, while some women went to school to snare those very same men.

Chapter 12

Life on the high seas was as exhilarating as he had remembered it. The problems suffered as a novice sailor were gone. Jack's sea legs steadied almost immediately to the pitch and roll of the ship, and the dirty oily jobs were welcome after the sterile confines of the classroom. This was *real* work for *real* men. The captain of this tub, the *S.S. Queen Helena,* permitted the men greater liberties and trusted their work ethic. On days when the South Pacific was calm, the sunlight reflected brilliantly off the water, the breezes were delightfully warm, and the bare-chested men worked in little more than skivvies.

With the ship at anchor, Jack and several crewmates confiscated several bottles of rum from the hold and imbibed enough to approach stumble-bum drunkenness. Jack's boisterous mates urged him to climb onto the ship's rail at the bow and to fly off like a sea eagle. Five of them bet three dollars apiece to Jack's one dollar that he wouldn't take the dare.

With arms spread like a bird and feeling a power beyond reason, Jack wobbled onto the rail, and then yelling *Geronimo,* dove into the cold ocean to a depth jarring him into sobriety. In the blue-black water he pushed upwards kicking, praying for his breath to hold out. With every push of his legs, he felt his lungs about to burst with a burning crushing pain. An interminable two minutes passed before he surfaced to gasp for air between coughing spasms. In a state of disorientation, he floated until he heard the crew shouting as they tossed a line and pulled him up onto the deck. Two crew members, to the wild applause of the others, hoisted him on their shoulders and carried him; one shouting, "Let's drink to the new champion deep-sea diver." Another shouted, "Let's see if he can fly off the stern like he did off the bow."

Yelling obscenities, Jack kicked and swung his arms. His shipmates forced him onto the rail and were about to shove him overboard, when a voice boomed, "Stop that goddamn shit now!" Furious, the captain ran to the inebriates who were quick to lower Jack to the deck. "All you drunken bastards get back to your stations and start mopping the deck, and when you finish, do it again."

Later, Jack confided to one of the crew. "That jump was one of the stupidest things I've ever done." The crewman said, "I thought you was gonna be meat for the sharks."

Like a typical old salt, Jack had acquired a parrot at an African port. The parrot with clipped wings perched on his shoulder and went everywhere with him squawking foul phrases it had repeated from its previous sailor-owner. Jack reprimanded it constantly but to no avail.

Seeing the parrot for the first time, the captain stopped to admire its bright green plumage and its stark yellow beak. "Polly wants a cracker?" he asked.

The bird cocked its head from side to side and replied, "Fuck you," a phrase he used to anyone seeking conversation.

The captain glowered at Jack. "That thing could wind up on a barbeque spit."

Frowning, the captain turned to leave. As he did, the parrot sang out, "Fuck you."

The painful necessity of getting rid of the bird was ordered by the captain who became infuriated when the bird relieved itself on a platter of food in the galley.

The squawking, defecating nuisance had to go immediately. Jack made apologies and hurried out with the bird giving it a few more invectives to add to its vocabulary. He shipped it home in December to his parents in Chicago where it survived one week, then died of pneumonia in a veterinary clinic.

During a year of duty, when he explored ports in northern Africa and shopped Middle East bazaars, Jack purchased artifacts with spirited haggling—an exercise in commercial intercourse he enjoyed. Among his acquisitions were African tribal masks, which ultimately found their way to Northwestern University, Ohio State University and one British museum.

Although this sailing adventure, like others, was filled with moments of excitement, he realized that the pleasures were only fleeting. From his shipmates, he learned sailing techniques and a language acceptable only to other sailors. In moments of reflection, he understood the necessity for seeking further education and marketable skills.

In the fall he returned to Northwestern with money he had saved as a seaman and was able to free himself of several previous jobs. Now he could do library research and spend time with friends, some of whom were the scions of wealthy families.

Wealth however, did not impress him; he found some of the wealthiest people to be the most boorish. Only the talented could earn his friendship. Among them were writers, poets, and performing artists. One classmate, Katherine Dunham, the charming black dancer, choreographer and actress shared delightful moments with him.

Miss Dunham's winsome smile and flirtations were meant to tease Jack. Both had been drawn to the other by a shared interest in anthropology but even more by animal instinct.

On a warm summer evening, a new lime-colored 1934

saucy Ford sport convertible coupe stopped behind Pa's stodgy 1926 gray Chandler sedan parked in front of his grocery store. Four young people, two seated in front and two in the rumble seat were singing as they spilled out of the car. They did a chain dance entering the store. Leading the line was the ebullient, Katherine Dunham. Jack held on to her gyrating hips while she snaked through the narrow aisles, and the men followed singing calypso tunes.

Ma and Pa, dumbstruck, watched while the dancing went on for several minutes. Jack, laughing and almost breathless, stopped to introduce his friends. "Ma and Pa this is Miss Katherine Dunham." He turned and introduced his male friends as well. Miss Dunham shook Ma and Pa's hands and said, "I see now where Jack gets his good looks."

"Katherine and I are classmates. We decided to take a ride in her new car and stop here for Cokes."

"Sure, sure." Pa hurried to the red Coca Cola cooler, slid the top to one side and told the young people to help themselves. Both Ma and Pa tried acting nonchalant, but the presence of this stunning young black woman caused an emotional cataclysm. Ma and Pa were not prejudiced in the manner of senseless rejection. They were accustomed to black people. After all, Ma had a black girl named Ada come in once a week to do house cleaning and the laundry. She liked Ada and respected her. But this woman was different. Ma could foresee a problem if Jack married this dancing woman. How could she face her family without shame? An even greater calamity came to mind—what about their children? She made a quick decision: she would love them, no matter what. God forbid.

Pa wasn't just anti-Negro, he was suspicious of *all* outsiders. An outsider was any non-Jew or any Jew born in Russia, Poland or Lithuania. Born in Romania, Pa was raised with the certitude that he was the son of a son of a son—as far back as Abraham—who was an adviser to the

King, one who would endow his sons and all their progeny with the inalienable rights and privileges of a high priest. Pa impressed upon his three sons that they possessed a vaunted heritage; they were Kohanim, members of the king's court. Were Jack to marry this black woman, the line of royalty would be broken—*fartig!*

Truth is, Pa was a relatively reasonable man who invoked the privileges of ancestry when it suited him. What happened five thousand or more years ago in the barren desert of Judea really mattered little to him.

CHAPTER 13

Professor Herskovits conducted the last seminar before the semester hiatus was about to begin. In the limited class, graduate students and scholars from other institutions were invited. He asked for a show of hands for those who had visited Africa. One hand, besides Jack's, went up. Dr. Herskovits asked the tall bespectacled man to stand and introduce himself.

The handsome stranger with cocoa-skin coloring, stood, smiled affably and said, "How do you do, everyone. My name is Ralph Bunche, and I'm here to learn everything I can about the Dark Continent and its people," he paused, "in case I get shagged out of this country and need to make a hasty retreat to the land of my forefathers." Polite laughter followed. After class, Jack introduced himself and both men took an instant liking to one another. This was the start of a long and eventful relationship filled with honor and accomplishment and ultimately with disappointment and shame.

Katherine Dunham, also a student in that class had to face serious decisions in her future. She and Jack parted company when she chose dancing over the continued study of anthropology, much to the dismay of her mentors at Northwestern and the University of Chicago. In time, she became the most famous interpreter and innovator of Afro-Caribbean dancing. And her performances with her troupe toured principal cities even as she championed the cause of freedom and civil rights for Negroes worldwide.

Summer 1934

Jack was given the opportunity of earning a good deal of money at the Chicago's World Fair. Among the selected group of university students, he was privileged to pedal a rickshaw-like tricycle for sightseers at an hourly rate of two dollars. That wasn't all profit since the pedalers shared fees with the equipment owners. On a good day, with generous tipping, he pocketed as much as twenty-five dollars, a king's ransom.

Jack stood and waited impatiently as Ma reached up to hand-brush a speck of lint from the epaulet of the blue cotton twill jacket with its white leather Sam Browne belt and bright brass buttons. Looking in the hall mirror, he adjusted the military-style dress hat with a white visor and slid the knot of the blue tie up against the white starched shirt collar.

In the late morning, Jack walked to board a bus going to the fair. The temperature kept pace with the climbing humidity. After twelve hours of pedaling and driving sightseers with his rehearsed spiel of points of interest, he returned home exhausted; his shirt collar unbuttoned and wilted from perspiration; his tie askew and the hat sweat band discolored from moisture. He staggered upstairs, undressed, bathed, and fell into bed, too tired to eat the meal Ma prepared.

At the end of the tour season, he had saved enough money for tuition, but he still could not satisfy his indebtedness to the student loan program at Northwestern where he owed several hundred dollars with accumulated interest. Jack's response to the loan officer's badgering was a promise of full payment at the time of graduation.

Another voyage as a seaman would permit him to save enough to stanch his debt with its grinding interest, besides, he wanted desperately to be on the high seas again. Another year-long run would satisfy his needs. He packed the barest essentials into his worn suitcase decorated with colorful ocean liner labels. An evening with Martha and a hasty goodbye to the folks fulfilled his social obligations. He boarded a Greyhound bus bound for New York to join the crew of a merchant vessel. This time he headed off as a well-seasoned shipmate.

After another year at sea, Jack returned to Northwestern to complete his studies and receive his baccalaureate degree.

Spring 1936

The normal four-year course of study had been stretched to six by his sailing episodes between semesters. He had no intention of attending the graduation ceremonies since he regarded them as outmoded customs of meaningless nonsense. Besides, he didn't want to spend the ten-dollar rental fee on the cap and gown.

While on the walkway, preparing to leave the campus for a visit home, Jack was stopped by a messenger.

"Mr. Harris? Jack Sargent Harris?"

Jack looked at the breathless fellow who had been running to catch him. He handed Jack an envelope "Is it that damned loan officer again? What's this for?"

The messenger shrugged and walked away. The note bore the Dean's name and the university seal. *I don't know the Dean, and I wouldn't be able to identify him in a line-up. What the hell have I done now?* Walking toward the administration building, he thought about his payments to the school's treasurer for his student loan and knew they were timely, so that couldn't be an issue.

"Come in, Mr. Harris." The Dean, middle-aged and balding, with a modest bay window and a politically fixed smile, shook Jack's hand and pointed to a chair opposite his desk. "I want to take this opportunity to personally congratulate you. Your adviser, Dr. Herskovits, and the committee on scholarship awards have selected you and several of your classmates to join a rather exclusive club. You've been elected into the Phi Beta Kappa honorary society." He positioned his head back displaying his double chin and smiled broadly as he awaited Jack's response.

Jack nodded and smiled, then said softly, "That's nice."

The Dean held up his own key along with others that dangled from a gold chain that looped across his dark vest. "You see, we're members of the same society. Wear your key proudly. You've earned it and the recognition that it brings."

Jack thanked him again and left. To him, the key was another trinket, not worth the purchase price and not worth the cost of a suit with a vest on which to hang it. Later, when Professor Herskovits congratulated him, Jack said, "They really had to scrape the bottom of the barrel to give me this."

"Nonsense, don't trivialize this. Your test grades, your attitude and class participation made that decision easy. Frankly, I'm willing to bet you'll contribute richly to the field of anthropology. Of that, I have no doubt."

Pleased with his Professor's blandishments, Jack smiled and said, "I hope I can live up to your expectations."

"You'll go on with your studies, and I want you to think seriously about going to Columbia and working with my old mentor, Dr. Franz Boas. You know of him from your studies; he's the pre-eminent anthropologist in America, perhaps the world. You'll be rubbing elbows and exchanging information with the likes of Margaret Mead and Ruth Benedict." Recalling his own academic comrades, Dr. Herskovits spoke with greater animation. "I'll write Dr. Boas and let him know that I am referring you to his post-grad program. By the way, I wouldn't be critical of Margaret Mead's work when you meet her."

Jack put up his hands. "Whoa, Doctor, I really appreciate all of this, but how am I supposed to live in New York?

There aren't enough dishes in all the restaurants for me to wash to pay my upkeep."

Herskovits smiled. "Jack, as resourceful as you are, I can't imagine you won't find a means for cadging a few dollars, or maybe you'll find a grateful dowager to put you up. Forgive my poor sense of humor." He smiled broadly. "We'll try to arrange a Social Sciences Research Council grant and maybe an additional grant or two." As though anticipating Jack's thinking, he added, "Please avoid the ships that might lure you back to the sea. The university is situated on the banks of the Hudson, and you'll be seeing plenty ships that might entice you."

Chapter 14

Evanston, summer 1936

Jack collected his mail on top of the Edwardian Period console in the entryway of his post WWI boarding house off campus. He eyed with anticipation a letter from the office of the Graduate School at Columbia. He hurried to his basement room, sat on his cot and ripped the envelope open.

It read:

Dear Mr. Harris,

The School of Social Sciences is pleased to announce your acceptance...

He read and reread the letter; his joy was tempered by the terms of a scholarship, which funded tuition only. He thought, *I'll get by if I don't eat, and I can find a cozy bench in the park for sleeping.* He wrote immediately to Dr. Ruth Benedict pleading desperate penury.

"...this is my problem: I have just received my B.S. degree from Northwestern University. I graduated with honors, distinction and some pressing debts. Since graduation I've worked on a construction gang in Evanston. With my earnings, I have erased some of my debts. Unfortunately, construction work has come to a standstill, and I can see nothing that will carry me through the rest of the summer and leave me enough for transportation costs to New York in the autumn.

Dr. Benedict replied to apologize for having less than

complete understanding of his type of scholarship. She had made the assumption that it would cover tuition as well as basic costs of living. She outlined a number of resources for additional funding.

Chapter 15

September 1936, New York City

Jack climbed the steps of the broad entryway past the tall Grecian columns, into the marble hall with its echo chamber reverberations and to the office of the registrar at Columbia University. In addition to class assignments in the post graduate division, he was given a key for lodging on the twelfth floor of the nearby John Jay Hall and told to report to the office of Professor Franz Boas in the morning.

His new home, a small tidy room, faced the Hudson. The room was filled with sunshine in contrast to the darkened little basement room he occupied in Evanston. He walked to the window and yearned to be on one of the gleaming yachts that plied the glassy waterway. In no time at all, he knew he would be on the shore talking with the people sailing those magnificent vessels.

Jack arrived fifteen minutes early and walked around the professor's cluttered office filled with memorabilia dating back to the turn of the century. Autographed photos of scientists and scholars including those of Albert Einstein, Madame Curie and Justice Benjamin Cardozo decorated one wall. Scenes and artifacts of the Northwest Indians, notably the Kwakiutl, about whom Boas had done much research, were displayed randomly.

Dr. Boas rushed into the room, a tall, slender man with

a bushy gray mustache and a receding hairline smiled with friendly eyes. With a firm handshake, he apologized for his tardiness. In his mid-seventies, speaking with a decided German accent, he bowed slightly as he said, "Welcome young man. Your sponsor, Dr. Herskovits, one of my favorite students, recommended you to our program." He hurried to take books off the chair for Jack to be seated; then he sat at his desk.

"Unfortunately, my days here are numbered. In another year, I'll have emeritus status, which means I'll be put out to pasture like a worthless old horse. Before I turn over the reins to a capable associate, Dr. Ralph Linton, I'll lay out a plan of activities for you. However, you must find your own financing if you are to live among the native people you wish to study."

I don't remember saying anything about studying native people. "Of course, I want to..."

"You are probably aware; I have devoted at least fifty years of research and teaching to validate my Theory of Relativism."

Jack's quizzical expression prompted the Professor to explain. "Without going into minute details, the theory essentially pooh-poohs the prevailing beliefs of some misguided politicians, and unfortunately so-called educators, who claim Western Civilization is superior to others. If you are thinking that is true, let me disabuse you of such beliefs right now. There are maniacal leaders like Herr Hitler who espouse the superiority of Western Man and particularly the Germanic and Scandinavian types. These psychotic, malignant militarists can do horrible things to western civilization unless they are stopped. I deplore violence, especially wars, but if peaceful negotiations with renegade nations fail, then..."

Boas threw up his arms. "Enough talk of this insanity. For now, you will help me do some research, and your salary will be paid by the National Youth Administration program. You will read my Tsimshian texts and extract culture from mythology. This is tedious and exacting work. The pay is $1.50 an hour, and if you find it boring, please do not complain to me."

In a letter written to Dr. Herskovits that month,
Jack wrote:

> *My financial problems have been beautifully straightened out with the help of Dr. Ruth Benedict who offered me a full-tuition loan sponsored by some fairy godmother in the department (whoever she is, bless her) which demands no interest and is quite sympathetic about repayment. (Incidentally, she is not the dowager you suggested that I might find.) I was able to cut through a flock of collegiate adolescents to see the head gal at the employment bureau. She literally flung all manners of jobs at me. I took the National Youth Administration program at $35 a month and another job as a part time secretary, which will average between $8 and $10 a week. With my room, board and tuition beautifully taken care of, and an income of about $18 a week, I feel well satisfied at the moment. However, I must remember I'm going to school, and every nickel must be accounted for.*
>
> *Phi Beta Kappa keys are a dime a dozen here at John Jay Hall. I sit at mealtime with a group of other grad students, and there is always high talk. The men speak after simulated meditation with ponderous words and precise intonation, their phrases slowly streaming forth and parading the table on stilts. Behind them we can see the professors whom they ape, and I am sure the same professors are gratified to know that they (the students) will pass the torch of learning to their prototypes who will guard their scholastic aristocracy with well-known conservative zeal. I know this is an immature form of protest, but I am often seized with an overpowering desire to belch or break wind*

in the middle of their well-formulated phrases.

Life here is exciting. It is most pleasant at last to feel that being a liberal or a radical injects one into the "in" group, and I know you can understand the healthy release I feel. There is no more necessity for vicious rationalizations, as I had to undergo in conversations at Northwestern. The pace at Northwestern was like a lilting Strauss waltz, while the pace at Columbia is like a rousing Sousa march. If students don't study here and don't participate in class work, it's their ass. There is no cosseting or cajoling. Here they're all mature, articulate and forever challenging. Make a mistake, and they're all over you.

All of the post-grads, with the exception of two or three are dirt poor. Money is at the top of their concerns — constantly. We'd go to Amsterdam Avenue or Broadway, spend a nickel for coffee and talk about trying to get teaching assignments, grants or civil service appointments. We'd discuss how best to answer questions to qualify for government jobs.

I miss Lake Michigan, but I go down to South Street every Sunday morning. The seamen's strike seems inevitable and the waterfront is in for a dirty time...I brought one of my old shipmates up here.

"You mean all these grown up guys are studying?" he asked. "Maybe it's all right, but I dunno. It ain't right just to sit down and read all the time." And on going up the John Jay elevator he said, "Jesus Christ, it smells like the YMCA. This is a helluva life. Don't you ever want to go back to the sea?"

"I do, but..."

A letter dated, December 6, 1936

Dear Dr. Herskovits,

Of course, you knew I couldn't keep clear of the waterfront...been there practically every night. Sure I picketed. Even tapped the department for donations. Dr. Boas was *splendid—he came through with $5 but the best part of that were his penetrating questions, which were better than the money.*

The entire department is planning to auction off some reprints. The proceeds will go to the defense of loyalist forces in Spain. Wonder why I feel remarkably alive here?

My classmates regard me as an oddball. To begin, I'm a Midwesterner among all those New Yorkers and Easterners. My background as a sailor and my occasional rough speech also set me apart. When I was asked whether I was a Communist, I answered that I was concerned with American seamen and their labor problems. I even picketed for them for better working conditions and decent salaries since I spoke with firsthand knowledge. I was also concerned with racial discrimination and women's rights. Actually, the communist views regarding certain inequalities were not far different from mine. To answer the question: I had no time for communists. I went to one meeting, after being persuaded by a zealot. They talked about piddling matters: collecting dues, places to hold meetings, paying for coffee— that sort of nonsense. Frankly, I detest organizations that rob me of my time; besides, I'm just not a joiner.

After a year of adjustment in the graduate program and finding a source of field study, I conferred with Dr. Benedict about living and working among the Wind River Shoshone Indians. With Dr. Benedict's help I received money from Dean Peagram at Columbia for research.

An isolated group of Indians in the Duck Valley Reservation that included Shoshone and Paiute intrigued me. Indian affairs informed me that there were 900 Indians on the reservation, 600 Shoshone and the rest Paiutes. The town was 100 miles from the nearest railroad, telephone or telegraph office. All supplies had to be hauled in and no utilities such as gas, electricity or running water were easily accessible. There was enough isolation with little of the white man's influence to make the study interesting.

Prices for most commodities were way up. Gasoline is 35 cents per gallon compared to 10 cents in New York.

One of my mentors, Ruth Benedict, is one of the loveliest ladies I have ever known. She is favorably disposed toward me, not in a physical sense, of course. I must have impressed her as being an eager beaver who was respectful and grateful. She, in turn, is exceedingly kind and goes out of her way to obtain grants for me, for which I shall be ever indebted. Her lectures are like poetry. She is a beautiful, graceful woman – one I shall never forget.

She and Dr. Boas managed to get a National Youth Administration grant for me to study the White Knife Shoshone in Nevada. Before that, however, I had been assigned along with another post grad to study some of the cultural traits of immigrants in this country. Nazi theories of race have been promoted here, and some pseudo-scientific academicians are espousing that nonsense. For instance, the Nazis claimed that inferior races used their arms and hands in gesturing while talking. Exclude the definition of race for the moment because the term has no validity here.

What we did was to go to Union Square and sit on one of the benches. I'd hold a newspaper and poke the lens of a camera through a hole in the paper and take footage of old Jews as well as old Italians speaking. Perhaps some were Greeks, Turks or Lebanese.

We'd developed the film and plotted on a graph the rapidity of movements of the arms, the relationship of the elbow to the shoulder, to the sides, the elbow to the hand and so on and coordinated with speech.

One of the most interesting illustrations of the relationship of gesture and speech was in an analysis of footage obtained from newsreels of the speeches of Mayor Fiorello LaGuardia. The colorful mayor of New York City spoke Yiddish, Italian and English, of course. Our footage showed six sets of gestures: when he spoke conversational Yiddish, he used one set of gestures; in a speech to a

Yiddish audience he used different gestures. This was also the case with conversational and oratorical Italian and similarly for English. The thesis was that gestures were based on cultures and not race.

We also showed generational differences. The gestures of immigrants were different from those of their sons. We went to Saratoga Race Track to clock the gestures of first-generation Italians and Jews who demonstrated modified, restricted and subdued gesturing, closer to American gestures. It was all fascinating for me. I'm not at all sure my mother or father would have shared my enthusiasm. My father would have called it kinderspielen or child's play—and he wondered why good money was used to teach such nonsense.

Some afternoons a few of us would go down to Broadway and over a cup of coffee we would discuss how to get teaching assignments, grants for civil service appointments. We'd discuss how best to answer test questions to qualify for government jobs.

CHAPTER 16

Winter 1936...Letter to Dr. Herskovits

> *Our marriage ceremony was brief but certainly more conventional than our first one seven years ago when we were in our teens, the marriage my father had annulled. Martha and I had a justice of the peace pronouncing platitudes for long life, happiness and fruitful bearing. Four of our New York friends bore witness to the union. I bring no monies to this arrangement, but fortunately, Martha is employed at a reasonable salary as a secretary to a political cartoonist for one of the large New York dailies.*

July 1937...Letter to Dr. Herskovits

> *We had little time to enjoy our newly acquired apartment in Manhattan when arrangements were made for me to gather data on the White Knife Shoshone in Owyhee, Nevada. Ruth Benedict managed to get me the modest sum of $500 to pay for informants, purchase a used car, and buy food and whatever else.*
>
> *Martha and I needed to live on the reservation. That was a grim assignment. The area was practically barren with scrub brush, wind, dust and little else. The evenings were biting cold, even in the summer. I would sit down with the elders, tired old men who had to prod their memories to tell me about life as it existed forty to sixty years ago.*
>
> *Martha interviewed the women and took excellent*

notes. *In that abysmal place she made life livable for me. The benefit of all that, at least to me, was that it prepared me for what I had hoped to do on my upcoming assignment in Africa. Also with this fieldwork, I plan to submit my thesis for a PhD.*

I returned the '30 Chevy coupe to the used car dealer and didn't lose much in the transaction. Getting around the reservation was largely by horseback. And I haven't been on a horse since, thank you.

Next week, my interpreter, who is worth a good deal more than I pay him ($1.50 per day), has to go to Carson City to act as a witness in court. During the July 4th celebration he acted as a special policeman and uncovered a few instances of romantic love progressing in the willows, and now he must go to federal court to tell his story.

I like to work with these Indians. They are simple, sincere and a little bewildered. They have few taboo terms and their stories are close to the fundamentals of life. Translation of their Indian names is like an excursion into pornography.

I insisted on giving my informant a present. There is no word for "present" among these peoples. They have taken over the white term "Christmas present" to denote a gift. After conferring with his wife, he asked me how long I had been married. I told him eight months. And now he insists upon returning, which he thinks, is a perfect "Christmas present" for us—a cradleboard that his wife is making. Entirely unnecessary, I must hasten to assure you.

We have a formidable amount of data that we'll be packing up for our return trip to New York and hope to find the time and money to collate it for my PhD.

One of the informants, a fellow who traveled in several bordering states and enjoyed a degree of sophistication asked if we were sufficiently warm during the cold nights. I told him we had difficulty getting warm even though we cuddled. I asked him if he found the weather to be extremely cold at night. He smiled and said, "It's colder than a well digger's ass in Wyoming." With that he laughed, an altogether rare event among these sober people.

The area is magnificent with mountains speckled with patches of tan where gold mines had been abandoned. Now and again someone pulls out ten or twenty thousand in dust or crude ore, and hope arises and the creeks and hillsides bustle with activity.

Our nearest town is about fifteen miles south, a mining town raised by the hand of Anaconda Copper which opened the fabulous Rio Tinto mine here a few years back. The place looks like a set on the MGM lot, ready to shoot a blood and thunder horse opera. You see it and you don't believe it.

Gambling is legal in this state as well as prostitution. Mix that up with a mushroom town fed by well-paid miners who have no other place to spend money, and you begin to see the picture. We never knew such towns existed outside the description of a Zane Grey western.

With the postal money orders chopped down to amounts not to exceed thirty dollars, I think Martha and I'll get by. Larger check amounts are difficult to cash. I'm hoping to get enough money from the sale of my car to get us back to New York.

Letter to Dr. Benedict, August 2, 1937

...socially and economically the Shoshone had been eased over to simple farming with little conflict, no clashing plans or previous patterns of sharp-societal segmentation to flame into opposition. Friendliness toward whites was prevalent long before reservation days and attitudes toward white civilization are now marked by mild approval and resignation. So far I have found few evidences of a thin layer of disapproval, mainly from the older people but no vicious flashbacks.

Mission work has been lax with infrequent itinerant mission workers leaving little favorable impression. Religious service attendance has dwindled, and it appears most Indians are apathetic.

Peyote recently appeared seems to be confined to a small group of Paiutes – those who migrated from Oregon in 1883 after their rebellion. One man on the reservation, an Oregon Paiute, has retained his long hair. The only other features of native dress are occasional moccasins and the cradleboard.

The Shoshone and Paiutes have freely intermarried and Mexican, Italian and Negro marriages are recorded. Not recorded are the children of the Basque sheepherders about here nor the Chinese blood planted by the freely sowing Chinese placer miners who had a community near here some years back.

We're about six thousand feet up, and it is the standing joke with the local wits that there are but two seasons: winter and the Fourth of July, but the sledding is not so good on the Fourth.

August 18, 1937... Letter to Dr. Benedict

I am on my last pennies. I sold my car to a local boy who has been paying me in installments; the car to be delivered after last installment – soon. No profit, of course, and the car is in almost constant need of repair on these primitive roads. I am holding on to Martha's transportation costs to Chicago. I will resort to an old transportation trick from more carefree days. The Basque firm of sheep men assured me that I could take charge of a shipment of sheep into the Chicago stockyards. The caboose accommodations are excellent; I knew them well.

I saved one boy seventy dollars on payments on a used car by writing a strong letter to the sales office in Elko. Word got around and the reservation "radicals" are just beginning to open up to me. I feel strongly that it would be a mistake to leave now. One hundred dollars, I think, would see me through until mid-September. I sincerely hope that the money is available. It will be well spent.

August 27, 1937...Letter to Dr. Benedict

Thank you for the two fifty dollar checks. The money will take us till the first of October, and I will be able to hire another informant who will provide information checks as well as additional information.

Some old-line anthropologists thought my field-work should have fit more neatly into the framework of long standing theories. I was interested in recording the manner in which these people had to scrounge for their food, and how that related to the family unit, and how they worshipped. If others wanted to pigeonhole their activities, that is fine. I was convinced that the family unit was determined largely by economic necessity.

I'll keep you informed.

Jack

January, 1938 New York City

Jack and Martha had settled into their miniscule Manhattan apartment to begin organizing notes. At Columbia, Dr. Ralph Linton, now head of the anthropology department, was able to get a grant for Jack from the Carnegie Institute to correlate notes which were to be included in Linton's new text book.

Herskovits at Northwestern encouraged Jack to seek a Social Sciences Research Council grant for fieldwork with the Ibo in West Africa. It was Herskovits's premise that certain cultural manifestations of the West African Negro could be found in some of the traits of the American Negro since most of the slaves had came from that part of Africa.

Early fall, 1938

Martha had worked late and stopped at the grocery to purchase enough food to fill two ten-pound kraft bags. After walking two city blocks on high heels she grew irritable when she reached the apartment. She balanced one of the bags against the doorjamb and fumbled for the keys in her purse. The door opened suddenly and she stumbled forward; one bag spilled its contents. Jack ran to retrieve the groceries then took the remaining bag from her. He guided her solicitously to the small dining room. "You okay, honey?"

"I feel lousy! I'm tired and achy, thank you." She unbuttoned her jacket and slumped in a club chair, her legs extended and spread apart. She closed her eyes, crossed her arms over her chest and sighed. She waited for Jack to say something.

He knelt beside her. "A grant from SSRC arrived today and guess what?"

She shook her head. "I can't possibly guess. What?"

"They've accepted my application. I'm getting $3500 to spend a year with the Ibo in Nigeria. Isn't that great?" Jack looked at her as though she might not have heard. "Honey, isn't that terrific?"

Martha pulled herself off the chair and walked to the bedroom. Jack followed. "What's wrong, Mart? Aren't you excited about going?" Before she could respond, he said, "We'll get our typhoid, and other inoculations; we'll go to Abercrombie and Fitch and get outfitted with pith helmets..."

Martha turned slowly to look at him. "Hold on, Doctor Arrowsmith. This is one Boy Scout trip you can do without me. Living with those Indians for three months was bad enough. I thought I'd die out there in that God-forsaken prairie. But to live in some jungle for a year with wild creatures...well, forget it." Her eyes narrowed and in a constrained voice, said, "Did you really think I would go with you?"

"I made the assumption that we'd sail to Europe, have a

holiday in London then head off to Lagos. We talked about it and agreed that if you found Africa too oppressive you could sail back home..."

"That's nonsense—absolute nonsense. To begin, there isn't that kind of money for me to accompany you, and then sail back home alone. And I certainly wouldn't take a tramp steamer." She reached for a cigarette from an open pack on the nightstand. Jack lit the cigarette; she inhaled deeply and brought her head back, then exhaled a long stream of smoke. "You make plans for yourself, Dearie, I'll manage somehow for the year. I'll go back to my family in Chicago. I'm certainly not staying here alone."

Despite his initial disappointment, Jack knew she was right, and he was not about to aggravate her.

Martha continued, her voice less strident but not completely conciliatory. "There are times when I wish you weren't so damned ambitious, so forceful; trying to bring the whole world together, to protect as you would say, the disadvantaged..."

"C'mon, Honey, you know that's not true. I want to observe these people—report the way they live, their means of making a livelihood, the way they interact. This is research that's significant."

"Yes, Sweetheart, I've heard it all before." She stubbed her cigarette on the ashtray. "Why couldn't you get a nice clean office job? Work with my sister's friend, Bernie Buchsbaum, in commercial real estate? I don't mean to sound crass, but the guy drives a Cadillac that's bigger than this apartment. He'd get you a job in his office..." Martha put her arms around his neck; her large brown eyes implored his.

He removed her arms from his neck. "Mart, it was never about money, and you know it. I love what I'm doing, and I'm naïve enough to think I can make a contribution toward understanding the way people treat or mistreat one another."

"Spare me the platitudes."

"I'm sorry this assignment pulls us apart. When I return

from Africa we'll have our whole lives to live together, I promise. We'll settle down on some university campus and live the genteel life. I'll teach, you'll raise the kids and do whatever a professor's wife is supposed to do."

Martha turned and walked away. "Sorry, Darling— we've discussed this before—no children—no way."

Chapter 17

November 1938 Aboard the Hollander
A letter to M.J.H.

The voyage to England was magnificent. Sailing as a pampered passenger has distinct advantages over sailing as a bloody swabbie. The salt air enhanced my appetite and the freely flowing Scotch was unresistable. I shall be forced to walk everywhere to burn off the extra pounds.

Your arrangements for my lecture at Cambridge before the Anthropological Club came off splendidly. The members showed a great deal of interest, and I am certain that was due to their ignorance of American Indian cultures, and their desire to hear a firsthand account. One of the attendees, Dr. Driberg, kept me up until two a.m. and wined and dined me almost to the hilt. I do like him; he lives in the anthropological tradition of lusty virility.

Your arrangements for me to meet with G.I. Jones, the District Officer, have expedited my travel by cutting through the usual red tape. He has advised me that he will meet me in Ozuitem after I call him from Lagos.

I look forward to the leisurely trip and the good food on this Dutch ship. The only good meals I had in London were eaten in foreign restaurants in Soho, there they do not boil every bit of meat overnight and, thank God, they remember there are such things in the world as herbs and spices: cloves, cinnamon, pepper, bay leaves and allspice. Furthermore, I had not been able to get out of a draft while

I was there.

Wouldn't there be a good article on the influence of the wars on the sex ratio in England and its consequences in the attitude, manner and behavior of the male sex? Every petty, prissy little jackass here has an exaggerated opinion of his own worth; the women seem to foster this, with the consequences that it is the men who sit like kings and walk like peacocks. To see one lighting and smoking a cigarette is like observing a formal ritual. And they're often so precious in their speech. This is all ludicrous now that England is fast becoming a second-rate power and continuing its stinking program of conciliation and peace with dishonor. So far, other than the avowed radicals, the only ones I have met who think Chamberlain might be wrong are the anthropologists.

December 3, 1938

Dear M.J.H.

This boat is giving me a splendid opportunity to see the coast. In two days we will be in Lagos. This is our third day in the Gold Coast, opportunity never offered by the mail boats. Two days ago I went to shore at Cape Coast and spent the night in the home of a native official. The town clerk gave me the use of his chauffeur and car, and we toured the countryside in it. I must say that I don't care much for the coast towns; the natives are too servile, too much saluting and salaaming as we pass and then that wicked sneering laugh as soon as our backs are turned, and there is something sad in their garb of phony Manchester batik.

The boat is dirty, old, small and has cargo strewn everywhere. In other words, it is a lovely thing, precisely what I wanted to travel on. There is none of this damned nonsense about dressing for dinner or shaving neither every day nor any of those trivial formalities, which can make life so annoying on the passenger ships. I am pleased to have this last respite before I go formal in Lagos and break out my startling new mess jacket and cummerbund. For the first time I have discovered that captains may be decent people, now that I no longer live in the fo'cs'l'e. Just to allow me to keep my hand in it, the old man lets me steer this wagon a few hours each afternoon.

After England, I again find myself in a quaint world of table manners. However, since I am an American and a priori somewhat mad, my eating eccentricities are generously forgiven, a courtesy which does not seem to be accorded to the two Englishmen aboard which secretly pleases me, for I distinctly remember the frozen glances I received in London one night when I mistook the fish knife for the butter knife. How was I to know?

I am saving this bit of juicy information for the last as it intrigued and annoyed the hell out of me, as I'm sure it should you. I sought some seclusion on the deck after the evening meal and took a last puff on my cigarette and tossed it into the sea. I was leaning on the railing watching the deep blue water with its foamy white caps slip along the hull of the ship when someone sidled up to me and also leaned on the railing. I turned to look at him; he looked familiar and yet I couldn't be sure. He had a military style haircut, and when I looked closely he appeared to be smiling or sneering. Then I realized who he was, a former classmate and one of your graduate students, Carl Betts. We spent a bit of time chatting and he said he had attended my lecture at Cambridge and made some flattering comments. All of which pleased me until we got on to the subject of politics and the world situation. The conversation took a nasty turn, and he infuriated the hell out of me. I had all I could do to keep from slugging him.

Were you aware that this guy is a Nazi sympathizer? When I heard that I found it difficult to believe, but I engaged him in conversation. I asked him why? How is it possible that a man exposed to the discipline, to the *years of intellectual pursuit of trying to understand man's development, his culture, ethos, his relationship with other human beings could possibly embrace the credo of hatred, the anti-intellectualism, the barbarity of those who would enslave the free world?*

The guy was completely unmoved by my questions and obviously had rehearsed answers to toss back easily. He said that much of what was being taught in our universities was speculative gibberish concocted by people, many of whom were Jews, who offered solutions to specious problems. Then he seemed to puff up and declared that western man had flourished by sheer physical power and superior intellect to solve problems. The Nazis, he claimed, had chosen to empower their thinking by gathering into their sphere of interest then ridiculing those who were mired down by notions of so-called democratic ideals, which in reality were socialistic or communistic doctrines.

I kept thinking of the precious hours wasted at the university by people like you who tried to make this guy a responsible and contributing member of society, and he turns out to be such drech. I would have engaged him in further conversation, but truth is, he made me so damned mad I couldn't stand talking with him. Earlier in our conversation, I asked him where he was going. He said he was making studies of the ports and adjacent terrain along the west coast of Africa, and then he was sailing south to Johannesburg. When I asked why, he gave me a cryptic answer. "It's an assignment."

Before we parted, I said, "Betts, you've chosen the wrong idol to worship."

He sneered then pulled aside his open jacket to reveal a holstered Luger, which he patted. "On the contrary, I think I've made the right choice."

"Betts, if ever we're at war, that is the U.S. with Germany, and we confront one another on the battlefield, *would you shoot to kill me?"*

"Hah! That's a highly unlikely scenario, but to answer you directly," he pointed his forefinger at me, *"you, my friend, would be a dead man."*

I didn't talk with him again and avoided the S.O.B. for the rest of the voyage.

With kind regards,

Jack

CHAPTER 18

December 15, 1938

In a letter to M.J.H. Jack explained why he chose to concentrate his observation of the Ibo in a relatively circumscribed area: an intensive study of one clan was sorely needed, after the initial and generally superficial studies of previous anthropologists. Working in two widely separated areas, as Herskovits suggested, the material would be discursive; furthermore there was a certain amount of expense involved in settling in two villages—costs that became prohibitive on a limited budget.

Jack discovered that unlike other West African societies, the Ibo had no kingdom, no highly centralized government with headquarters many miles away and no priestly clans to exert influence from outside the immediate clan. The Ibo were the largest tribe in all of Africa and provided the largest source of slaves for the new world. John Adams in 1790 said that of twenty thousand slaves sold annually, sixteen thousand were Ibo. Slaves came from independent groups who did not participate in highly formalized societies such as the tribes of the Benin, Ashanti, Yoruba or Dahomey.

He wrote, "Because of the importance of this material, I shall stay in Bende for the next ten days or so in an endeavor to obtain information about the slave trade from old residents in the area, because Bende was the largest slave market in the entire territory. Unfortunately, the most famous of the recent traders who participated in the last phases of the trade died only last year (1937), although I am now attempting to round up his relatives, friends, and other inhabitants of this immediate area who can offer information." After considerable effort involving baksheesh, Jack contacted a distant relative of the slave trader. He was reluctant to divulge information, or he had little actual information to offer.

From Lagos, a large port in Nigeria, Jack moved inland to his designated village. Determined to ignore preconceived notions about the people, he immersed himself in their everyday activities. His written impressions indicated that they had a vibrant culture and exhibited an enormous difference from the sad Shoshone of Nevada. The Ibo village was tremendously exciting, full of the things he had read about. There were religious figures, native doctors who actually worked cures, spirit possession that one could see, work parties and lively meetings of village elders. And oh, the dancing! The night drumming and the singing with leaders and chorus, well...I needn't go on.

He continued to write that unfortunately, I arrived in the Ibo country at a most difficult time. The women (and men also, this time) were again demonstrating and refusing to pay the annual tax. For a short, tense period it appeared as though there might be a recurrence of the infamous Aba riots of 1929. After a few baton charges by the police troops and the fear of the very presence of police, the trouble appears to have subsided, although no one seems quite certain.

Orders came from Lagos that because of the possible danger, I was not to enter the disturbed area. I stayed far away, not because of the warning, but because I had no desire to be associated with the police or the disagreeable task of tax collecting. Taxes have been levied only since 1927. In 1929 a number of natives were killed and wounded by the police and Frontier Force. Afterwards groups of natives led by the women had burned and destroyed European factories and government property. Since that time, taxes have been collected with difficulty and the people are eager to seize upon any rumor by which they might avoid this levy.

The area I've chosen to investigate is inhabited by approximately 6,000 people living compactly in clusters within a radius of 24 square miles. Transportation has been costly: travel to this place from Lagos by boat, train and lorry has cost over 10 pounds. The nearest European factory is six miles away (by foot), although I can get boys to bring in my supplies at sixpence per load. The country is too rough even for a bicycle, so I look forward to keeping fit by footwork.

Herskovits had written an introduction for Jack to take to the district officer, a Mr. G.I. Jones. Jack wrote to Doctor Herskovits to explain that after having met Jones, he found him to be not only a charming host but intelligently interested in Anthropology and was a former student of social sciences from Cambridge, England. He served as the British District Officer for Western Nigeria for several years. In his mid to late thirties, at 5'7", Jones was slender and moved with an air of authority, just short of a swagger. He wore the typical British pith helmet, Bermuda shorts and knee-length argyle stockings. A Leica camera hung from his neck and bounced against his chest as he walked to greet Jack.

Jones offered his home to Jack while Jack's home awaited construction. Jack took advantage of Jones's generosity, which included food, domestic help, and an ample supply of liquor.

Traveling with Jones to a number of villages where Jones held court in his capacity as district officer and designated judge, Jack got an introduction to Ibo life and some cultural variations. Jones thought the Ozuitem was a good village to start because it was small. Some of the elders gave permission for Jack to work there. They agreed to build his house for about thirty pounds, a reasonable cost for labor and materials. It would have a veranda for eating and working, a bedroom and behind that a kitchen. A separate building would be built for servants' quarters. The latrine, about fifteen yards from the main house, would consist of a small outhouse with one hole.

With Jones's recommendation, Jack hired an interpreter who learned English at a mission school and could speak it fairly well. Sometimes Jack would remonstrate with him when after a long spiel by an informant; the interpreter would relate in too few words what was said.

In the spirit of communal participation, Jack worked with the men on their farms; he took off his shirt and shorts and in a loin cloth with a towel around his neck cut the thick bush with a machete. On his first day on the field he was unprepared for the army of pinching ants that came in a column several feet wide and two hundred or more feet long and destroyed all organic matter in their path. When they got inside clothing they moved without detection until at a certain point, as if by a signal, they all started to bite at once with their pincers. When the ants bit him in the crotch, Jack threw his machete down, did a high-stepping dance, flailed his arms and pulled off his clothes, all the while he yelled obscenities to the amusement of the natives. After that, with every three strokes of the machete, he flicked the ants off with his towel in timed precision.

Following the completion of his house, constructed of bamboo and raffia, the palm branches used in an overlapping and interlocking pattern to make the roof rain- proof, Jack inspected and approved the project and prepared to make final payment to the chief. With his translator, he approached the large home of the patriarch who sat with crossed legs in his recreation room. Jack estimated the chief's age at sixty-five to seventy, but he appeared older with withered black skin clinging to boney parts like crinkled cellophane. Creases radiated around his thin lips and a mere four to five brown/black-eroded teeth projected from his lower gum. His current primary wife, tall and plump, stood behind him while several other wives stood on either side. They all smiled and welcomed Jack, a favored visitor, to chat and join the chief in pipe smoking. The ritual afforded time for further inquiries about tribal life.

The chief's pipe had a long stem and a large bowl. Jack offered him English tobacco, which he accepted after smelling and rubbing it between his thumb and forefinger. He filled his pipe with the moist tobacco and tamped it down with his long bony finger. He sucked on the stem, and then accepted a light from Jack's cigarette lighter.

Puffing forcefully until he was sure the tobacco burned well, the chief set the pipe aside and spoke as the interpreter translated. He spoke in measured phrases to give the translator time.

Peering into Jack's eyes, the chief said, "You are a young man and a good man. You work hard and show respect for our people." He paused. "But a problem arises—one of great importance."

Looking askance at the interpreter, then at the chief, Jack asked, "What is the problem?"

"The problem is, you are alone."

"Why is that a problem?"

"It is not healthy or normal for a young man to live in a house without a wife."

Jack smiled dismissively. "I'm fine living alone, and besides I *am* a married man. Unfortunately, my wife could not accompany me; she was not well when I left the States." *Truth is, she never could have survived this primitive life style for a whole year.*

The chief spoke deliberately. "Your marriage to one

woman in the States has nothing to do with your need for a woman here."

"Chief, with all due respect, in my country—our customs are different."

"Your customs do not prevail here. In order to live among us in harmony, you will accept a wife, one we have chosen. One who will see that you are properly fed and who will tend to all of your needs."

"But chief, really I can't..."

The chief arose. "It is settled. She is the young widow of a fallen hunter. A childless woman, strong and blessed by good spirits. She will comfort you and make your stay here fruitful."

Fruitful? What in the hell does that mean?

"We have arranged for you to meet her and her family and the wedding will be planned soon."

The chief left the room. The women who remained approached Jack and his interpreter. They all spoke at once, giggled and made little dance steps.

Jack burdened by this latest complication, a contravention to his customs and morality, sought advice from G.I. Jones.

"I've never been placed in that position, Yank. I think your Judeo-Christian concepts of decency and transgressions must be put aside here for purposes of your research. If you were a Mormon or Muslim you would have no constraints about polygamy."

A mother approached tugging her reluctant daughter who appeared to be about seventeen years of age. She was slender and tall at about 5' 6". Her head was bowed; her cocoa-colored unblemished skin was tinted: her eyebrows darkened with wood ash and her lips reddened with vegetable coloring. She raised her head and smiled. When ordered by her mother to reveal her teeth she smiled broadly and displayed pearly, perfectly aligned teeth. Her outer garment, a strapless sack with horizontal rings of vivid colors, revealed prominent conical breasts. Her lower legs and feet were bare but unscarred, a rare condition among adults who were constantly exposed to thorns, razor-sharp leaf edges and machete swipes. She wore wristlets, earrings, necklaces and rolls of *jigida* (beads) around her waist. Like most barefoot natives her feet were broad.

Introduced as Jack's bride-to-be, *Adachi*, lowered her head again to show submission. Jack remained uncomfortable. An inchoate state of polygamy was not to his liking but could not be rejected without causing a breach in the tribal social framework and a rebuff to the chief's authority. If he chose not to participate in the folkways and mores, he might be considered an outsider, a leper banished from the family he wished to enter.

The chief advised Jack that marriage is not an accommodation to sexual fulfillment but an obligation to beget children. The woman's position in the family remains highly unpredictable until she gives birth to a child, particularly a male child.

Any postponement of the wedding ceremony would not be tolerated except for the intervention of pestilence, fire or deluge. The whole village, but particularly the women, was in joyous anticipation of the glorious occasion. They prepared foods and decorations in a bustling activity accompanied by humming and singing. Festive clothing was assembled and gold and silver trinkets were polished with fine pumice.

Chapter 19

On the wedding day, Jack was introduced to Adachi's sister and brother as well as several aunts and uncles. Her parents, handsome people, were dressed in freshly washed clothes reserved for special occasions. The men wore skirt-like garments and the women plain sack-like dresses with shoulder straps.

Two tables were laden with a variety of foods: yams, kolanuts, plantains, roasted ears of corn and barbequed goat and lamb.

Women guests sat on the ground with small straw mats while the men sat on animal skins. Jack, his bride and her parents sat on hand-carved wooden stools, and they balanced woven plates on their laps. They used their fingers for feeding. Weddings such as this were happy occasions; they provided a legitimate reason for feasting on animal protein, a rare commodity in this community.

A leg of lamb or goat, the prized morsel of meat, was served to Jack as the person of honor and then to his bride. The bride's parents watched Jack to see if he approved of the food, then the singing and swaying among the wedding party started as all moved to the rhythm and beat of the drums. Following the meal, the area was cleared for dancing. Men and women danced separately and Jack participated in the dance characterized by stomping and arms extended outward and bent upward at the elbows. For one dance step the men placed their arms on the shoulders of the one next to them and formed a large circle. They moved in one direction and then reversed that. All the while they sang in a low chant.

A fermented drink in a bowl was passed around to the men and the dancing pace accelerated to the point of frenzy as the beat of the drums increased.

With an intermission in the dance, the interpreter was signaled by the bride's father to have him bring Jack to his side. This was in essence a father-to-son message affirming the importance of the marriage commitment. Without hesitation the father explained to Jack the importance of the male-female union: a childless woman after a year of marriage is regarded as a freak, not truly a wife but rather a wife in anticipation. She is subject to ridicule as one who has not fulfilled her responsibilities. When she bears a child she meets her obligation to the community and is accorded the status of a true woman, not one who merely appears as one. The message, which Jack had heard three times before, acted like a vacuum sucking out the revelry of the party.

Jack was admonished that his obligation for having this fine tall woman as a wife was to aid in producing a child. Listening to this, Jack felt a revulsion, a betrayal to his principles based on his upbringing in a monogamous society. He had rationalized his role in this venture but made the chief, the bride, and her family aware of his prior marriage and the limited time he intended to remain in Africa. His explanations were received without reproach, concern or question.

The chief, by way of assurance, mentioned that he had five wives that served him well. Of course, he was obligated to care for all their needs: food, clothing and beds. Divorce or separation was not complicated nor did it result in social upheaval. The community had known that when Jack departed, no angst would surface; he was to leave his house and furnishings to his wife, and if she were with child, his duty for the care and development of the offspring was left to his conscience and honor. A number of itinerant business men who made yearly trips to this region left sums of money with women who had borne their children. Jack vowed that at the end of the year he would have no such obligation.

When the nuptials ceased at sunrise Jack and his bride retired to Jack's home. The mosquito netting around his bed had been decorated with leaves and petals, and a fertility goddess with a bloated abdomen and a sizeable hole in the entry of the reproductive canal had been placed on the nightstand.

Jack joined his new relatives and neighbors in farming chores, in social gatherings and with his interpreter joined discussion groups necessary for research data. He in turn was asked about his own country, its people, the government, social prohibitions and customs.

He answered all questions respectfully and in terms that did not confuse or demean. Because of his supply of medications including the newly available sulfa drugs, he was asked to treat sicknesses and injuries. He was not completely comfortable doing this since a medicine man with salves, herbal nostrums and incantations was a member of the community and had been treating the natives for a number of years. Many tribesmen knew Jack's medicine was more effective; he could lance a boil and dress a wound like a real doctor.

One day while working with a machete in the field with his neighbors that included women, Jack stopped to listen to the sound of distant humming, a buzzing like an approaching convoy of lorries. The men and women listened momentarily then ran screaming to their huts. Jack bewildered by the activity watched as the workers emerged almost immediately with brooms and palm fronds. An ominous dark cloud, miles wide and long descended with a crescendo of droning and blanketed the area. It was an invasion of locusts of biblical proportions that blocked out the sun. Both men and women swung their brooms and palm fronds with remarkable force and skill. The locusts perhaps discouraged by the rebellious activity stayed but minutes and moved on as rapidly as they had approached.

Sacks of cloth were used to collect the dead locusts that provide protein for several meals. When the locusts were fried in palm oil they became crunchy and tasty like French fries if one kept his eyes shut while eating.

When an epidemic gripped the community, Jack was expected to serve as a doctor, not to supersede the village's medicine man, but rather to supplement his efforts. Still many villagers viewed Jack's healing powers suspiciously.

A virulent strain of staphylococcus caused high fever, nausea and pustular skin lesions. The chief prevailed upon Jack to treat the victims. Although reluctant to assume medical responsibilities, Jack could not refuse. He stressed the importance for all members of the community to wash their hands before eating and after defecating when leaves or dried grass was used to remove fecal material from the rectum. Jack's limited supply of poor quality toilet paper meant for his use alone could not be distributed.

While the rampant siege infected over half the village, Jack, Adachi and the interpreter worked over twelve or more hours a day with no rest and little food. With three days of constant care to the natives, Jack succumbed to the virulent infection with the onset of fever, nausea and dizziness. Multiple skin lesions with rodent-like burrowing characteristics erupted on his face, chest and abdomen. He fell into bed exhausted, with a burning temperature and delirium.

The chief learning of Jack's condition dispatched a runner to fetch the only British trained medical doctor who was in permanent attendance at a leper colony eight miles away in bush country. An Evangelical missionary, the doctor nearing retirement age, trudged with his medical bag behind the runner. "You go on, Bucko. I'll be there in two hours or so if these old sticks hold up."

Dr. Guillaume Miller a tidy 5'6" Scotsman wore a pith helmet, khaki shorts, a long sleeved shirt, calf-length socks and thick-soled hiking boots, stopped at the entry way and leaned against the door jamb. He removed the helmet, wiped his sweatband with a handkerchief and blew out a weary sigh. "Where's the patient?" he asked Adachi in clear Ibo dialect. She led him to Jack's bed, lifted the mosquito netting and fanned Jack's face distorted by lesions. Dr. Miller grimaced when he looked at Jack. "Lad, you've got the scabrous marks on your face like a rotting piece of carrion. You won't look any better when I'm through with you, but you might start to heal." He asked Adachi to undress Jack and prepare boiled water. He studied the multiple lesions on the head and chest, then shook his head. His eyes focused on the groin, and he raised the penis and scrotum. "Good. No bubos."

Bending over to speak into Jack's ear, he said, "How in the name of all that's holy, did you manage to muck up your face with all that corruption?" Jack opened his eyes but said nothing and appeared confused. "No man walking the face of this God-forsaken land, trying to do some good, should suffer like this. No sir. Now let's have the lady here bring us the boiled water so I can wash around these pustular lesions before I lance them."

Dr. Miller slipped on rubber gloves then reached for a syringe with Novocain. He hummed an unidentifiable tune and interspersed it with comments in an effort to distract Jack's anticipation of pain. "This bit of Novocain will deaden the pain and allow me to drain the cesspools of pus, yes sir. Did you know Dr. Sigmund Freud was responsible for the development of this wonderful anesthetic agent?"

Before Jack could reply, Dr. Miller had given the first

injection near a large lesion on the left chin. Jack's head reared back. "Jesus Christ!"

"Glad to hear your response, Lad, but you mustn't take the Lord's name in vain."

"I'm not! I'm hoping he'll help me here."

"Heh, heh, heh, your sense of humor rises like the sweetness of lilacs from the depths of offal and corruption."

The first incision into the boil-like lesion was made, and Jack felt no pain, but he did feel the liquid contents run down his chin to his neck. Dr. Miller sponged the area. "That damnable bugger won't give you anymore fits." He summoned Adachi to hold a sterile cloth against the incised boil while he examined and prepared to treat more infected areas.

After forty-five minutes of treatment both the patient and doctor were sweating profusely despite the constant fanning efforts of Adachi and the interpreter. Jack still in a weakened condition wore cloth bandages that encircled his face from his chin to the top of his head and from his forehead to the back of his head. The doctor advised him to remain in bed for a week, but Jack challenged the advice and attempted to stand. He shook, waddled, then fell backward onto the bed. "Damn, you were right Doc, I'm dropping anchor right now. What do I owe you for your trouble?"

"Not a bloody farthing, Lad. The church and the government reimburse me just fine." He whispered into Jack's ear, "The government robs these poor souls; the least they can do is pay for the supplies and services of those who help these poor exploited devils." He was cleaning his instruments: a bistoury, scissors and syringe when Jack had the interpreter bring a bottle of Bushmill's Irish whiskey, a rare commodity in this area, hidden in a storage bin.

"Bless you, my Son. I don't ordinarily imbibe, but I do find this good for medicinal purposes, you know arthritis and an occasional cough. Unfortunately or fortunately, the medicinal purposes are coming around more frequently."

He laughed as he nestled the bottle into his medical bag and pulled out a bottle marked, *Sulfanilamide*. "Here's some medicine that will help cure those nasty buggers. One day we'll have a cure for those poor deformed creatures I treat at the leper colony. Yessir, there'll be medicine for every ailment of humankind except for man's crazy obsession to cheat, beat, kill and fornicate with his neighbor."

"Doc, you obviously don't consider yourself a part of the parliamentary establishment."

"Lad, you can close your eyes to unspeakable offenses and live the good life, or you can speak your mind and be tossed on a dung heap. I've told the bloody magistrate what I think of John Bull's treatment of these Darkies. For my unsolicited opinion, I've been cast into a leper colony. But I thank the Lord every day that I'm allowed to bring some wee measure of succor to these poor souls—these children all but forgotten by the Almighty.

When you leave this place, Lad, don't forget these poor devils who have been robbed, flogged and cheated of their freedom to evil masters."

Late winter 1939

Dear Mel:

I've been moseying around in a Vauxhall sedan borrowed from the District Officer, Jones, and I explored the clans around here. At only a distance of twelve to fifteen miles, the clans showed startling differences. For instance, a clubhouse in one of the villages strictly forbids women and is enclosed by a tall fence that women cannot cross. In contrast, another village welcomed women, and I saw them chatting with the men. When I asked the chief in my compound why this was so, he gave me a simple answer: different villages have different customs—that's all. Behind all this, these clans were even more isolated before World War One when there were practically no roads to accommodate lorries.

I was under the impression that most of the clans were patriarchal in structure and was surprised to find that one of the villages had a matrilineal organization. It will be interesting to learn how these differences are resolved in any social exchange between the village members.

The Vauxhall carried me over areas of tremendous topographical diversity. I drove over a hundred miles to the town of Onitsha in western Iboland in order to establish my letter of credit in a bank that the Social Sciences Research Committee had arranged for me. I stayed overnight and took an entire day each way with stops wherever I was inclined. There were striking changes in the land from that of deep verdant valleys and rolling country of eastern Iboland to that of monotonous, brown flatland in the west as I neared the Niger.

My own compound of four structures consists of my own house, that of my boys', the cooks house and a small cluster of outhouses. A corps of women comes by monthly to rub the mud walls and freshen the paint decorations along the veranda.

My boys are laying out a garden while my cook has built a chicken coop for the fowl we keep. With the neighbor's goats wandering through my compound I feel quite domesticated. My cook deserves every bit of the thirty shillings I pay him. He was outraged when some Ozuitem people asked nine pence for a chicken that could be bought for eight pence in Bende. He has therefore arranged to have one of his hangers-on walk the better part of the day to Bende to take advantage of the enormous savings in the market place.

I found a water source and hired a boy to fetch it at ten bob a month which is the government wage for ordinary labor a grown man would be pleased to work for. In contrast to the government scale of four pence a day, the natives themselves pay tuppence a day for men to work on their farms (although they also supply two meals). Though

I pay only four servants, they have brought with them their wives, relatives, their own servants and sundry hangers-on so that my compound boasts of a shifting population of ten to fifteen persons.

Previously I mentioned the invasion of millions of locusts and how for several minutes they droned over our heads and were the object of constant beating to provide a much-needed source of protein. The desire for any kind of meat is desperate. I inquired about beef and was told that it is exceedingly expensive because the cattle must be driven down here from the north and the tse tse forbids their staying long in this area. An occasional leopard is killed by a hunter (sometimes visa versa) and then there is great rejoicing, but for the most part meat must come from fowl and domestic goats and sheep, but rodents such as bats and rats are other sources of protein.

There was cause for celebration in the village when a motorcar arrived and had managed to negotiate a road over which only a Nigerian lorry driver would have attempted to drive. It was a phenomenon for the Ozouitem, for it meant that centuries of isolation from some areas had at last been broken, and the villagers envisioned it as a highway to markets, a road leading to prosperity.

One village was mainly responsible for construction of the road; its young men rushed through the clan market place waving their shovels, machetes and firing their old daneguns, and a number of them danced the abu agha, the traditional dance of the victor in battle, for it was their victory. They had built the road over which the first lorry had passed—the same dance they had performed when they had vanquished the fierce Abam warriors almost a generation ago. The women danced and made up their own lyrics saying in effect that the motor has come at last. Much palm wine was drunk, a goat was sacrificially killed, and the dancing continued until sunset.

CHAPTER 20

Spring 1939 (notation from daily log)

The work is exhausting but the people are delightfully friendly and helpful. At the end of the day I have little trouble falling asleep after I block out the scratching, scraping and squeaking sounds of rats scurrying in the roof and the croaking of the toads jumping around my floor.

Large critters are of even greater concern. Quite frankly, most animals don't bother me, but I must admit to some antipathy toward snakes. There was a rumor of a large snake slithering around the men's communal latrine. Last week one of the boys seated in the latrine spotted a ten-foot boa constrictor as it wriggled toward him. The boy stuck his foot near its mouth. The snake inched forward, opened its mouth and proceeded up the boy's leg to his knee at which point the boy used his knife to slice the snake from its mouth downward as far as he could reach. When the snake finished writhing, the boy summoned help and he and his friend slung the snake over their shoulders and brought it home where it was later eaten by a grateful family.

Jack had recovered sufficiently from his massive staph infections to confer with the tribal elders but had not regained enough strength to work in the fields. He enlisted the help of five families in a patrilineal line to report on various aspects of their daily routines. They answered most of his questions but circumvented some, which might have exposed embarrassing situations. The following points were pursued:

Markets An analysis of the weekly market place was recorded as to what was sold, bought, prices paid, where vendors came from, which Ozuitem women attended, the incidence of haggling and boycotting and when prices were too high.

Money In the past there existed bartering capability with native salt, several varieties of yams, and women's own crops. English coins supplanted metal bars but cowries (mollusk shells) used for generations are still in use.

Feasts and Ceremonies were a large part of the life of the Ozuitem and each entailed gift giving. The host considered himself unfortunate if he did not receive in gifts as much as he had spent in preparing the feast.

Annual Income and Expenditures This was not done easily since various methods of acquisition are used. Women's income and expenses were a delicate matter to unravel and one of the areas of greater secrecy.

Food It should be pointed out that relatively few yams were eaten considering their bartering importance among the crops. Much work was lavished on them because of their importance in ceremonies and feasts. Few are eaten in comparison with coco yams and cassava.

The investigation stressed an important point: the respective roles of husband and wife in feeding each other and their families. The husband feeds his wife (or wives) and children only from the digging of the new yams until the clearing of the bush for the new crop—a period of roughly four months. The wife's burden is to feed her husband and family for the rest of the year on other foods she gathers from her garden or purchases in the market place. The woman's failure to feed her family can lead to a marital breakup.

Labor Studies include not only the actual number of hours that each member of these five families devote to farm work, trading, work at home, etc., but it also includes material on the organization for work: village groups, extended family groups, secret and non-secret societies, age grades, hired laborers, itinerant workers, wages, etc.

Farming and Land Tenure Recorded are the types of soils, land rotation, and crops each grow best—a fact intimately linked with the rental of land. The women here grow twenty-one crops on their farms, three crops at home and they gather nine kinds of food plants in the bush. Men, on the other hand, plant only one crop exclusively—yams but as matter a fact, nothing is exclusively planted; some women plant yams, and some men to insure their own food supply in the event of a quarrel with their wives, maintain "Women's farms." These are called, "Farm of man who has no mother," since a man usually relies upon his mother to feed him when he quarrels with his wife. In addition, men can plant nine crops near home and another two crops in the bush. Then there are twelve crops, which both men and women can plant and harvest on the farm and at home and which either may gather in the bush.

I've also traced out the system of land tenure (and this was a hellish job); also the rent, pledge and sale of land as well as minor forms of tenure. Some men owned individual plots of land and this may have been true only for certain areas of the Ibo country. Don't allow anyone to label this a primitive society. The bookkeeping of transactions can be quite complicated.

If I feel the need of a holiday, I'll walk into Bende and stay with G.I. Jones for a few days; listen to the gramophone and swim in his inflatable swimming pool, then I'll try to round out the material I've written above. Should I accomplish a reasonable amount of work, I'll reward myself with a snifter or two of Jones's Scotch and allow him to tell me of his triumphs meting out justice among competing native factions. When he becomes long-winded, we can kill a bottle easily.

Letter to M.J.H. dated September 1939

There have been certain repercussions here due to the war in Europe. Troops of the native Frontier Force have been shipped out to defend the Cameroons. Lagos, Calabar and other important coastal towns have been rushed through air raid precautionary measures. All the Germans in the Colony have been interned. The Govt. issued an order forbidding food hoarding, so immediately the native traders bought all available supplies of stock-fish, rice and salt which sent the prices to profiteering. The canning factories are now rationing food provisions to Europeans at higher prices. It's devil's own job to get lard, and I'm now on my last tin of flour. Neither affects me very much since I've used palm oil before which makes an effective though stinking shortening.

The reaction of the natives in Ozuitem to the war is one of impatience with the Whites. Whites had stopped the natives from headhunting and conducting wars and now the Whites, the blasted hypocrites, are having a grand war of their own. Nor can the natives understand why Great Britain allowed Germany to rearm after being beaten in the last war. What seems to concern them most, however, is whether the price of palm oil will again rise as it did after the last war, so that they may again enjoy prosperity.

The church people here are saying that Cineke (God) is on the side of the right and the just, and therefore the British will soon win this war. Reactions, you see, not very different from those of the so-called civilized nations.

Suicide here is a recognized way of getting out of difficulties. It is an old tradition. Slaves used to hang themselves after murdering or beating their masters to escape harsh punishment for these crimes. Murderers are given recourse to suicide. My records show the occurrence for suicide is related to incurable illnesses, frustrated love, incest and other intolerable situations. Suicide is so uppermost in thought that I find it occurs as a line in at least one popular song: "If my mother's lover continues to mistreat me, I will hang myself." Of course, this is a violent society. There are few natural deaths; most are the result of sorcery, wrath of the ancestors or deities or through some infectious agency. The incidence of murder is about as high as that of suicide while that for rape is probably higher although my list of cases is small because of the reticence of women to publicly announce what has happened. Wife beating as well as husband beating is common, as is divorce.

A Bende official visited with me last week and brought his portable gramophone and a selection of jazz records, both "hot" and "sweet". Unfortunately, he brought no classical music, but to the jazz the natives responded favorably, they liked it. On my invitation a woman of about forty, an acknowledged good dancer, danced in perfect time to two widely different tempos—"Caravan" (slow) and "Hot & Bothered" (fast) with feet, shoulder, head and facial movements that would be recognized at the Savoy in Harlem. Next, I asked another good dancer, a man of about twenty-five, and I also put on two contrasting records. Again, perfect time. One step was almost a "buck and wing", and at one stage there were the jerking movements of the head known in Harlem as "peckin'."

The following day I asked various people about the white man's music. They all liked it but asked what it meant. There is no Ozuitem music played merely as music; all music has words and meaning. They couldn't grasp the concept of music without words even though their own lyrics were not always appropriate to the occasion.

The war now makes my return uncertain. I assume

that it will be impossible to return by way of Europe. That means I will have to rely upon the non-passenger cargo boats from the States, which come every two months from either the Gulf or Boston. Such a sailing will mean a return either earlier or later than I expected.

Incidentally, I'm getting damned tired of chicken twice a day, every day for the past 280 days. Now that I've gotten over my fever attacks, I'm plagued with a bloody case of diarrhea.

CHAPTER 21

Jack sat on his veranda, typed notes, swatted the occasional insect and sipped Scotch and water. One of his new native aunties with several of her village friends stopped by, ostensibly to chat. The occasion was unusual since these people, although friendly, rarely initiated conversation. Jack and his interpreter usually engaged them in conversation for the purpose of collecting data. She apologized for disturbing him but insisted that they talk. Jack made sure his interpreter listened carefully as she spoke rapidly to him.

Jack looked at the interpreter. "What was that all about?"

"She is telling you that your status would be greatly enhanced if you could demonstrate your prowess as a fearless hunter."

Jack's expression turned anxious. "Hunting what? The only hunting I've ever done was shooting rabbits and squirrels with a borrowed air gun, and I wasn't very good at it."

The interpreter laughed. "This lady is talking about big-time game—killing a leopard." Jack's eyes widened. "Doing that would reward you with membership into the prestigious Leopard Society."

The thought of hunting big game filled Jack with loathing and his reaction was apparent.

His auntie, noting his expression, held out her hand and waved it from side to side, a signal telling him not to be concerned. If killing a leopard was not to his liking, she said he could prove himself in another way.

Jack looked at the interpreter for further explanation. He explained to Jack that if he did not care to kill a leopard—he could kill a man.

"What the hell does that mean?"

The interpreter said that a man guilty of an unforgivable crime, who was held prisoner, had the choice of committing suicide or facing death by community action. If he chose community action, Jack would be his executioner: the shooter. Jack didn't care for that choice and without hesitation agreed to kill a leopard. The ladies nodded their approval. Jack looked at his interpreter and peppered him with questions: How, when and where? Jack turned to his auntie for further explanation. She assured him that the chief and his hunters would contact him and explain everything.

After the women left, Jack looked at his interpreter in frustration. He too assured him. "Don't worry, these people look upon you as a family member, a nephew and a good person. They will not allow the leopard to maul you to death or eat you."

On the day of the big shoot, the villagers were abuzz with excitement. Adults and children gathered in the square and stared at Jack and the hunting party. The children held sticks like rifles on their shoulders and marched about with exaggerated steps. Three out of the six hunters accompanying Jack carried 30 aught 6 Remington rifles. The party trekked into the bush for about two miles. With high humidity, the bush was steamy. Jack wore a pith helmet, dark glasses and binoculars that dangled from his neck. His rifle was carried by one of the men. Perspiration created wide moist areas under his armpits and dampened his shirt. The hunters guided him around obstacles and critters he did not see or hear. They would crouch suddenly and become still, warning Jack to do the same. Their eyes searched, their ears listened and their noses sniffed.

The party walked stealthily, the lead man stopped at a point about fifty yards ahead of them. Using sign and body language, he signaled Jack to prepare to shoot. An adult leopard lay high on a tree branch almost obscured by leaves and shadows. A hunter at Jack's side checked the chamber of his rifle, then handed it to him. They walked slowly until the animal was clearly visible in Jack's scope. Given the nod to shoot, Jack pulled the trigger slowly and steadily as he had been taught. The recoil almost knocked him over, and the blast caused momentary deafness. A second rifle discharged almost immediately. The animal jerked then fell to the ground. One of the hunters with a rifle approached the fallen leopard cautiously to verify its death.

The animal's front and hind legs were bound then tied to a pole and carried out of the bush back to the village. Amid shouting, clapping and a burst of spontaneous dancing, the villagers welcomed the hunting party. Adults and children ran close to the suspended leopard, pointed at it and cheered. The children crowded around Jack; some held onto his legs as though his body could confer magical powers upon them. That constituted Jack's initiation into the Leopard Society with all its privileges and secrets. The greatest good from that venture, Jack thought, came from the animal protein provided for the patrilineal group.

CHAPTER 22

G.I. Jones's tired Model A Ford pickup stopped in front of the chief's house. Jones reached into the bed of the truck and hauled out a bolt of linen and two tins of tobacco. The real reason for his visit to the chief was to discuss labor problems among tribesmen who were objecting to the long hours of work in the British owned palm oil canning factory. After his meeting, Jones walked a hundred and fifty yards to Jack's compound.

He knocked on the doorframe and was greeted by Adachi who exchanged greetings in her Ibo dialect. She invited Jones in, then led him to Jack's den where he had been typing notes.

In his clipped British accent, Jones said, "Well, how's the intrepid Yank getting along with the Crown's loyal subjects?" Jones looked around, put his hands to his throat and said, "I'm absolutely parched. There's not a drop of bloody moisture between my lips and my gullet. How about fetching a bottle of Bushmill's and we'll toast to that molly-coddled old bugger, the Prince of Wales and his skinny harlot, Mrs. Wally Simpson. After that, we'll toast Mr. Roosevelt and his lady friends." He shook his head. "Now, there's an ensemble of corkers who won't allow world affairs to get in the way of their fornicating."

They clicked glasses, then Jones sat heavily in a chair. He sipped the whisky then smacked his tongue against his pallet. "Aah-h, if there's one thing the Irish do well, it's making whiskey—that and making trouble for the Crown. The bloody bastards wouldn't survive if we didn't support them. By God, we're keeping half the world afloat with our sterling.

Jack threw Jones a quizzical look. "You really believe your government is the great benefactor to all the people it has subjugated?"

"Well I think we've done a damn good job. Surely, you observed that we, that is the Crown, brought worthwhile change to a completely primitive and socially undeveloped people."

Jack turned a critical eye toward Jones. "I'm not at all sure I agree with you."

"Come off it, Old Boy. You have only to look at their civil court system, the commercial banking network and the means for marketing their resources. You can't be blind to all of that. We'll be making more changes. All we need is a few more tax dollars and more time to get the work done."

"Jones, your country men have had over four hundred years to make changes. Frankly, I think they've taken much more than they've given."

"Yank, are you suggesting we've been exploiting these poor devils?" With tongue in cheek he glanced sideways at Jack. "You're right on both accounts, but we can live through all your criticisms providing you don't tell the rest of the world what bloody bastards we are. We British guard our resources quite closely, thank you. Furthermore, I believe you Americans are envious of our colonial empire. Too bad your government couldn't participate in the division of this Great Dark Continent. It was here for the taking."

"We have our own sordid record on how we appropriated and enslaved these people."

Smiling wryly, Jones said, "That social consciousness of yours is admirable, Old Boy, but if you flaunt it, some vipers will attack and swallow you whole. Your battle cry for freedom, liberty and equality for all people will remain a mockery." Jones pleased with his assertions continued, "Seventy-five years ago your well-meaning President Lincoln was assassinated for seeking freedom for your Africans. Heaven forbid you should meet such a fate. If you find yourself being verbally attacked, remember the advice you got from this lowly district officer."

"Thanks for the warning. I'm hopeful that the world has changed sufficiently so that..."

Jones interrupted. "Only your youth and optimism can make you think the way you do. Men with small minds and covetous motives will try to sway you—and make no mistake; they're out there, constantly. They present themselves as righteous, God-fearing people preaching the virtuous life." Jones had become more serious; the lines around his mouth drew downward. "Some may be sincere in their confused thinking, but most are scoundrels bilking the uneducated with solicitations for donations or votes and always appealing to the primitive instincts of fear and vengeance."

Jack pondered Jones's pessimism. "You're not suggesting that most politicians are self-serving?"

"Yank, that's exactly what I mean."

"Then you'll agree that the Ibo have legitimate complaints about their tax payments—payments that do not benefit them, at least, not directly. They're not favorably disposed to the notion that their taxes pay for the upkeep of the colonial government. They complain the government does bloody little for them. They see the police and courts as oppressive agencies that are miserably corrupt and do little to provide law and order. When they are told that their taxes pay for paving the streets in distant cities like Bende while their own roads remain rutted and beaten-up—well, that makes no sense to them, not at all." Jack's comments were not immediately rebutted.

"I can assure you, Yank, if you tell the world what

bloody bastards we British are, you will have only a few allies, the Blacks and Commies will agree with you, of course, but the rest of the colonial world will do everything to deny what you say. They'll do anything short of killing you. Come to think of it, I can't be sure they won't." Jones laughed. "Sorry, that's a bad joke, but they won't let you go unscathed. First, they'll emasculate you, then hang you out for the buzzards in the newspapers and radio to pick your carcass clean." He pointed his glass at Jack for emphasis. "Be careful how you tread, Yank."

"Jones, my observations on these people will probably appear in some obscure anthropology journal that holds little interest to the world at large."

Jones nodded. "Listen, Yank, I've read some of your preliminary findings, and in spite of what I said about few caring what you say, you've written enough to indict the British Foreign Office for its exploitation of the Ibo. It's enough that we and the natives have a precarious relationship; we don't need any more uprisings like that last one in 1929 when the women burned our factories and refused to pay taxes. We couldn't imprison the bloody lot of them."

"Seems to me the solution would be to treat them honestly and stop regarding them as children or lesser beings. Stop forcing them to do labor for shamefully little remuneration."

Jones assumed a patronizing air and shook his finger at Jack. "That's precisely what I mean, Yank. You don't seem to have the foggiest notion of the work we've done to maintain this fragile relationship, one we've cultivated..."

"You've had five hundred years to cultivate your relationship—a failed relationship, I might add."

Jones cut him off. "Now wait a minute, Yank..."

Jack interrupted. "Would you like to conduct a little test?" Before Jones could answer, Jack said, "Let's go out on the village square and ask your grateful subjects if they enjoy being governed by the Crown."

Both men hesitated a moment, then laughed. "Yank, you've got me there. That's a wager I'm bound to lose."

"One day Jones, this magnificent empire of yours is going to collapse; everyone of your colonies is going to revolt including that Jewel in the Crown—India."

Jones shook his head. "No, no, Yank. That'll never happen. They all need us too much. Even *you* depend on that munificent stipend my government gives you for doing your research. Don't you?" Jones threw his head back and gulped the last of the whiskey then set the glass down. He covered his glass when Jack offered more. "No, dear boy, "I'll be too smashed to negotiate that goat path they call a road. It's bad enough when I'm sober." He glanced at the paper in the typewriter. "You've been here over a year, that's longer than you intended to stay. Who's picking up the tab for your extended vacation?"

"The Carnegie Institute."

"There you have it, another former British subject, although a Scot, is responsible for your subsistence."

Jack smiled. "But he's a U.S. citizen who made his money in the good old US of A."

Jones shook Jack's hand. "I always enjoy talking with you even though we don't agree on all political matters. Let me know when you're ready to leave this Garden of Eden. I'll drive you to the harbor in that faithful old Ford produced by another American capitalist."

Jack smiled. "I'd appreciate that, and may the gods provide you with an unlimited supply of good old Irish whiskey."

"Amen."

CHAPTER 23

Jack crammed his belongings, a typewriter, notebooks, texts and clothing into two battered suitcases and two empty wooden whiskey crates. He addressed and glued labels on two sides of each crate. His houseboy hauled them out and placed them in the bed of G.I. Jones's pickup. Jones shoved some boxes aside to make room for Jack's things, then flung a canvas tarp over them and secured the tarp with rope to both sides of the truck.

Jack embraced Adachi who wiped tears from her cheeks with the back of her hand. Standing beside her, both the interpreter and the houseboy appearing melancholy took turns shaking Jack's hand. Speaking in his native tongue, the interpreter translated his message afterward. "Goodbye, good master. May you live many years with good spirits to guide and protect you."

Villagers gathered to watch. Young children hiding behind their mothers' dresses peeked around them to watch the sorrowful farewells.

"Well, Yank, take a good look about you. You may never see the likes of this God-forsaken place again," Jones said.

"I don't know if this is God's forsaken place, but it could be if your government continues to exploit these poor souls. These people are kind, intelligent, tolerant..."

Jones waved his hand dismissively. "That's about all the preaching I can take from your bleeding heart, Yank. Now get in and let's get on our bloody way."

Jack sat in the dusty, mud-spattered pick-up that showed wear beyond its years. The smell of gasoline permeated the cab. "Jesus, did you pour gasoline around here? Aren't you afraid this thing will blow up?"

"No, Yank, you're sitting behind a slightly leaky petrol tank. Just don't light up."

Jack surveyed the cab with dismay. A part of the torn headliner hung down reaching the top of his head. He rolled up the window half way to allow air to circulate but not enough to fill the cab with road dust. The narrow road, constructed of composite materials, gaped with cracks and depressions causing bone-jarring shaking. The engine noise made conversation difficult. Adding to Jack's discomfort, a broken seat spring kept jabbing him, causing him to sit forward and brace himself against the dashboard.

Jones avoided the larger craters that might have caused an axle to break. The speedometer did not register, and the horn button was gone, but Jones had mounted a Klaxon horn on the cowl to warn away animals or natives. The passenger floor mat was worn away and one of the missing floorboards allowed Jack to see the road they were passing over.

Jones sensed Jack's insecurity. "Yank, don't worry about this little four-banger getting us there. It's a reliable cuss. I put in a liter or two of oil every month, fill 'er up with petrol and water and she turns over every time—not like the fussy V-8s. If the radiator doesn't boil over and the carburetor doesn't get mucked-up, we'll be all right. Of course, if we get a sudden downpour and this road turns into a wash, we could be bloody-well marooned."

"Any chance of a big cat calling on us if we get stalled?" Jack's question begged a reassuring response.

Jones laughed. "No, not at all. Those cats will have nothing to do with this tin monster. Besides, they want shelter from the downpour, too."

"But if they're hungry?"

Jones pointed to the back window. "There's a

sawed-off-Winchester on the window ledge that'll take out a rhino or elephant. But if you mean only to scare them, there's an air rifle for shooting them in the arse. The choice is yours."

The ride continued slowly as the roads showed no signs of improvement. They headed toward Bende on the way to Lagos where Jack expected to board a ship for the States. He thought about the past year and his travails but also the pleasant experiences with the Ibo. His study focused on the economic problems of sixteen individuals. The thesis would propose the importance of economy as the major factor in determining the organization and acculturation of the people. Previous studies emphasized culture as the determinant in daily living activities.

The vehicle lurched as it struck a large pothole. Jones grabbed the steering wheel as the pickup veered to one side. "Goddamned sorry roads," he said. "All right, I'll admit, we haven't looked after the roads as well as we might have, but we're getting around to that. A few more tax dollars will do it."

That's their mantra—increase taxes, increase taxes, increase taxes.

Jack held onto the instrument panel to maintain his balance as the vehicle careened from side to side and jolted up and down. He watched Jones who studied the road to avoid the larger ruts and deeper holes. Jack's voice took on a staccato quality as the vehicle bounced along the washboard surface.

The radiator hissed when the vehicle stopped at the wharf. Jones removed the tarp; he and Jack pulled the luggage off as porters eager for tips picked them up and carried them onto the cargo ship. Jack shook Jones's hand and thanked him for his many courtesies over the past year.

Placing his hand on Jack's shoulder, Jones said,

"Remember Yank, some bastards, probably my own bloody British colleagues, will try to debunk your findings and chew out your naive arse. If you stick to your convictions, you could lose more than you might hope to gain. I, for one, don't play the role of crusader or reformer. I do what I think is expected of me—no more, no less. That way no one gets hurt too badly. Do I make myself clear?"

"Jones, we differ. I see the world with its blemishes, the pock-marks of injustice, the raw welts on the backs of slaves..."

Jones interrupted, shaking his head. "C'mon, man, stop your bloody preaching. I've heard it all before." He turned his back to Jack and remained quiet for a moment, then turned back. "Forgive me Yank, I know deep down you're absolutely right. Go ahead; let the world know that changes must be made and that these creatures are entitled to a better life. Do what you will, but be warned again: you'll face powerful enemies who'll want no part of your world and will fight you."

Jack smiled. "I'll remember that, old friend."

CHAPTER 24

1939 Return From Africa

Jack emerged from the Yellow Cab at 42nd Street and Park Avenue in front of the massive gray edifice, the New York Grand Terminal. He yanked out his suitcases with their colorful ocean liner badges placed to conceal scratches and tears. Although he had been in this terminal before and knew it by its old name, Grand Central Station, he remained in awe of its size and elegance: the wide expanse of its marble hall, the magnificent curved stairways and the giant brass clock. Through the high arch windows, the sunrays cast oval areas of glistening light on the polished floor.

The crowds and sounds contrasted with his recent memories of the African colony. All that seemed like a dream, a fantasy that filled his head and heart with a fondness as he recalled the friendship of generous and courteous natives who accepted him as a son. He would miss the lush and verdant valleys and the magnificent sunrises and sunsets.

Once again, he found himself in the so-called civilized world with its jarring abruptness, shattering noises and nervous inhabitants. In a slow-moving queue he waited to purchase his ticket from a sullen clerk annoyed with questions regarding departure and arrival times. Jack placed the ticket to Chicago in his wallet and walked into the men's restroom to find more lines.

At the washbasin, he brought his face close to the mirror to study his scarred and pockmarked complexion, reminders of the lanced infected boils resulting from his treatment of the natives. Pulling the skin on one side of his face, then the other, he stared until an impatient traveler behind him cleared his throat. "Sorry, "he said, then hurried to find his way underground to long parallel rows of trains and the gate for the Chicago-bound express.

Out of New York City, the Diesel-powered train sped through towns with large stretches of farmland. Nearing each crossing, the train sounded its warning with a horn blast, unlike the high-pitched mournful whistle of the old steam engine, a sound now gone, but one remembered with longing. His world had changed in so short a time, and with that change came gnawing anxieties.

War threatened Europe, and he knew it would eventually involve the United States. What would he do if there was a general call to arms? Conscription had already started, but he would volunteer if war was declared. None of this was to his liking, but the issues lay clearly defined in his mind. He had thought about offering his services to the Freedom Fighters against Franco's Nationalist Forces in Spain several years earlier, but the opportunity had been lost by his research projects and the objections of his wife.

Martha, his wife of less than three years was on his mind, and he was eager to see her. More than a year had passed since they had been together. Her letters to him in Africa were pleasant but too infrequent. She had written about seeing this one and that one, attending cocktail parties and meeting interesting people...carrying on an innocent flirtation, now and then. Jack pondered their relationship and reluctantly recognized that time and distance had diminished the intense ardor and the constant yearning for her.

He wondered: somehow her letters had failed to convey the sparkle and excitement of their earlier romance. Did she truly understand his single-minded dedication to research? Maybe not. She was a beautiful woman who turned heads, and she must have yearned for male companionship—perhaps a cocktail and conversation over a cigarette. And why not? He gazed absently out the window and thought: I'm about to face other problems: getting a teaching assignment and making a living wage. God knows, it was time to settle down.

He placed his anthropology publication on the seat beside him and walked through several cars to the club car at the rear. Several passengers sat with drinks, smoked and made quiet conversation. The black bartender wiping the bar counter looked up and smiled. "Fix you a drink, sir?" His name badge read, *Sam*.

"Crown Royal on the rocks, please." Jack took his drink and sat on a barrel-back chair and picked up a discarded *New York Times*, dated September 1, 1939. The headline read, *Nazis Blitzkrieg Poland*. The follow-up story revealed that the Polish cavalry, men and horses had been completely annihilated in an onslaught by German tanks. Hundreds seeking to flee the country were mowed down by relentless waves of diving Stukas. The border was described as a scene of unimaginable horror as men, women and children lay massacred. Chamberlain, the British Prime Minister and Daladier, the French President, were expected to declare war within twenty-four hours. *This is the beginning of the big one!* Jack read and reread every detail. His heart pounded against his chest wall and his breathing deepened.

Seated next to him, a disheveled man, perhaps in his early-thirties, had slumped in his chair; he held a drink in one hand and a cigar in the other. With bleary eyes, he turned toward Jack and pointed his cigar at the newspaper. "Those Nazis haven't had any serious opposition yet, but I gotta admit they're damned good." He swiveled in his chair to look more closely at Jack. "You look like an able-bodied guy." With slurred speech he said, "You could be called up by the military any day, you know."

Jack said, "I'll be ready. How about you?"

"Me? Go into the military? Not if I can help it." He sneered. "C'mon, this is a phony war. Hitler will take out a few second-rate countries, kill a few hundred Jews and settle down to his schnitzel and beer." He waved his hand dismissively at the newspaper. "None of that crap means anything." He looked around then leaned toward Jack and in a show of confidentiality said, "That crazy Charlie Chaplin look-alike can kill all the fucking Jews, Polacks, and Pope ass-kissers he wants, and I for one would back him up. He'll be doing the world a favor, you know." Then in an afterthought, he said, "He can do the same to niggers." His voice became louder; he looked around seeking approval.

Jack swirled the ice cubes in his tumbler and stared at the man. "You sound bitter—in fact, I think you're obnoxious and just plain stupid."

"Hey, who you calling stupid?" The man put his drink on the side table and from his slouching posture wriggled upright, then with support from the chair arms pushed himself to a standing position. Jack stood in front of him. The man picked up his drink, brought it back to toss into Jack's face. Jack sidestepped the slow-moving drunk and grabbed the tumbler from his hand. The man stood transfixed while Jack threw the liquor into his face. He blinked and his jaw dropped.

Jack nudged him so that he fell backwards into his chair. Bending over him and pointing a finger in his face, Jack said in a soft but menacing tone, "Keep your big mouth shut, and if you can't, you can expect to get the shit knocked out of you."

The bartender walked toward the two men. "Look, gentlemen, we can't have any trouble here. Fighting on the railroad could get you arrested. What seems to be the trouble, anyway?"

"Not much, Sam. This fella was getting all hot and bothered and needed a quick splash to cool off."

Sam nodded. "Yessir." He leaned toward Jack. "I heard

some bad things..."

Jack took a deep breath, reached for his drink. "He was slandering certain cultural and racial groups. He thought so-called lesser people should be destroyed by superior beings—superior, like the Nazis. Let's hope he has a change of heart—at least for the rest of this trip. Maybe a cup of strong coffee would help."

Sam looked at the cowed passenger who blinked repeatedly while remaining drops of liquor fell from his face and hair onto his shirt. "Yessir, I think you're right." Sam's concerned expression changed to a broad smile. "Strong black coffee might be just what he needs."

"What he really needs, Sam, is to try spewing hateful garbage to a black Jew in some dark alley in Harlem."

Sam nodded. "Yessir, that would be just fine. Uh-huh, yessiree, that should suit him just fine."

CHAPTER 25

January 1940, Columbus, Ohio

"Look around Mart, this is going to be our new home town. What d'ya think?"

Martha was slow to respond. "Not as charming as Northwestern's campus, but it'll do—for now."

Jack drove slowly on Lane Avenue in the recently acquired, used 1937 Dodge Sedan as it entered the campus of Ohio State University. The avenue had been cleared recently of snow and mounds of it obscured the curbs.

"Do you think there are any decent clothing shops here?" She asked.

"I'm going to see Dean Kincaid, head of the Social Science Department to get my assignment. After that we'll check out one of the apartments set aside for incoming instructors. It's kind of exciting, isn't it?"

"Uh-huh. I guess so. I'm going to miss my family."

"You're just a few hours away by train."

"...would have been nice if Doc Herskovits found you a job in his department at Northwestern."

"He would have if a position had been available."

"Maybe and maybe not. You might have been too much competition for him—a challenge to his role as head honcho."

"Mart, that's a strange thing to say."

"Is it? My intuition, which is more finely-tuned than yours, tells me that's a distinct possibility."

Jack miffed by her conversation, said, "Herskovits wrote

compelling and gracious letters on my behalf to the dean at Penn State and the Department of Land Conservation, and recommended me highly for this teaching job. I don't understand your thinking."

"Don't concern yourself about it now. Let's find our apartment and pretend to be a happy couple in this dismal little burg."

"Are there any further questions before we end class?" Jack stood in front of his Anthropology 101 class when a hand shot up from the back row.

"I mean no disrespect, sir, but what is the relevance of this course considering the situation in the world today? I mean, with Europe preparing for war and the Japs rattling sabers and all of that?" The student in a R.O.T.C. uniform stood while the eyes of twenty-eight classmates turned toward him.

"Your question is timely. But before I answer, I should like you to give me a definition of this course as you understand it. We're several weeks into the semester, so you must have formed some impressions of what we're trying to accomplish here."

The student fidgeted with his overseas hat folded over his belt. "Anthropology is the study of man, that is, his physical and cultural characteristics." He stopped and waited for Jack's response.

"In a narrow interpretation, that is correct. A more complete answer would include man's origin, his customs, social relationships, cultural development and his behavior. The key words are: cultural developments and behavior in a given social structure. What is so-called normal behavior and why does the abnormal occur and what are its consequences'? You must understand the concept of normal before you can comprehend the abnormal. How and why does a reversion to tribal ferocity for instance occur in a highly complex and civilized society? Take Germany for instance..."

The bell rang and the students left their seats. Several gathered around Jack to engage him in further questioning. Their interest flattered him, and he answered questions until the next class and its instructor arrived.

Jack's class drew larger enrollment numbers, and he was asked by the dean to give extra classes to accommodate those who had been turned away. Conducting more classes encroached upon his home time during which he corrected test papers and prepared material for future assignments. And what of his own research projects? There simply weren't enough hours in the day.

Martha felt more isolated as Jack's evenings were taken with more schoolwork. She started to knit but grew increasingly resentful at being shut out of his world. She had shown no interest in Jack's courses and refused to attend his classes even though she had been invited. Her interest in academic matters waned and money became ever more important. She wanted to know why he had not been given a raise or been promoted from assistant to associate professor after a year.

December 7, 1941

Martha's sister phoned from Chicago to tell her that Pearl Harbor had been bombed by the Japs, and the American fleet in the Pacific had been wiped out.

"Where the hell is Pearl Harbor?" Jack turned on the radio.

"...at approximately 8:00 A.M., a wave of Japanese planes flew over the U.S. Naval Base at Pearl Harbor and destroyed several warships: the U.S.S. Arizona, the U.S.S. Ohio countless seamen are presumed dead and many injured. Planes at Higgins Air Field were destroyed leaving the island defenseless..."

Jack slumped in his chair and held his head in his hands. "How in the hell is this possible? I can't believe it!"

Martha placed her hand on his shoulder. It's awful. But what can we do about it?"

Jack's jaw muscles tightened. "I don't know, but I've got to do something. I'm not going to teach a classroom of girls while young men are going off to war. I've got to volunteer my services somehow." He snapped his fingers. "Ralph Bunche is in Washington with some outfit like the Coordinator of Information. Maybe he can get me into some unit. At the very least I should be able to qualify for O.C.S."

"Unless your medical record prevents it." Martha said.

"I'll sign a waiver. I won't hold the government responsible for any malarial relapses or recurrent bouts of anemia."

"I don't think they work that way, dear. Once you're in uniform they assume responsibility for your health."

"As soon as the university breaks for a winter hiatus, I'm going to D.C....I'll call Ralph and set up an appointment."

CHAPTER 26

In the office of the Coordinator of Information, the secretary glanced at Jack's driver's license and university ID card, then at her appointment book. "I'll tell Dr. Bunche you're here, Dr. Harris."

Both men smiled broadly then engaged in a bear hug. Bunche took a step back and looked at Jack. "Tell me all about yourself and Martha. I haven't seen you two in at least three years, but I've heard good things about you from Mel Herskovits."

The men exchanged pleasantries and spoke about mutual friends, some who had already entered into government positions or military service.

"Jack there's a crying need for someone who knows anything about Africa. I wanted to volunteer my services but the White House wants me to remain here. Would you believe we have only a hand full of qualified Africanists? Three of them are retired from the State Department and too old to be pressed into service. Another is a pacifist and refuses...then there's you and me."

"Where do I go to sign up?" Jack smiled and pulled a pen out of his jacket pocket.

"Wild Bill Donovan has been put in charge of a new department, the O.S.S., Office of Strategic Services, a cloak and dagger outfit. My bet is that he'll roll out the red carpet for you. I'll have my secretary call his office now, if that meets with your approval."

"Just tell me where to report."

Bunche's voice became somber. "Jack, you might be put in harm's way. Are you sure you want to do this? You could ride out any conflict with a deferment—teaching is an essential..."

"Ralph, a youngster in class asked me about the relevance of anthropology in this time of crisis. This is a better response than the gibberish I gave him."

Jack S. Harris in Costa Rica 1930 (Age 18)
Shore leave from a merchant vessel

Seaman "Russell Sumner" April 1936
Aboard cargo ship with parrot

In Nigeria 1938 (Age 26)
Living among the Ibo for one year

With Ibo child in Nigeria 1938

Dr. Jack S. Harris (Age 29)
Before entering the OSS

On United Nations assignment in Tanganyika

With the United Nations (Circa 1950)
Secretariat

Executive and Director of Manifold Industries
San Jose, Costa Rica (Circa 1956)

Dancing with Shirley
San Jose, Costa Rica (Circa 1958)

Jack and Shirley with Micheal and Jonathan

"Don Jack" in San Jose, Costa Rica
2004

Chapter 27

Spring 1942

The olive drab 1940 Plymouth sedan moved slowly along the serpentine lane shaded by an archway of tall poplars. The wooded area opened abruptly onto a sun-lit expanse of velvety green extending for acres.

Seated next to the p.f.c. driver, Jack said, "Get a load of this, will ya? What is this place?"

The driver, smiled. "It's your new home. Used to be a congressional retreat and golf course. Not bad, eh? You got yourself a limited-time membership here but don't expect to play golf. "

At a rock-faced guard station, the vehicle was approached by an MP who asked for Jack's papers; he looked at them briefly, then waved the driver through. Jack pressed the driver for information about the camp. Eager to talk, he explained the arrangement of buildings, many of them newly constructed and others under construction. After a quarter of a mile, the vehicle stopped in front of broad steps leading to an imposing lodge-type edifice perched on a hillock. "Okay, buddy, this is your stop." Taking Jack's suitcase, he escorted him up the steps and into the spacious lobby with a vaulted ceiling supported by rough-hewn timbers. Jack gawked while the driver kept up a steady stream of chatter. "You must be some kind of special guy to be seeing the Big Man here. Hardly anyone but VIP military brass gets to see him." They walked along a long hallway to an unmarked office door. "Knock and wait to be called in," the driver said and left. Jack cinched his tie, pulled at his jacket sleeves and pushed a few strands of hair back before knocking.

"Come in!" The voice was firm and loud. "Wild Bill" Donovan, sitting at a wooden desk with three phones, an intercom and stacks of manila folders, held a phone in one hand and motioned Jack to come forward. He reached for the sealed dossier Jack held, placed it on his desk, and then pointed to a chair. Donovan completed his phone conversation, opened the sealed dossier and scanned several pages. He looked up. "So you're Jack Sargent Harris, eh?" He rubbed his chin with the back of his hand and said, "You look like an old friend of mine. His name was Ben Wilson. Does that name suit you?"

"That'll be fine, Sir."

"Good. Be sure you destroy any cards, clothing, and stationery, anything that shows your old name. It's Ben Wilson, now. Get used to it."

Donovan, a man in his late fifties, wore G.I. fatigues with an almost inconspicuous single star on his wrinkled collar. He turned the pages of the dossier with a lip-moistened forefinger, then looked up and smiled. "I knew there was something I liked about you the minute you walked in." His folksy manner dispelled the stiff formality Jack had anticipated.

Donovan continued, "You're a Columbia graduate—like me. Fine school. Of course, I was there thirty years before you. I knocked off a B.A. degree and two years later a law degree. I'll have to admit, I wasn't the greatest scholar, but by God, I enjoyed my time there. Got a medal for oratory and played substitute quarterback. Became a big man on campus." He pointed his thumb backward to a portrait on the wall. "Our commander-in-chief, FDR, was there at the same time, but we didn't socialize—too entirely different backgrounds. He was high society. I was riff-raff." He smiled broadly. "I met some awfully good-looking fillies who were eager to trot. They thought I was handsome. Believe it or not, I was." Patting his waist, he said, "Look at me now. I'm a dammed pear-shaped, balding gray-haired old fart. But in my day I had enough adventure and success for three lifetimes. Yes sir, but let me assure you," he paused, "the greatest adventures are yet to come—for both of us. We've got wars on both sides of the world. Ain't that a bitch?" He closed Jack's dossier. "Do you know anything about me?"

"Sir, I know you had an enviable record as a hero in World War One."

"Yeah, that's what they say. Caught a Kraut's bullet in my leg—almost bled to death." He continued nonchalantly. "But I recovered." He leaned back in his chair. "Tell me what you know about the Allied and Axis positions in North Africa."

Speaking tentatively, Jack said his information came from newspapers and radio reports. He had read about the fluid battle lines of the German, Italian, and Vichy French forces clashing with Montgomery's British forces in the African territories bordering the Mediterranean.

Donovan, impatient, stood and turned to the wall behind him to pull down a rolled map of the African continent. Pointing to the northern border of Egypt with his pen, he said, "The British 8th army is going to open an offensive here at El Alamein. We need information on Axis troop numbers, the type of weapons they have and where they're deployed. We'd like to know where their oil depots are and how much fuel reserves they have."

Jack concentrated on Donovan's every word. The realization that he might be in the thick of battle made his heart race; his eyes widened as they followed Donovan's pen on the large map.

"We'll need you to get this information or as much as you can." He leaned across the desk and in a subdued voice said, "What I'm about to say is top-drawer stuff. I wouldn't be telling you this, but eventually you'll need to know." He returned to the map and circled an area around Tunisia and tapped it with his pen. "We're going to land troops here—a massive invasion involving several armies to push the fucking Nazis and Italians into the Mediterranean or into prisoner-of-war camps. The enemy is expecting us to land in Western Europe. They're amassing troops in France along Normandy and on the Eastern front near Stalingrad." He paused to assess Jack's reaction. "Don't look so worried, son. The war effort doesn't hinge on your intelligence alone. We have our sources of information, but yours will be important since you know the territory and the people."

Jack's familiarity with Africa was not the Mediterranean coastal region but the Nigerian coast two thousand miles south and west of the anticipated battle zones. However, he was not about to make an issue for fear of losing his assignment.

Donovan's voice became more animated. "Your cover will be that of a university professor gathering"—he stopped to read the printed paper on his desk—"gathering ethnological data or some such thing on native desert people." He looked up and said dismissively, "Hell, make up your own excuse for being there. Your assistant will be a radio operator, a young fellow I yanked out of the signal corps from Camp Crowder, Missouri. He'll join you later. For now you'll share quarters with another anthropologist.

"The radio operator who will join you is Danny Miller. He's a crackerjack encoder and decoder able to whip out sixty words a minute with good accuracy. Those are his good points." Donovan hesitated as though reluctant to go on. "He's young, I'm told he's a little impulsive. Be patient with him. He's a kid eager for adventure and might have a tendency to be less than critically cautious. Be a big brother and look after him."

Jack nodded.

"Your credentials will show that you're Doctor Ben Wilson, an Associate Professor of Anthropology from Northwestern

University. You've been teaching for two years. That cover-up has been confirmed with the university in case someone gets nosey. ID cards will be printed and treated to simulate signs of wallet wear."

Donovan started to pace and his speech became staccato-like. "The Brits are up to their asses in intelligence. They're not well coordinated. They have Military Intelligence, the M16, and British Secret Intelligence. They don't share anything among themselves. And damn little with us. We need someone who can scrounge information. Get it to Washington pronto. That's where you and Danny Miller come in.

"The Vichy French can fall under German control at any time, and the French ships would be commandeered. We can't let that happen. In neutral countries like Spain and Portugal, the Axis influence is strong. Those neutrals are being exploited for espionage, propaganda and submarine assistance. There's an urgent need for information on military maneuvers, topography, political sentiments, and fifth-column activities, things like that. Try to get information but don't expect much help from the British or Free French. Brown nose them if you must. Wheedle as much as you can out of them."

"Sir, would they expect information from me? What would I give them?"

Donovan looked up. "Preferably, something they already know. We'll decide that later.

"Jack, excuse me, I meant to say Ben, another word or two before you leave. When you've finished your training here you'll be embarking on a risky assignment. You'll be putting your life on the line. What's more: you'll not be in uniform which means there will be no Geneva Convention rules to provide a safety net. The Nazis will give you no quarter. Being a spy or saboteur can mean torture—even death. Among your survival items is a lethal capsule, cyanide." He smiled sardonically. "That's a hell of a note: survival and cyanide in one breath." Donovan turned and rolled up the map, then looked at Jack. "By the way, what did you get your doctorate in? What was the subject of your thesis?"

"Some aspects on the agrarian and economic development of the White Knife Shoshone of Nevada."

Donovan nodded, then looked at the papers on his desk again.

Jack said, "I hope my background is no deterrent.... I have no desire to sit behind a desk..."

Donovan interrupted. "Sitting on your ass behind a desk is not what we're about here. That's for pot-bellied officers fighting from behind the lines. Your job is to keep us informed while keeping yourself and your partner safe. Should the opportunity arise, try creating a bit of shit for the enemy. Any more questions?"

"Can I get in touch with my wife or my family?"

"There are no phones for the candidates. All outgoing letters will be censored. You can write that you're in an army training camp. Give no specifics and avoid using clever codes or subterfuge. We know them all. A violation results in automatic incarceration. Nobody outside this camp is to know your location or your type of training. Is that clear?"

"Yessir."

"Anything else on your mind?"

"How long is the training program, Sir?"

Donovan hesitated. "I'd like to say two months, but we need you desperately in the field." He ran his hand through his thinning hair and shook his head in frustration. "There isn't enough time for in-depth training. Those Krauts and turncoat French aren't going to let up. We've got to know what they're doing in North Africa and what the Nazis are doing in South Africa. We're depending on fellows like you. I'd rather have a half-dozen thinking PhDs than a battalion of ass-scratching officers. "

From his quasi-military training in the CCC camp, Jack was about to salute when Donovan put up his hand.

"Saluting is not necessary. In fact, I'd rather you didn't. You might come across some G.I. pain-in-the-ass officer demanding army protocol, but for the most part those regulations are not observed here. You'll find the training intense, but enjoyable for the most part. The mess hall is open all day if you can find time to use it, and the food is good, maybe too good. Plenty of fresh fruits and vegetables, steaks and eggs, all you want and rich desserts." He patted his belly and said, "Don't get this soft."

CHAPTER 28

Jack left headquarters and walked to a newly constructed single-story clapboard building designated *Quartermaster.* Inside he found long tables with neat piles of trousers and jackets in olive drab wool, fatigues in heavy cotton and khaki pants and shirts. On shelves were stacked underwear, shirts, ties, socks and shoes.

"Your waist size?" The corporal behind the counter asked.

"32"

"Collar size and sleeve length?"

"16 and 35."

"Shoe size?"

"13 ½ ."

"Did you say 13 ½?"

Jack nodded.

"We've got nothing like that here. We'll put in a requisition for them. Should be here in a few days. In the meantime, wear what you've got."

With his arms filled with clothing, Jack walked to his designated barracks, one in a line of six. He opened the door, balancing clothing between his flexed knee and chin.

While hanging his clothes on a rack behind the head of his cot, Jack heard the door open. A tall, balding man approached him. "Hi. Are you the unfortunate guy who's my new roommate?"

Jack set the remainder of clothing on his cot to shake his hand. "Hi, I'm Ben Wilson. And you are?"

"Here, they call me Bill Bailey." At age twenty-eight, a year younger than Jack, Bailey appeared older with a paunchy abdomen and early baldness. With a firm handshake and an easy smile, he spoke with a drawl that Jack figured came from Kentucky or maybe Tennessee.

"What was your field of expertise?" Jack asked.

"*The Acculturation of South Africans by Boer Immigrants.* I spent a year in and around Johannesburg..." He trailed off. "When I start talking too much remind me to shut up." He changed the subject abruptly. "They're going to have to give this here old boy some real physical training to bring him up to fighting condition. 'Course, they won't have to show me how to fire a rifle or a pistol—I know all about that, but I'm not much on hand-to-hand combat or knife throwing, and I never tossed a grenade. With my heft, I don't know how I'm going to uphold their motto of 'to see without being seen.' Man, I'm just not built like that."

While Jack was placing newly-issued socks and underwear in a foot locker at the end of his bed, Bailey continued, "I agreed with that young Lieutenant, Rex Appleyard, this morning before you arrived; he gave his method of pistol shooting known as 'instinctive firing' or 'point shooting'. Yes sir, that's the way to bring down a sonofabitch who's about to blow your ass apart." Bailey squatted with his feet spread, whipped out an imaginary gun, extended his hands in a shooting position and shouted, "Bang, Bang! Yessir, don't waste time taking aim, just fire where you're pointing." He stood and placed the imaginary gun in an imaginary holster on his belt.

Bailey looked at his watch. "Don't get too comfortable, pal, we're due in Dangerous Dan Fairbairn's class in ten minutes."

"Who's that?"

"Probably the most famous instructor in all O.S.S. training camps, that's all. He's a Brit army captain, an import who's supposed to be the world's foremost expert on close combat. Like I said, if I ever get close enough to a

Nazi, I'll shoot the bastard. To hell with this hand-to-hand bravado crap."

They walked to Area B, a single-story building where a number of candidates, fourteen in this group, stood facing a slight, gray-haired, bespectacled man in starched fatigues. He looked around and counted heads. "Good, we're all here. Let's start."

Fairbairn spoke with a lilting Scottish brogue that gave no hint of menace. "Men, the thought I want you to take away from this session is that you are to forget about fighting like gentlemen. Rules of the Marquis of Queensbury don't apply here. I teach what I call 'gutter fighting.' This is fighting that will save your life. There's only one rule to be observed." He paused, then in a shrill voice startled the group with a yell, "Kill or be killed!" He paused to let the message penetrate. "You heard me right. Forget about your polite American sportsmanship. The enemy will show you no mercy; he doesn't give a damn about rules of engagement. Unless you know how to beat him, *he will kill you!*" He paced before the group.

"Let me give you a brief history. Many years ago when I was a young man I left Scotland, to enlist in the Royal Marines and was sent to the Far East. There I joined the British-led Shanghai Municipal Police Force. One day, I responded to a melee caused by warring Chinese gangs..." He began to speak slowly to emphasize the next few phrases. "I jolly well got the shit beaten out of me. I had broken ribs, a punctured lung, a fractured arm and a ruptured kidney. When the medics first saw me, they thought I was dead. I spent two months in the hospital.

"From that time on, I vowed I would never let that happen to me again. I mastered jujitsu, Chinese boxing and martial arts. I engaged in hundreds of street fights afterwards, and even though I've got scars to show for it, nobody got the best of me. I organized anti-riot squads and designed my own system of defensive/offensive maneuvers. I call my method *Defendu*, that's described in my book, *Get Tough*. I have copies for all of you. Take the book to your barracks and read every page. The next time we meet you'll practice on each other."

Jack tilted his head toward Bailey and whispered, "This little guy looks about as vicious as an interior decorator."

Fairbairn saw Jack whispering and signaled him to step forward. "All right, laddie, come over here. The instructor with legs slightly parted and arms hung loosely, said, "Throw me your hardest punch."

Jack shook his head. "I can't do that, Sir. I've got no reason to..."

In a lightening movement, Fairbairn kicked Jack in the groin. Jack bent over and groaned; a grimace of pain transformed his beet-red face. With fiery eyes, he lunged at the instructor who stepped aside, caught Jack by the arm, flipped him onto the mat facedown, and then twisted his arm behind him.

With a controlled smile, he helped Jack to his feet, turned to the stunned onlookers, then back to the aching and embarrassed Jack. "Laddie, don't expect your enemy to treat you as cordially."

CHAPTER 29

Lieutenant Appleyard held a roster and stood before the group of fourteen. He called, "Wilson—Ben Wilson." There was no response. He looked around. "Come on fella, respond to your name." Bill Bailey elbowed Jack.

"Here, Sir!" Jack blurted out. *Am I ever going to get accustomed to this name?*

"All right men, listen up, I need your undivided attention. We've got a lot of ground to cover." Appleyard looked at his watch. "In ninety minutes we're going to the firing range to test your skills. Gather around the table here to look at these firearms. By the end of the day, you will have fired most of the small ones, and you'll be able to disassemble them, then put them together—blindfolded."

"Blindfolded?" one of the volunteers asked.

"That's right, blindfolded. If your piece jams in the dark, you damn-well better know how to fix it, pronto." He walked along the table and stopped to name each firearm and explain its advantages and disadvantages. "This is the M1 rifle, a good choice for long range purposes. Obviously, you can't conceal it when you're among the enemy." He picked up a Colt .45 revolver. "This baby is a favorite for shorter range targets. It's not as efficient as some of the newer semi-automatics but still preferred by many. It never jams, so it's highly reliable." He pointed to the British Sten, two submachine guns, a .50 caliber Thompson machine gun and an anti-tank bazooka. "These larger firearms you won't be using, but I show them because you might see them on the battle field. If you pick one up, you might want to use it."

He looked at the roster of names again. "Bailey, come over here and demonstrate how you'd shoot the enemy at two hundred yards with the M1."

With confidence borne from handling guns at an early age, Bailey gripped the stock and pointed the barrel downward. He balanced the rifle in the crook of his right arm, opened the chamber to check for ammunition, and then slid the chamber closed with a snap. He positioned the stock against his right shoulder, supported the barrel with his left hand, and then cocked his head to aim with his right eye. The group gathered around to watch.

Appleyard said, "You can see this man has had considerable experience. He handles the weapon like it's an extension of his arm—and that's as it should be. However, if you were to stand as he does and wait until the enemy is right where you want him, you would probably be shot dead." He paused. "Remember, the enemy might have you in his sight also. You'd better be camouflaged or hidden. Again, this is not sport—this is war."

He approached Jack. "All right, Wilson, let me place you in a situation: you're in enemy territory and you see someone at about fifty to a hundred yards away sending messages or talking on a field phone, and he has a Luger in his holster or on a table near his hand. You know he's up to no damn good. You're faced with a decision. Two questions: number one: what type of firearm do you use?" He waved his hand across the array of guns on the table. "Number two: what do you intend to do about the enemy?"

"To answer your first question, Sir," Jack pointed to the Colt .45 revolver, "this would be my first choice—maybe with a noise suppressor."

Appleyard nodded. "I'll go along with that. Now, what are you going to do?"

"I'd keep my gun on the enemy and take him prisoner."

"NO! Goddammit!" Appleyard pounded his fist on the table. "Think! You're in the middle of a war. You don't need a prisoner when you're out there alone. They're needless baggage. You kill the sonofabitch because he sure as hell would kill you. Got that?"

"Yes, Sir! It's just that I thought interrogating him would be important."

Appleyard paused, grimacing. "Maybe under ideal conditions, if you're with a group of men in a relatively safe territory, you might be able to bring the bastard to HQ for questioning. But on a one-to-one basis—out in the field? Uh, uh. Too risky. Understand?"

"Yes, Sir."

"Good. Remember, just get rid of the sonofabitch— that's all."

Daylight was disappearing with storm clouds moving in. A light drizzle developed into a wind-driven rain that buffeted the trainees' fatigues. Several men looked to Appleyard for relief, but he gave no sign of curtailing the firing range exercise. The different abilities of the trainees became obvious with the firing of the various arms at one, two and three hundred yard targets. After two hours of practice, some rubbed their aching shoulders from rifle recoil; others blew into their cupped hands for warmth, most were sulking because of the miserable weather.

Jack muttered to Bailey, "Doesn't this guy have the God-given sense to get us out of the rain? No damn-fool enemy is going to be shooting at us in this kind of weather— they've got to be smarter than that."

Bailey looked over Jack's shoulder then cleared his throat audibly. Appleyard, standing behind them, raised his voice above the howling wind. "Wilson, show me how you shoot this M1 in the wind and rain." He thrust an M1 at Jack, and said, "I'll make a deal with you. Hit that two hundred yard target, and I'll call the practice off, then we can all go to the mess hall for coffee and sinkers. But if you miss after six rounds, we'll stay out for another half hour." The trainees listened and moaned, then gathered behind Jack to watch and give encouragement.

With his handkerchief, Jack wiped his nose and the barrel of the rifle. He gasped when he lay prone on the rain-soaked tarp. The cold wetness penetrated to his skin. He blinked, took aim, held his breath and squeezed the trigger slowly. In rapid fire three bullets found their mark in the middle circle of the target just above the bulls eye.

Appleyard, who had been watching with binoculars smiled, then broke out into open laughter. The group yelled and applauded as if for a major victory. Appleyard bent over and slapped Jack's back. "Damn good shooting, Wilson." Jack got off the tarp; the front of his drenched fatigues clung to his body. "Got any shooting secrets you can share with the rest of us?" Appleyard asked.

Jack nodded toward Bailey. "He taught me to compensate for wind and rain deflection; he calls it the 'Kentucky windage factor.'" Jack handed the rifle to the lieutenant. "If you don't mind, I'll skip the coffee and doughnuts. I want a hot shower and dry clothes." Jack, or rather Ben Wilson, enjoyed the temporary popularity that would last until the next course of training.

CHAPTER 30

The new camp commander, Vance Gray, a full bird colonel, with a reputation for strict military protocol that preceded his arrival, stood at the speaker's stand. Until his arrival, organizational routine had been relaxed in the park-like camp located outside Baltimore; spit-and-polish compliance had never been required. A certain informal attitude was tolerated by the cadre since the typical O.S.S. candidate was older, well-educated or skilled for a different type of warfare. He was not held to the rigorous standards of regular camp life.

The colonel drew his shoulders back and held his head high to give his introductory speech in the auditorium that accommodated two hundred men. He reflected West Point correctness; his blouse and trousers held knife-like creases and his overseas cap tilted at a proper angle. The flying silver bird insignias glistened on his shirt collar and cap. His clipped speech offered no hint of familiarity or humor. "Men, you have learned skills of the utmost importance in this war against a ruthless and clever enemy. You have been trained to send signals and decode messages. You have been taught to blow up military installations and to disable vehicles. Furthermore, you have acquired techniques in hand-to-hand combat and the ability to shoot and kill efficiently.

"Some of you will be shipping out to Fort Benning, Georgia, to become parachutists fighting behind enemy lines. I envy your opportunity. Others will go to posts in the European Theatre of Operations, Pacific Theatre or to Africa. Before you leave here you will have learned proper military decorum, and while I'm in command you will conduct yourselves accordingly.

"In one more week you will have completed your training, and you will act in organized groups. We're going to put you through trial runs, actual wartime situations. There will be no spoon-feeding or coddling. You will be divided into groups. Each group will have a leader." The colonel paused as his eyes encompassed the length and breadth of the assembly. "Men, now hear this: failure to accomplish your mission is not an option—failure is totally unacceptable."

He strode off the podium and the men stood. Bailey turned toward Jack. "That old boy is just full of plain old Kentucky chicken shit. He thinks he's talking to a bunch of boy scouts. I don't see him lasting long around here."

Because of his proficiency on the target range, Jack had been chosen group leader of six men. His group met in a side room where Lt. Appleyard, their advisor, had the men form an arc in front of him. He placed a thick roll of blueprints on the table. "Men, this is your assignment: you are to disable a small airplane-parts factory in an industrial park outside Baltimore. Remember, you are to disable it, not destroy it. During actual combat conditions you will have the option of destroying or disabling a facility. The prevailing conditions will determine what you do. This is a plant essential to our needs. Again, you will disable it, not destroy it.

"This is not a prank; there is risk involved, injury, possible death. Plan your job meticulously. Execute it, then high-tail out of there. This will be your final exam. Pass it and you go on to greater glory. Screw up and you might still go on to greater glory." He laughed in front of the unsmiling group.

Bailey, out of the corner of his mouth, mumbled to Jack, "Is this guy trying to be funny?"

The lieutenant continued, "Remember, your existence here and this camp's whereabouts are unknown to people on the outside. If you get caught, don't admit to anything. You'll be given a phone number to memorize. That number will set the wheels in motion for your rescue. However," he paused and made eye-contact with each trainee, "get caught and you'll be tossed out of here and transferred to a regular army unit. If you do get caught sabotaging in enemy territory you'll be interrogated, then probably killed." Several trainees cleared their throats and coughed nervously.

He continued, "You'll make an early A.M. approach to the factory. It will be guarded by at least one armed watchman and protected by an alarm system and high–intensity lights. In addition, there's an eight-foot Cyclone fence surrounding the property."

"We talking Fort Knox here?" One of the men asked.

The lieutenant ignored the question. "I have here copies of the blueprints of the plant taken from the city's Department of Engineering Records and Data." He handed the rolled blueprints to Jack. "You and one of your men will reconnoiter the plant during the day and make mental notes. No written details or instructions. Any questions?"

"Yeah. How do we get there, and what about our clothes?" one of the men asked. "What equipment will we need?"

Another asked, "Does plant management know about us?"

"No, of course not. That's the purpose of this mission. To answer your other questions, we'll give you a civilian-type sedan, and you can wear your own civvies, those you wore when you came to this camp. As for equipment, you'll have to decide that after you case the factory. We'll supply any of your needs. Don't request a cannon or TNT," he chuckled. "If there are no further questions, I'll leave you to discuss this among yourselves." He looked at his wristwatch. "By the way, you have exactly seventy-two hours to complete the assignment." Appleyard turned to leave and called out, "Good luck."

Jack took the blueprints, rolled them out on the desk and said, "Okay fellas, let's get to work."

CHAPTER 31

June 5, 1942

Bill Bailey flew into the barracks with a newspaper under his arm. "Hey, Ben you gotta see this—right here on the first page." Bailey spread the first page of the *Baltimore Sun-Times* on his cot. Jack looked at the paper over Bailey's shoulder. The heading of the column read, "*Local Defense Plant Sabotaged.*" The article went on to say that the American Aviation Hinge and Screw factory located in the suburban industrial park outside Baltimore..." They laughed and jabbed one another.

"Well, Ol' Boy, you pulled it off, just as you planned it," Bailey said.

"*We* pulled it off just as *we* planned it," Jack said. "But that poor guard didn't know what the hell hit him when Casey tackled him from behind. Both of them flew about twenty feet."

"Yeah, that was sort of chancy." Bailey shook his head. "My adrenaline went stratospheric. If that guard got hold of his gun and shot at us—that would have been all she wrote. Three of us got on him like flies on dog turd. Of course, we were damn lucky there were no other guards."

Jack scanning the article again, said, "It says that the attempt to disable the plant was a definite act of well-planned sabotage. The machinery within the factory was not damaged, and no evidence existed that the building had been broken into. Four exterior lights had been shot out. Empty cartridges had been recovered and were sent to the FBI for analysis. The Cyclone fence surrounding the factory revealed no damage suggesting that the saboteurs climbed over it, then over-powered the guard.

"The guard was found by members of the morning shift. He had been huddled in the protective recess of the plant entrance with duct tape covering his mouth, his hands tied behind him, and his ankles bound with tape. An emergency crew repaired the severed wiring in the high voltage transformer located inside the Cyclone fence.

"When questioned, the guard told reporters that the job was strictly professional and well-planned. The men knew exactly what they were doing, although he could give no reason why the factory had not been broken into. 'Once the transformer was knocked out, and I was tied up, they took off,' he said.

"When asked what the men looked like, the guard shrugged and said, 'Oh, they were clever, all right, they wore masks and gloves. Funny thing though, they didn't talk like yeggs. More like educated guys, ya know? They apologized for *inconveniencing* me. Can you believe that? I was glad they didn't bust me up except for the bruises I got when they tackled me. Jeez, I thought I was hit by a freight train. My side still hurts. One of the guys emptied my pistol and stuck it back in my holster. But they took my ammo clip.'"

Bill Bailey was cutting the article out of the newspaper when a knock at the door preceded a recruit who barged in. "Ben Wilson? Bill Bailey? Colonel Gray wants to see you guys in his office, ASAP."

"What for?" Bailey asked.

"How would I know? He doesn't share confidences with me." The messenger turned and left.

"Think he wants to congratulate us for a job well done?" Bailey asked.

"Either that or he's signing our transfer papers for basic training and wants the pleasure of chewing our asses before we leave," Jack said.

Both men, in fatigues, stood before the seated spit-and-polish colonel who glowered at them. "Don't you men know how to approach an officer?" He sprang out of his chair and walked in front of them. "Remove your hats! Stand at attention! Now salute! Haven't you been taught *any* basic military courtesy?" He stopped in front of the unshaven Bailey who stood four inches taller than he. "Answer me! Haven't you been told about personal hygiene? Shaving daily?"

"No, I sure haven't," Bailey drawled. "If I had, I just don't remember."

The colonel froze; his eyes shut, his fists clenched tightly. "*No* is not an answer," he shouted. "The proper response is, '*No, Sir!*'" Sputtering, his face twitching rapidly, he walked behind his desk where a newspaper lay open. His forefinger stabbed repeatedly at an article.

Both men remained at attention, but Bailey's eyes shifted sideways toward Jack. The colonel glared at them. "Will either one of you geniuses tell me what in the hell you were trying to do at that airplane-parts factory?"

"Well, sir..." Bailey said.

The colonel interrupted. "That was the most ill-conceived, needlessly dangerous, absolutely stupidest caper I have ever..."

"But, sir, we were told..." Bailey started again.

"Don't interrupt! That guard could have shot or killed one or all of you, or you could have killed him, a perfectly innocent man." His voice rose even higher. "The newspapers would have learned all about this camp, and our whole operation would have been in jeopardy."

Jack started to say, "This mission was sanctioned by..."

"Dammit! Don't *you* interrupt." The colonel's face turned crimson, spittle formed at the corners of his mouth. "Get your gear and prepare to move out. We don't need your ilk around here. The clerk will cut your orders. You

both carry too damn much wise-ass liability for this outfit."
He sat at his desk, crumpled the newspaper and threw it in
a wastebasket. "Now, get the hell out of my sight!"

The men saluted, did an about-face and left the office
hurriedly. Outside, Bailey started to apologize to Jack for
irritating the colonel.

"No need for apologies. That tight-ass martinet had no
business reaming our asses."

"How did he get wind of our mission? I thought it was
a guarded secret."

Jack said, "Gray has his informants. Appleyard might
have tipped him off hoping to get a promotion. I can't imagine
Wild Bill Donovan responding like that jerk Gray did."

"You're right about that." Bailey ran off and called over
his shoulder. "Ben, I'll see you at the barracks."

Jack gathered the few items on the shelf above his cot
and those from his footlocker and placed them in a duffle
bag. He was sorry about the whole damn fracas. Truth
was, he didn't understand the reason for the colonel's flare-
up. The team had accomplished its mission: the factory
had been disabled according to the directive; no one was
injured, and the plant became operable after the wires to
the transformer were replaced.

Bailey, breathless rushed into the barracks. "Hold the
phone, Ben, I just came from Donovan's office. We're not
going anywhere until ol' Wild Bill says so. In fact, there's
a good chance that the chicken-shit colonel will be leaving
before we do. Donovan's aide got in touch with him. Seems
like there's been too many complaints about Gray. Turns
out, he's the wrong man for this job, just like I said he would
be. And if that doesn't scald the cat's ass, Wild Bill wants to
congratulate us on a job well done. He's breaking precedent, giving us three days furlough before we ship out. Hot
damn! The only stipulations are that we say nothing about

our training or the camp, and secondly, that we don't get the clap or something worse. For me, I'm shackin' up with my gal Mary. I'm gonna' give ol' willie here such a workout; he's not going to see the light of day for twenty-four hours."

Bailey started humming, *Deep in the Heart of Texas* while placing a pair of fatigues and toilet articles in his duffle bag. He tossed an anthropology journal on top of the bag. "I'll take this to read in case I get bored with screwing, but I doubt that'll happen." He stopped and looked at Jack. "Hey, Ben, here I am prattlin' away and not even having the courtesy to ask where you'll be going. You're welcome to join me at my folks' digs in Paducah. I'm going to rent a car and drive like mad to get there. You can share the ride. Their place isn't exactly the Ritz, but Ma keeps a spare room handy. I can ask Mary to introduce you to one of her girlfriends; we could be real cozy-like."

"Thanks, Bill. I think I'll go to the library at Columbia, do research on the coastal cities of North Africa. I'm certain my marching orders will take me there. The Allies are going to be invading the northwest—" Jack stopped. "Jesus, I don't know why I said that. Forget what I said."

"Didn't hear a word." Bailey started to gather his belongings, then stopped. "Can't you meet your wife somewhere? You might not get to see her for—hell, who knows when? I'm saying hello to my folks, giving Ma a kiss on her cheek and shaking Dad's hand; then I'm heading over to Mary's to fuck my brains out. If I come back acting like an idiot, you'll know what happened. I hope she's strong enough and doesn't have the rag on. What d'ya say, Benny-boy? Change your mind?"

"I can't chance waiting around for a military flight to Chicago from Paducah or getting back here on time. Thanks anyway."

"Sure enough, Ol' Buddy. I'll probably be sent to the south end of Africa...oops! There I go shooting off my trap. Forget what *I* said about Africa. Maybe we can meet along the coast and have us a good ol' time between sabotaging tricks." Bailey stopped and sounded serious. "When you think about this, it's all kind of surreal, isn't it? Here we are, two grown men, assistant professors, no less, playing at being spies..."

"Who the hell's playing?"

"You're right. Sometimes I lose perspective." Bailey threw his duffle bag over his shoulder and walked toward the door. "See you back here in three days, Ol' Buddy, when the real fun begins."

CHAPTER 32

Northwest Africa, spring 1942

Danny, somewhat short of stature, jittery and quick-moving, with ruddy cheeks and closely-cropped hair, came from a farming community near Elyria, Ohio. He maintained a constant stream of nervous chatter, complaining about the weather, their driver and his vehicle. His youthful exuberance at times, Jack thought, could be refreshing albeit wearying.

Because of his aptitude in telegraphy, he was plucked out of basic training and sent to O.S.S. His expertise gave him military importance, which was recognized by Bill Donovan.

In his hometown, his Uncle Lyle, the railroad ticket master, allowed Danny to root around the depot storage room where unclaimed baggage and old telegraphic equipment moldered on shelves. Danny's fascination with the telegraphic keys and their clicking sounds captivated his imagination, and he spent hours sending make-believe messages. His uncle was amazed that he had mastered the Morse code within days.

At age eighteen, Danny volunteered for military service. His accelerated program at the Signal Corps at Camp Crowder, Missouri, left him little time to socialize. Like any young fellow with a normal allotment of hormones, he was ready and eager to connect with a woman. On a weekend pass to Joplin, he was cajoled by three barracks buddies to join them in a visit to a *cathouse* and get his ashes hauled.

"Gosh, do you think it's okay?" Danny asked. "Sure I'd like to go. I won't get the clap or syphilis or anything like that, will I?"

"Wear a rubber, you'll be okay," one of the buddies replied. "I just wouldn't swap spit, that's all."

"What about a blow job? Is that okay?"

"Jeez, Danny, how the hell would I know? Either you come with us and get laid or ya don't."

"Okay, I'll take my chances. I'm comin.' I wouldn't miss this for nothin.'"

The following day Danny seemed to strut and swagger just a bit.

Jack had remembered what Wild Bill Donovan said about Danny being a fine radio operator, but a kid who was socially immature. Jack was confident that Danny's competence as a radio operator wouldn't be impaired by erratic behavior, and that he could be kept in tow.

Akim, an Egyptian with mahogany skin and a black beard, was hired to drive Jack and Danny north toward Tunis. He placed Jack's two suitcases on the roof of the 1931 black Citroen four door sedan. With coarse hemp he fastened the suitcases to the spare tire in the back and to the headlamp stanchions in front. Jack sat next to Akim while Danny sat in the back with his suitcase that contained a radio transmitter and receiver packed among clothing.

Akim, middle-aged, and lean, had classic Semitic features, a prominent aquiline nose and piercing black eyes. His nasal hairs merged into his thick and end-curled mustache. He wore a soiled turban and a long gray-striped night shirt-like garment, a caftan. His English, although accented, was easily understood.

After approximately 250 kilometers on rough roads, in the warm afternoon sun through the monotony of the desert scene and the sleep-inducing hum of the vehicle's motor, Akim startled the passengers with a pronouncement from his high- pitched voice. "The road ahead is blocked by a sentry. I cannot go beyond that point."

"Why?" Danny asked.

"The Vichy camp is ahead. The sentry will stop us."

"Go around him." Danny demanded.

"That, my friend, is certain suicide. I suggest we wait until evening when it is dark; then perhaps we can plan a different route. For now, maybe we can find a Bedouin who will offer us the hospitality of his tent—maybe a tasty leg of lamb and some tea." With a sly smile, he said, "Take my advice: do not attempt to sleep with one of his wives or one of his daughters, or you may have your testicles prepared like shish kabob." He laughed and pounded the steering wheel but stopped abruptly when neither Jack nor Danny seemed to appreciate his humor. Akim snorted up a mucous wad and ejected it out the window. "I wished only to make a joke."

"We'll take our chances with the sentry," Jack said. "Remember, we're non-combatants, scholars and our credentials are in order."

The driver mumbled into his beard. "May Allah be merciful and bestow upon you quick wisdom to spare your lives."

The vehicle stopped about fifty yards short of the sentry's post. The sand and accumulated dust and mud had reduced visibility through the windshield to almost complete obscurity. Akim picked up a soiled rag from the floor and got out to clear enough of the windshield to permit better vision. With Akim out of the vehicle, Danny leaned forward and whispered to Jack, "That guy stinks like a pole-cat that keeps whiffing us. How can you stand sitting next to him?" Without waiting for a response, he continued, "These people are goddamn filthy."

Jack turned towards Danny. "Don't be so judgmental. He may have a sour stomach and is just farting to relieve pressure."

"Farting, my ass! I bet he's got a load of shit in his diaper."

"We have more serious problems right now."

Akim returned to the driver's seat. "I don't like the looks of this. That guard could make trouble, and I don't want them to take my car."

Danny looked around nervously; he snapped open his suitcase and felt around the clothing until his hand clutched the Smith and Wesson. He lifted it out, opened the safety, then set it under his right thigh.

Akim drove slowly and stopped at the gate, then waited until the sentry, an older French non-com in foreign legion uniform approached from the kiosk and spoke to him in French. Akim conversed easily for several minutes then turned to face Jack. "He wants to know who you are and what you are doing here. He wants to see your identification."

Jack, as Ben Wilson, reached for his wallet and removed his driver's license, then took a letter from his packet. The letter stated that he was a scholar seeking information on the cultural patterns of nomadic people in the Mediterranean Basin.

The sentry looked at the license and the letter, then removed his hat and scratched his head. He asked the driver to explain the letter's meaning. Akim translated the letter to the suspicious sentry who peered into the vehicle. He conversed further with Akim who in turn said to Jack, "He respects your noble purpose but wonders if you know that there is a war going on. Besides, he says, you are an enemy alien, and you have no right being here. He is obligated to call his superior officer who will order the arrest of both of you."

Jack turned around to see Danny concealing his gun. He put his hand on Danny's wrist to restrain him. There had to be a peaceful way to deal with this sentry. Money? Of course. Jack leaned toward the driver and said, "The sonofabitch wants baksheesh. Tell him we'll give him American dollars—five of them, if he lets us through. We got reservations at a hotel in Kasserine."

Akim gave the message to the sentry who listened, then shook his head and glowered.

Danny leaned toward Jack. "What the hell are we gonna do, Ben? We're in the middle of a goddamned desert with a zillion enemies who probably have us in their gun sights already."

While Akim and the *gendarme* haggled like a bargain seeker and a peddler in a Mid-Eastern bazaar, Danny became increasingly agitated. He wiped perspiration beads from his brow and neck and strained to listen to the conversation in French, which he did not understand at all. He reached for a cigarette from a pack of Camels and lit it with his Zippo lighter. Taking short nervous drags on the cigarette, he looked at Jack. "Ben, you want a smoke?"

Jack shook his head absently while he watched the animated conversation at the sentry's post. He turned to Danny. "How many packs of cigarettes do you have?"

"Two cartons. Why?"

"Quick! Give me a carton." Jack yelled to Akim and waved the carton. "Tell him we'll give him these." Jack knew American cigarettes had long been a favorite among foreigners who paid dearly for them. He watched as the sentry's eyes widened. The sentry pushed Akim aside and headed for Jack's outstretched hand holding the carton.

The sentry snatched the carton, opened the cover and counted the ten packs, then hurried back to his kiosk to raise the barrier. "*Allez! Allez!*" he shouted and saluted as Akim put the car in gear and sped, its squealing tires spewing dirt and sand.

Danny looked out the rear window. "Jeezuz, that was close. My ticker's still thumping." He wiped his brow again.

Jack said, "Listen, I say we make no more stops till we get to that damned hotel." The road known as the Kasserine Pass was hardly a modern highway. Actually, it was a narrow ribbon of earth cleared of boulders and rocks. It curved around the foothills of the barren Atlas Mountains as the automobile continued to bounce over rough terrain. From on high, the vehicle presented an easy target for a marksman.

Jack turned to look at Danny slouching in a subdued state, breathing slowly. Danny aware that Jack was looking at him, sat up and asked, "What's up, Ben?"

"I've been thinking: can you imagine what a trap this would be for an army moving through here? There's no way to take cover. Planes could strafe columns of men. Hell, it'd be a bloody massacre. Why don't you take some pictures of this? You have your Leica and that Bolex motion camera...start taking photos. Someone will want them at Allied Headquarters, I'm sure."

Danny lowered the soiled window and took a number of 35mm still photos; he placed the camera on the seat and picked up the motion picture camera, then leaned out the window to direct the lens forward to show the condition and formation of the Pass. After five minutes of shooting, Danny brought the camera inside the sedan to re-wind the motor. A sharp metallic ring startled him as well as Jack and the driver. Quickly he wound up the window, then looked about and saw a bullet hole in the metal window frame next to him. He jerked away from the window and shouted, "Some sonofabitch is aiming to kill me!" He grabbed his Smith and Wesson and started to roll the window down.

Jack turned to face him. "Dammit, put that gun away. Hit the floor. Now stay down. There's a good chance that whoever is shooting got off a lucky shot."

"Yeah, lucky for me." Danny huddled below the window holding his pistol with both hands.

Turning toward Akim, whose normally dark complexion had taken on an eerie ashen shade, Jack said, "Can't you go faster than 45 kilometers an hour?"

Akim shook his head. "Speed will stir up rocks on the road. I have already replaced a gasoline tank and a fuel line this year. " His explanation, however plausible, did not relieve his passengers' anxiety and eagerness to get away from the shooter.

"Get this crate the hell out of here!" Danny demanded from his cramped position.

"If I speed, we might not get to the hotel before we run out of petrol." He pointed to the instrument panel. "Look at the gauge; you will see that the fuel needle bounces between low and empty."

Jack shook his head and moaned.

Danny more vocal, said, "Goddamnit! Why the hell didn't you fill a few cans before we started? You knew there would be no service along the way." He uttered more invectives as he lay huddled on the floor.

"Allah will provide," Akim sounded confident. "As soon as we find more shelter, we shall stop."

"I hope you're not thinking of pissing into that tank," Danny said.

Akim laughed. "My friend, you overestimate my power." He continued to drive at an agonizingly slow pace while Jack glanced frequently at the gas gauge needle that hovered ever closer to empty.

The ominous sound of the sputtering engine occurred just as the sedan rolled to a stop on the shaded side of a hill. Akim tried to start the car several times, but only the hollow whirring of the starter motor could be heard.

"Shit! Now what?" Danny's frustration led him to kick the back of the front seat. "Are we just gonna sit here and wait to be picked off by some fucking, crazy Kraut, Frog or Ayerab?" He grabbed his gun, held it at his side, peeked out the window and surveyed the hills for a shooter.

Akim walked to the rear of the vehicle.

"Now, where's that crazy sonofabitch going?" Danny asked Jack who shook his head and shrugged. Both watched Akim as he opened the large boxy carrier fastened to the luggage rack at the rear of the car. He struggled to lift out a five-gallon jerry can, set it on the ground, opened the gas filler cap, and then poured in the contents. The sound of fuel splashing into the empty tank was reassuring. Danny remained skeptical. "I hope this damned crate starts."

Akim, smelling of gasoline, pumped the accelerator pedal several times, turned the ignition key, then stepped on the starter. The starter motor cranked but the engine did not turn over. Akim got out of the car again and started to rock it from side to side.

"What is this, some kind of Arabic ritual to scare this heap into starting?" Danny asked.

"No, it is to move the gasoline to the engine." Akim returned quickly to the driver's seat and depressed the starter button. The engine roared to life while a cloud of black smoke belched out the tail pipe. Akim smiled broadly. "Allah be praised."

Danny sat back. "Where do I go to change my religion?"

Chapter 33

No further incidents occurred as the mud-spattered Citroen pulled up to the elegant porte-cochere of the Bel Air Kasserine Hotel. Jack and Danny carried their own suitcases into the lobby. A number of Vichy French officers were milling around, smoking, drinking, laughing and giving the impression of relaxing in an upper echelon military retreat. There appeared to be no evidences of a war zone.

Danny, admiring the art nouveau décor, said, "This is more like it. I would enlist in this Frog army—if I could speak the lingo."

At the registration desk, Jack was filling out forms when Danny tapped his shoulder and whispered, "There's a delegation of the French Foreign Legion coming toward us." Jack turned to look.

A major in dress uniform accompanied by two non-coms approached them.

"Pardonnez moi, monsieur, avez vous une cigarette, peut-etre?" The major's steely eyes made a rapid assessment of Jack.

"You'll have to forgive me, Sir, my French is poor. If you'd like a cigarette, I'd be happy to oblige." Jack reached for his pack of Pall Mall but had already decided that the request was a ruse. *This guy with his immaculate uniform and smooth manners really wants conversation and more probably, he wants information.*

The major accepted the cigarette that was immediately lit by one of the non-coms. He inhaled deeply, lifted his chin to exhale a gust of smoke. *"Merci, Monsieur."* He looked at the cigarette in his hand. "American cigarettes are the finest. Our communication will be no problem. I speak English fluently. Would you be so kind as to follow me?" Before Jack or Danny could resist, the non-coms closed in on them while the major made an about-face. Jack and Danny wanted to pick up their suitcases, when the major said, "No, no. Leave your valises. We will bring them up to your room later. For now, follow me, *s'il vous plait."*

"Hey, wait a minute! We need our suitcases. Danny protested. "We can't leave them behind. We've got valuable stuff in them." He resisted being prodded by the gendarme and looked over his shoulder at the suitcases left unattended near the registration desk. He started to turn back but was pushed forcibly and made to follow the major. "Watch who you're shovin', Frenchie."

The major walked on ignoring Danny's protests, then stopped in front of one of three elevator doors. When the door opened two officers stepped out and nodded to the major. The five men stepped into the elevator, and before the door closed two men in mufti hurried to enter. One of the non-coms spread his arms to bar their entrance. *"Prenez l'autre,"* he said tilting his head to direct them to another elevator. He stepped back and pushed the button marked three.

"You must forgive our abrupt manners," the major said. "Our leader, the man we are going to see upstairs is pressed for time, and we cannot detain him." When the elevator stopped, the major led the group down a long hallway decorated with art nouveau wall sconces. The major halted the group in front of an unmarked door and rapped three times, paused, then knocked twice more.

The door opened, a corporal saluted the major, then stepped aside to permit the group of five to enter an anteroom. The major removed his hat, placed it under his arm, and followed the corporal to another room with a closed door.

Before entering that room, the major dismissed his non-coms.

Jack and Danny looked about the spacious anteroom furnished with objets d'artes and pictures on the walls. The remaining corporal stationed himself at the closed hallway door and watched the two men. Jack studied a smaller copy of the famous David portrait that hung in the Louvre showing Napoleon with Josephine at his side as he was being crowned Emperor of France. Jack's ostensible interest in the painting belied his worries about what was happening beyond the closed door, and what were the possibilities of Danny and him escaping.

Danny moved closer to Jack and whispered, "What the hell do you think is going on in there? They gonna use us for target practice?"

"Calm down. Remember we're anthropologists studying the culture of the nomadic tribes. Act nonchalant—not like you're a scared rabbit."

"Are you kidding? I'm scared shitless." In an attempt to conceal his fear, he pointed casually to a portrait. "Who's this old walrus?"

Jack looked at the printed card below the painting. "That's Marshall Henri Philippe Pétain, Premier of Vichy France, another kiss-ass puppet for Hitler."

A knock on the hallway door preceded the entrance of a soldier who said something in French to the corporal, then walked to the closed door through which the major had disappeared minutes ago. The soldier knocked, waited for a response, then entered the room and closed the door behind him.

"I hope that's our last-minute reprieve," Danny said.

"Reprieve from what? You're jumping to conclusions. We're here to do academic studies for the university. Now, like I said—relax."

Danny whispered again into Jack's ear, "We're enemy aliens—remember? They could shoot our asses out of a cannon if they wanted to; there's no one here to stop them."

He looked at the corporal standing guard, then looked at Jack. "I'm telling you right now: I don't like this. I'm not waiting around for them to chop me into some fuckin' French fricassee."

The door to the inner room opened, and the soldier who had entered a moment before left. The major standing in the doorway signaled Jack and Danny to enter.

At a large ornately carved desk, an elderly officer in immaculate attire sat and glared as Jack and Danny entered the room. His jacket stacked with bars of multi-colored ribbons and gold battle stars attested to many campaigns. His sleeve cuffs had half a dozen gold embroidered rings. The major, standing to his left, pointed to two chairs in front of the desk for Jack and Danny. A large photograph on the wall behind the desk was that of the man seated in front of them. The engraved title below the picture read, *François Darlan, Admiral de la flotte.*

Jack remembered from his orientation lectures on current affairs at the O.S.S. camp that Admiral Darlan was the *de facto* head of the Vichy government and was regarded by the Allies as a despicable enemy. He was described as a wavering opportunist, a pompous, untrustworthy ass who always acted in his own self- interest. On more than one occasion, he would form an alliance with the Allies, change his mind and collaborate with the Nazis. Churchill did not trust him to make the French fleet based in Africa available to the Allies, so he ordered the Royal Navy to attack the French Fleet. Torpedoing several of the French warships, the British caused the deaths of thirteen hundred French sailors. Darlan developed a bitter hatred for the English and their allies from that time on.

Jack recalled that only the year before, 1941, the Nazis became suspicious of Darlan's vacillating position and forced him to surrender many of his responsibilities back to Pierre Laval whom he had succeeded as Prime Minister. Darlan, however, retained his post as commander of the

French Armed Forces. With unconcealed contempt, Darlan looked at the two Americans sitting before him.

Pointing to Jack, and speaking English with a thick French accent, Darlan asked, "What are you doing in this country?" Before Jack could respond, Darlan looked at Danny and said, "And what is your interest here?"

Jack's well-rehearsed spiel about research among the nomadic people was received with skepticism by the admiral, who closed his eyes and shook his head slowly. Perceiving the admiral's negative response, Jack had a sense of foreboding; his speech slowed to a stop. At that point, Darlan's eyes narrowed and he leaned forward. "Aha, monsieur, even you cannot go on with that charade." With a strident voice he shouted, "You are lying. You are engaging in a deadly game. You and your partner are spies, *n' est-ce pas?* You are aware of a spy's destiny?" He stared at the squirming Danny. "Of course, you are. You will be hanged or shot to death."

Danny sat on the edge of his chair and fidgeted while beads of perspiration formed on his brow. He looked at the admiral's smug demeanor and then at Jack, praying for a sign of relief from a dreadful heart-pounding anxiety.

"Admiral, you are mistaken about us," Jack said. "We come here as..."

The admiral cut him off. "Young man, do not insult my intelligence."

Jack tried to maintain his composure to conceal his mounting alarm. Danny blanched; his shoulders sagged as the admiral continued.

Darlan looked at a paper on his desk. "The soldier who came into my office minutes ago gave me a list of rather curious objects found in your suitcases downstairs. Among the items were: radio equipment for sending and receiving messages, guns with U.S. Army identification and cameras with telescopic lenses." He handed the list to the major standing to his left, then glared at the captives in front of him. "We have every right to kill you as spies. First, we will interrogate you, and depending on your cooperation, we may merely have you put in prison. But if you do not cooperate we will have no alternative but to put you before a firing squad. Is that understood?"

The admiral was interrupted by the ringing of his desk phone. Listening briefly, he said, "Oui," then stood, took his hat off a coat rack and ordered the major to follow him. The major ordered the corporal in the anteroom to guard Jack and Danny. After the officers left, Danny whispered to Jack, "Let's jump this sonofabitch and get the hell out of here."

Danny approached the non-com. "Parlee vooz, English?"

"Non!"

"That's good," Danny said, 'cause you don't need to know what I'm saying."

The puzzled soldier struck a defensive position and reached for his gun when Danny taunted him with shadow-boxing maneuvers. Distracted, the soldier allowed Jack to slip behind him and apply a sleeper hold with his forearm across the throat that cut off the soldier's breathing. Jack kneed him in the back; the force caused an audible crunch like a fracture of a vertebra or rib. The soldier crumpled; his eyes rolled upward, and his gun fell to the floor.

Jack lunged at the gun while the soldier started to regain consciousness but exhibited breathing difficulty; his complexion turned chalky; he grimaced with pain and shut his eyes tightly.

"What the hell do we do with him now?" Danny asked while going through the soldier's pockets.

"Get that braided rope from the window drapes." Jack grabbed the rope from Danny and tied the soldier's wrists behind his back; he cut the rope with his pocketknife and tossed the remainder to Danny. "Tie his ankles."

Danny about to tie the rope ends, said, "I don't have enough to make a square knot."

"Tie his boot laces together. But dammit, hurry!

Someone'll come through that door any minute."

The soldier began moaning. Jack pulled his lower jaw downward to force his mouth open. *"Ouvrez la bouche!"* He remembered enough classroom French to shout the command. "Danny jam your handkerchief into his mouth." He took his own handkerchief and tied it around the soldier's mouth and neck. "That ought to keep him quiet." Looking around, Jack focused on the closet door. "We'll put him in there. Grab his feet. I've got this end."

With the soldier in the sitting position and the closet door closed, only his muffled protests could be heard. Danny looked at Jack. "C'mon, let's get the hell outta here. They could be coming back with a firing squad. Jeezus, I don't want to die out here with all these fuckin' heathens."

Jack ran toward the hallway door and opened it enough to peer in both directions. The major and a non-com were walking out of the elevator, a distance of about 100 feet.

Closing the door hurriedly, Jack turned the lock on the door then tilted a chair under the knob. "Let's go!" He ran toward the window facing an outside balcony with a wrought iron balustrade. He remembered seeing the hotel from the outside with its balconies on all three floors. They encircled the hotel making it look like a three-tiered layer cake. "Danny, quick, give me a hand with this window." Straining to pull the window up proved futile. It was painted stuck to the sill and the sides.

Frantic, Jack looked around the room, grabbed a chair and smashed the window. Both cleared enough of the jagged glass to crawl through the space. On the balcony they heard the rattling of the hallway doorknob.

They walked at a normal pace so as not to arouse suspicion. Jack said, "They'll be looking for two men. Let's separate. You walk ahead, find an exit, walk north for a city block or two, then wait for me outside some hotel entrance." Jack looked at his watch. "Let's plan on meeting in a half hour or so. If I don't show up in an hour, take off. Act like a tourist. Don't panic if you're stopped and questioned—and for God's sake, don't pick a fight."

Tense and wary, Jack knew he and Danny would be the object of a massive manhunt. They had violated the dictates of Wild Bill Donovan's two cardinal rules: first, don't get caught by the enemy; second, kill the enemy before he kills you. *Sure, that's easier said than done.*

Jack tried to recollect what had led them to their predicament. They'd had no warning that Vichy officers would be lying in wait when they entered the hotel. Then he remembered that the sentry at the roadblock had a telephone and probably had informed the post command of their intended arrival. As for the need to kill the enemy, they hadn't been able to kill anyone, not even the non-com they'd left bound in the closet. And why kill him? He was no threat. They had neutralized him.

Jack's heart thumped as he struggled to maintain a normal walking pace. Like a hunted animal, he became keenly aware of his surroundings. Strangely, nothing of an extraordinary nature was happening—no frenzied yelling, no general alarm and no soldiers rushing about. The cliché about the quiet before the storm kept bouncing around in his head. A red arrow at a door indicating elevators and stairs drew him inside. He looked down the hallway in both directions before stepping into a waiting elevator. Before pushing the down button, he stepped out of the elevator thinking the stairwell was a safer option.

Racing two steps at a time, he reached the main floor where he opened the door partially and saw soldiers stationed at each of the three elevators. He closed the door quickly and continued downstairs. A sign on the wall read: *beismant,* an underground parking facility. He surveyed the area for an attendant. No one was there. Crouching among the cars, he tried opening the doors of several before he found one that was unlocked, a late model Peugeot sedan. Among the tricks taught at the O.S.S. camp was the art of hot-wiring a car.

As he lay on the seat looking under the dashboard, he heard footsteps of two or more people approaching. *Now what?* He held his breath until the footsteps stopped... car doors closed... a car started and left. Beads of perspiration dripped into his eyes clouding his vision. Using his sleeve to wipe his eyes and forehead, he looked under the dashboard for the wires. Only blackness. *Be patient, your eyes will adjust. Ah, here it is, the wire loom.* He located the ground wire and the wire to the starter motor. With his pocket knife he scraped the insulation off to twist the wire ends together. As soon as the wires touched, both he and the car jumped as the engine turned over. Untwisting his torso to sit behind the steering wheel, he put the car in reverse and slowly backed out of the parking space.

A traffic signal at the first intersection made him stop. Nervous and still sweaty, he looked around; nothing appeared unusual until he looked in the rear view mirror. The lights on a police car were flashing. *"Dammit."* He pounded the steering wheel and cursed. When the signal changed, he drove across the intersection and veered to the curb where he waited in dread anticipation. *This was no time to be questioned by the police.* The police car followed closely, then suddenly sped past sounding its repetitive sing-song two-note siren. Jack's near panic subsided until he heard continuous and multiple siren sounds that seemed to be converging toward him. *They're back. Are they coming for me after all?* He slumped back and down in his seat attempting to hide. Two police cars rushed by. *Thank God, they're gone.* Another thought gripped him: *what if they're responding to something that happened to Danny? He was capable of trouble with little or no provocation.*

When that last police car sped past, Jack pulled the Peugeot away from the curb and continued slowly scouting for Danny. He watched each hotel entryway, then stopped in front of one to wait and look about. Before moving on, he heard the right rear door open. He looked over his shoulder—a beaten and bloodied Danny lay sprawled on the seat.

CHAPTER 34

Jack, shaken by Danny's bloody and beaten appearance, drove for about two hundred yards before stopping. He jumped out of the sedan to look at Danny's prostrated form on the back seat. "God Almighty! What in the hell happened to you?"

"Never mind that!" Danny waved his hands in protest. "Let's get the hell out of here! Those sonsobitches mean to kill me." Blood dripped from his nose and swollen split lower lip. "Got a handkerchief?"

"No. We used them on that soldier back there. Use your shirt sleeve."

Jack jumped back into the driver's seat and drove at the posted speed limit of forty kilometers, so as not to be noticed by the police.

Danny's red swollen left eye had turned violaceous. His lacerated lower lip left a trail of partially congealed blood that dripped off his chin onto his shirt along with the bloody mucous from his nose. In a paroxysm of sneezing and coughing, he sprayed blood onto the back of the front seat and onto the floor. With a grunt he sat up to survey the surroundings. "Where'd you get this fancy crate?"

"Someone was considerate enough to make it available."

"Uh-huh." Danny looked out the side window and watched German and French soldiers and sailors walking along the avenue—most with women of convenience. "This goddamned place is crawling with Krauts and turncoat

Frogs. I bet they're busting their balls looking for us. What d'ya say we ditch this crate, hole up somewhere and get in touch with the cavalry?" He paused. "Without my radio gear that won't be easy."

Jack looked at Danny in the rearview mirror. "I've got the name of a contact in Sidi Bou Said, about fifty miles from here. While you clean up, I'll get us some clothes and dark glasses. Now, tell me, what in the hell happened to you? You look as though you took on a whole regiment."

Danny ran the sleeve of his bloodied shirt under his nose again. "Yeah, but you should see the two sonsobitches who started it all."

Jack drove for several city blocks before noticing a vacancy sign posted on a dilapidated hotel with bastardized Moorish architecture. An arrow indicated parking in the rear of the building. He drove into a garbage-strewn alley, parked near the back entrance of the hotel. Nearby, an open trash bin swarmed with flies and reeked of stinking organic decay. Reaching under the dashboard, he pulled apart the wires to stop the engine. "Let's try our luck in this palace. Will you be steady enough to walk?"

"Hell, yes!" Danny climbed out of the car and held onto the door for balance, then stumbled. Jack caught and guided him forward.

"We parted company a little over an hour ago. How did you manage to get so damned beaten up?"

"Lucky, I guess."

The rear entrance, a patched-up screen door, squeaked as Jack opened it. Both walked into a dark passageway smelling of stale beer, whiskey and cigarette smoke. Crates of British and American liquors as well as boxes of German beer were stacked against the walls of a hallway that opened into a dimly lit lobby. The furnishings, drab and worn, added to the oppressiveness. Two sleeping elderly bearded men, occupied opposite ends of a sagging sofa.

A heavy-set black-bearded clerk with a turban sat

behind a marred wooden counter under a yellowing sign that read: *Registration*. A cigarette dangling from his mouth dropped ashes on his beard and on his gray-striped cotton caftan. Under bushy brows, he glanced at Jack then studied Danny's battered, bloodied face and clothes. When Danny returned the stare, the clerk looked away and turned the guest registry toward them. In an accent influenced by several imperfectly learned languages, he asked with sarcasm, "Would you gentlemen prefer the presidential suite or one of our customary deluxe units?" Before Jack could respond, the clerk added, "Payment is expected in advance—ten dollars a day."

Jack shook his head. "That's a bit excessive, don't you think?"

In a smile partially concealed by his beard but showing irregular, tobacco-stained teeth, the clerk said, "Good friend, there is a war going on, as I'm sure you are aware. Hotel rooms are scarce and costly."

Jack drew dinars from his wallet but was stopped when the clerk placed his hand on Jack's. "The management prefers American dollars—in fact, they insist on it." He tilted his head and raised his eyebrows. "Otherwise, our prices are much higher—you do understand, I'm sure."

"Oh, I understand all right. We're in the land of *Ali Baba and the Forty Thieves*."

The clerk found no humor in the comment.

Jack leaned toward the clerk and signaled him to bring his head closer so he could whisper in his ear. The clerk raised his brow, nodded and withdrew as he placed a room-key on the counter.

Taking the key numbered 207, Jack and Danny walked to the ancient birdcage elevator. Once out of earshot, Danny asked, "What the hell did you say to the Aga Khan back there that made his eyes bug out?"

"I merely told him that if any police or military were directed to our room, some of our friends would bomb this

firetrap, and his fat ass would reach Allah before the rest
of him did."

CHAPTER 35

"Jeezuz. Look at this shit-hole, will ya?" Danny sat and bounced on the thin lumpy mattress and looked around the dingy room with peeling and faded wallpaper. The worn rug showing wear in patches of exposed threads and irregularly shaped splotches, revealed years of accumulated spillage. Dead flies lay belly-up on the dusty windowsills. Danny sniffed the mattress. "I can still smell the cum on this bed—like some fucker missed the mark." He walked into the washroom with its low-wattage bulb hanging from a high ceiling, and its cracked enamel basin discolored by rust from a dripping faucet. Studying his image in the pitted mirror, he said, "Jeezus, those sonsobitches did a real number on me."

He moistened a washcloth, dabbed his face gingerly and spoke to his image. "That's all right, kid, we took care of those two Supermen. Bet I gave 'em a pair of blue balls. They won't be bringing their legs together for a month." He tried smiling but his face hurt too much.

Listening to Danny absently, Jack walked to the side of the window facing the street. He pulled the curtain aside to watch for police or suspicious-looking characters entering the building. *Hell, they all looked suspicious.*

Danny continued talking into the mirror. "After you and me separated, I walked into this hotel called the Tunis Oasis or something like that. I sat at the bar listening for scuttlebutt—you know, troop movements, personnel strength, things like that. And wouldn't you know, as soon as I sat down, this broad sashays up to me and says in a Frenchy-kind of voice, 'Would you like a little company?' Man, she didn't have to ask twice. I stood up and introduced myself, gave her my phony name and all, a real con job. I figured she was impressed with my gentlemanly ways. Anyway, she sat down; we ordered drinks, a gin and tonic for her and a beer for me. She swiveled outward, hiked up her skirt and crossed her legs—Jeez, the sexiest gams I ever seen, I swear, and she's wearing a garter with a little silk flower. When I seen that I almost creamed my shorts. Know what I mean?"

Jack said nothing and continued to look out the window.

Sensing Jack's disapproval, Danny said, "Look, I haven't been with a broad since I left Joplin over two months ago, and I've been having a lot of wet dreams lately." Eager to continue, he said, "She reached for my hand, looked at my palm like she's reading it and told me I'm strong and smart, and she suspected I was a ladies' man. I knew she was putting me on, but hell, I liked it, anyway. Before we finished our drinks, she took my hand and walked me over to the elevator. We went up to the third floor. She opened the door to a room that just about knocked me out—trimmings like I never seen before. I mean gorgeous white and pink fluffy furniture and a four-poster bed about a mile high. I knew when I got on it, I'd sink to the floor below; the place smelled like a bunch of lilacs and roses. Oh, man, I thought I was in heaven. Know what I mean?

"All the while she's smiling at me, she's taking off her earrings, necklace and bracelets. She started unbuttoning her blouse, tossed it on the bed, and her brassiere was barely holding up two cannon balls with a mile-deep crevasse between 'em. She bent over to wiggle outta her skirt, and there was this little flimsy thing barely covering her crotch. She signaled for me to start undressing 'cause I was standing and gawking like a dumb ox with a hard-on like a baseball bat."

Without turning his gaze from the window, Jack asked, "What does all this have to do with you getting beaten up?"

Danny held the damp washcloth to his eye and lip and leaned closer to the mirror. He ignored Jack's question and responded in his own tempo and sequence. "I think her name was Marlena—looked like a French broad, maybe with Arab blood mixed in—long black hair, dark dancing eyes and a killer smile. Anyway, she was sizzling. Do I think she was a hooker? Oh, yeah, but a high-class one— any fool could see that.

"She helped me off with my shirt and reached for my belt, but I didn't need no help taking off my pants or my shorts 'cause, man, I was ready for action. She was on the bed, put her arms up to pull me down, and her eyes went kind of dreamy and she smiled like *the Moaner Leezer*. Oh, man, I could taste it. I was hoping I wouldn't have a prenatural emasculation—or whatever it's called."

"Premature ejaculation."

"Yeah, that's it. Anyway, I was just about to put the bricks to her when the door flew open. Shit! I jumped up and covered my gazonga with both hands when two gorillas in black leather coats and black fedoras came at me. They started yelling something in heine-talk. I told 'em to fuck-off. But that didn't stop 'em. I grabbed my shirt and pants when all of a sudden one of the gorillas smashed his fist into my eye and knocked me against the wall. Man, I didn't know where I was. I seen stars in colors—honest-to-God. But I got my bearings quick, and I picked up a lamp off the nightstand just as the sonofabitch pulled out his Luger. I crashed the lamp down on that sucker's noggin, and he crumpled like a stale cracker. While I was fumbling with the goddamned Luger, the second sonofabitch lunged at me swinging. I spun around just like Fairbairn taught us and the heel of my shoe caught him in the balls—he went down screaming, holding his jewels."

"Wait a minute. You're naked but wearing shoes?"

"Hell yes! I keep 'em on ever since I got caught in that Joplin cathouse when the M.P.s barged in. When I jumped off the bed I jammed my foot on the bedpost. It hurt like a sonofabitch. I got hauled back to camp and got company punishment. That wasn't bad, but the damn toe hurt for two weeks. I swore I'd never take my shoes off again while I'm getting laid.

"Getting back to those two bozos who were attacking me in the hotel—one's on the floor nursing his crotch, the other was laid out cold with a crease in his head. I grabbed my clothes, and Marlena pulled the bed sheet over her like nobody would know she's there. I grabbed the Luger and tore outta there, left my undershirt and shorts behind and put my pants and shirt on while running down the hall. My nose was leaking like a damn faucet. I ran down the stairs, through the lobby and out to the street. Man, was I ever glad to see you pull up along the curb." Danny stopped and frowned. "Think they'll be able to identify me from that laundry mark on my shorts?"

"That'll be the least of your worries."

CHAPTER 36

"Wonder what happened to Marlena?" Danny asked of his image, then pulled down the lower lid of his swollen discolored eye to examine the hemorrhage. "That baby's angry looking."

"Get out of your bloody clothes and wash up," Jack said. "I'll go downstairs to buy us some Arab-type clothes and dark glasses at the *souk*. I'll make a call outside the hotel to our contact and hope he can get us the hell out of here."

Within twenty-five minutes, Jack returned carrying two bundles wrapped in Arabic newspapers tied with coarse hemp. He tossed one of the bundles to Danny. "Here's your *dishdhasha* and *kufi*."

"My what?"

"That's their names for a robe and headgear. I had the merchant wrap this rag on my head, the way it's supposed to be, then I left it intact." Jack removed two pairs of dark glasses from his pocket and handed one to Danny.

"What did you find out from our contact?" Danny asked.

"Someone will pick us up in an hour."

Danny backed away from the mirror. "So, Ben-Boy, what was our big contribution to the war effort here?"

"Not much, but at least we didn't cause an international crisis."

Danny tore at the bundle and pulled out a wrinkled, striped-cotton robe along with an intact headpiece. He smelled the robe and wrinkled his nose. Standing nude, he put the robe over him and looked in the mirror. "I look like my crazy Aunt Tillie, but ya know, this sure makes pissing easy or taking a crap. Outta be convenient too for a quick lay." He pulled up the back hem and turned to look at his buttocks. "Maybe these heathens ain't so dumb after all."

Jack listened absently to Danny as he resumed his watch through the window. He jerked his head away and left the curtain fall in place. In a loud whisper he said, "Looks like three Frogs just got out of a staff car. The one in the middle is hidden by an umbrella."

"If they're after us, we're shit out of luck. There's no way we can get out of here—not like that get-away from the Bel Aire Kasserine," Danny said.

"Relax, we're not dead yet. Get your gun and cover me from the washroom." Jack reached for the semi-automatic taken from the French soldier they tied up in the closet two hours before. He motioned for Danny to remain in the washroom while he moved to the side of the hallway door. With his back against the wall Jack listened.

Danny leaned against the washroom door jamb and watched. With both hands, he held the gun at his side. In the eerie quiet, the only sounds he heard were the thumpings of his heart. Beads of perspiration formed on his forehead.

The clanging of the closing elevator door preceded the high-pitched whirring of the motor on the ancient elevator as it ascended. Jack and Danny stiffened in anticipation. The sound stopped, the elevator door opened then slammed shut and the cadence of several walkers grew louder. Jack and Danny braced themselves and held their cocked weapons. The footsteps stopped at their door.

A voice commanded, "Ouvrez la porte! Open up! We know you're in there!"

Jack put his finger to his lips. Danny nodded.

The voice became louder. "Open up! We want to talk with you. You are no longer our enemy. Admiral Darlan has signed a treaty with your General Mark Clark and

General Eisenhower. We are allies once again."

Motioning Danny to stay out of sight, Jack jumped to the other side of the door to be behind it when it opened. He reached forward to release the door lock. The door opened slowly and three people entered the room. Jack kicked the door closed and shouted, "Don't move! Keep your hands high."

Danny leaped forward with his gun. "You heard the man. Now keep your hands up."

The spokesman for the three spoke English with a pronounced Gallic accent. "All right, Monsieur Tom Mix or Buck Jones or whoever you are, we're here, as I said, not as enemies but as allies. All we need is some information. Please, put the artillery away."

Jack kept his gun aimed. "First, tell us who you are and what you want."

"We are from the Department of French Military Intelligence, and we have a person of interest with us."

Standing between two men, a dark-eyed woman concealed in a black hijab and burkha watched with apprehension in her expressive eyes. Given a harsh command by one of the men, she reluctantly removed her burkha to reveal her face.

"Marlena!" Danny yelled.

She lowered her head and attempted to step backward, but was held by the men on either side.

The spokesman for the three, said, "Aha. So, Magdalena here, not Marlena, as you call her, seduced you and brought you to her apartment." Danny listened, amazed. The Frenchman continued, "She collects information from those who foolishly succumb to her. You have already identified her. Your sexual performance was interrupted by two Gestapo goons, *n'est pas?* We found them in her room: one bent over, protecting his gonads, the other holding a bloody towel on his head."

He continued to address Danny. "You were agile enough

to evade capture, and I might add, quite fortunate. They could have killed you." He turned to look at the woman beside him. "Madame Magdalena has turned out to be a double agent. She is a courtesan, supposedly in our employ, but now we know she gives information, among other things, to our enemies. We will deal with her appropriately."

Danny's head turned alternately from the Frenchman to Magdalena.

"We brought her here for your identification," the Frenchman said. "She has expressed a desire, after friendly persuasion, to return some cards removed from your wallet while you were otherwise engaged." Danny quickly reached for his wallet in the back pocket of his pants draped over a chair. The Frenchman removed three dog-eared cards from his own wallet and gave them to Danny. "We have no further use for these. In spite of your efforts to conceal your true identity, we know who you are and for whom you work. Since we are allies now, we have no reason to detain you further." He paused, then said, "A word of advice, my young friends—leave this area, it is dangerous."

He and his partner escorted Magdalena to the door when he stopped and turned around. "By the way, thank you for not killing Private André, the one you tied up and put in the closet, at Admiral Darlan's headquarters. My superior officer, Colonel Francoise, would like to extend his most cordial felicitations to General Bill Donovan. They were comrades during World War I when they fought side-by-side against the Bosch."

Danny tried to conceal his Luger but found no pockets in his dishdhasha and held the gun awkwardly at his side. He said to the Frenchman, "We can't send or receive any messages without our radio equipment."

"But of course, monsieur. Your equipment remains at the Hotel Bel Air Kasserine. Sorry for the inconvenience. After you pay for the replacement of the broken window, your equipment will be released to you." He studied Danny for a moment and smiled. "Incidentally, monsieur, you're wearing your caftan backwards, but it becomes you."

CHAPTER 37

Jack and Danny boarded the army air transport, a Douglas C-47 Skytrain filled with crates and duffel bags stacked against the fuselage creating a narrow central aisle. Two crates served as seats for them. Two other men in mufti came aboard and sat opposite them. Danny shouted above the roar of the engines warming up, "You fellas got an assignment in Johannesburg?"

The men looked at one another but said nothing.

Danny glanced at one, then the other. "Well, do ya?"

"Yeah," one said and looked away, a signal that he wanted no further conversation.

Jack elbowed Danny and shook his head almost imperceptibly. "What's with you? You've been warned against idle chatter with strangers."

"Hell, I just wanted to be friendly. I'm not giving away any secrets. Maybe these guys know a broad in the big city, someone who's clean and willing. Know what I mean?" He remained silent for a moment, then said, "Willing is more important than clean right now 'cause I carry a Pro Kit. After I get laid, I squirt the magic juice up my pecker. It's a little messy, but it's worth it."

Jack frowned and turned away. He was reminded that the O.S.S. had a strange assortment of members, and Danny was certainly one. Unlike most, he was young, brash, unsophisticated, and obsessed with sex. Only his remarkable skill as a radio operator qualified him for the O.S.S. Jack recalled

General Donovan telling him to be patient with Danny and to guide him. They had barely survived a frightening ordeal in Tunis, and Jack hoped Danny could somehow manage to avoid another life-threatening fiasco. The purpose of their mission to South Africa was to detect and report enemy activity along the coastal waters, particularly U-boat incursions. In addition, they were to monitor industrial diamond purchases needed for metal grinding and note shipments of rare metals, oil and radioactive materials.

Still posing as anthropology scholars doing field research on the folkways and mores of native tribes in South Africa, Jack and Danny had been warned of strong pro-German sentiment among the Boers. The Boers, descended from Dutch settlers, had been defeated by the British a mere forty years before in a war that lasted four years. Anti-British sentiment simmered among the Boers who were supportive of the Germans in the present war. They had placed a puppet leader in a recently formed Bund. Jack was to observe Bund activities and report acts of sabotage and fifth column infiltration.

Allied informants had succeeded in locating harbors where German U boats lay in wait to prey on Allied shipping. The safe passage of enemy subs had to be directed by land-based lookouts, radio operators who worked under cover of darkness and camouflage.

As the pilot circled the landing field, he cut the engines and the intrusive droning stopped. Danny lowered his head and said nothing as he felt his pockets for his gun and knife; then he leaned back, his head rested against the fuselage. He remained quiet and introspective.

"What're you thinking?" Jack asked.

"If—if anything should happen to me..."

"C'mon, kid, nothing's going to happen to you. Relax."

"Wait just a goddamn minute. I said, *if* anything happens to me—promise you'll get in touch with my ma and pa and tell 'em I love 'em, and I always wanted them to be proud of me."

Patting Danny's shoulder, Jack said, "Enough melodramatics, kid. You can tell them yourself what a hero you are when you get back."

At the Johannesburg Airport, the four passengers and pilots walked across the broad tarmac with suitcases and duffle bags to a waiting unmarked black panel truck, the type used to convey military corpses.

CHAPTER 38

Jack and Danny emerged from the panel truck parked in the porte-cochere of the Glendora Hotel, a converted Victorian mansion set on a hill. At the registration desk in a lobby furnished with antiques of the fin de siècle period, Danny whistled low, then said, "Man, this sure beats sleeping in a tent." Jack made payments with Thomas Cook checks and with the concierge made arrangements for renting a vehicle; then he and Danny carried their luggage to an assigned room.

After placing his suitcase beside a twin bed, Danny fell on the quilted bedding and folded his arms under his head. A beatific smile transformed his weary expression. "Wake me up, Ben, when the war is over."

"Before you take your beauty rest, Buddy-Boy, get your crystal set out and contact headquarters. Let them know we've arrived. Maybe they've got new directives for us."

"Jeez. Don't you ever wanna rest?"

"Ask those poor bastards in foxholes that same question."

"Okay, okay, don't make me feel guilty." Danny stood up and arranged the radio equipment recovered from the Bel Air Kasserine Hotel. He looked around the room as though noticing it for the first time. "This is one hell of a room, Ben. 'Course I'd like it better if we had a naked broad or two here. Why don't we ring for two babes like the ones downstairs at the registration desk?" Before Jack could respond, Danny continued, "If you don't mind, I'll take the one with the big tits. Man, I'd like putting my cock between those boomers after I nibble on 'em for a while. Know what I mean?" He made sucking sounds with his lips.

Jack shook his head. "You're like a goddamned horny teenager fantasizing about the boobs and ass on someone like Betty Grable. Forget that. Put the damned headset on and send off a message."

Danny assembled the equipment on the desk, put his headset on and adjusted several dials. He sent a message in code then listened for several minutes. His hand shot up to stop conversation while he made rapid squiggles on a pad of paper. "Here it is Ben—our new assignment." He pulled a map out of his briefcase, unfolded and flattened it on the desk. His forefinger ran along coordinates near the coastal waters. "U-boats... spotted here." He tapped the point with his finger. "...an area approximately two miles beyond the shore line near Port Elizabeth. Radio messages go out to a receiver in Brest, France, then triangulate to Nazi ships and subs. The messages give information on Allied shipping coming into nearby ports."

Jack looked over Danny's shoulder and ran his finger from the suspected submarine positions to a forested area off Cape Town. He circled an area about a half dollar in size. "This could be the site for those signals. Someone is communicating with enemy subs and ships from this point."

Re-folding the map, Danny said, "Okay, so what's the plan, boss man?"

Looking at his watch, Jack said, "In less than two hours it'll be dark. Pack up the equipment and let's start reconnoitering."

Danny reached for his Luger on the desk and checked the ammo clip. "All set here, Ben-Boy. Maybe this little caper will make up for the Tunis fuck-up." He started to pack his radio equipment, then stopped. "Suppose we find the sonofabitch sending signals to a boat or sub, what do we do about it?"

"What do we do about it? You tell me. I'll use the old

Socratic method from O.S.S. training. Think about your question, then give me the answer."

"They can take their Socratic method and shove it." Danny's movements became more deliberate; he positioned, then re-positioned his equipment and became contemplative. "I know we've been told to destroy the enemy and their equipment, so I guess…"

"No guessing, Kid—but don't worry about that now." Jack anticipated Danny's inner conflict and sought to relieve his anxiety while attempting to reassure himself. He smiled. "We'll figure out what to do when we get there."

Danny, uncharacteristically quiet, nodded and picked up the suitcase with the radio equipment. He followed Jack out of the hotel to the rented Opel near the entrance.

Sun bathers and swimmers were leaving the beach with their folding chairs, food chests and umbrellas as the glowing orange-yellow sun slipped below the horizon drawing the light and warmth out of a cloudless sky. "In about twenty minutes there'll be only moonlight. With some luck we should be able to pick up light signals *if* a sub is out there," Jack said.

They walked down a grassy slope toward a rock wall that separated the slope from the sandy beach below. Sitting on the sand with their backs against the rock wall, Jack and Danny watched the rhythmic movements of the waves lapping the shore. Danny set up his equipment on a towel spread over the sand and made contact with the South African Allied Command post.

Jack held the high-powered binoculars and scanned the sea with expectation.

"How do they get stuff out to the U-boats?" Danny asked.

Jack tilted his head to the right. "There's a maintenance path about one hundred yards from here where a truck can come off the road and go to the water's edge. From that point, a motor boat carries the stuff to a sub, easy maneuver."

Danny scooped up a fist full of sand and let it pour slowly out of his hand. "What kind of stuff?"

"Espionage data... contraband of some sort." Jack continued to sweep the horizon slowly with the binoculars.

Danny looked at Jack. "Ever been in one of those subs? They're like sardine cans. Hardly room to fart, much less haul any extra crap."

As Jack scanned for the silhouette of a cargo ship, a sub's conning tower or periscope, he said, "A few bags of commercial-grade diamonds don't take up much room. They can be squeezed into any space—like an empty torpedo rack."

Standing among the butts of a half-dozen cigarettes he had smoked, Jack directed his binoculars away from the sea toward the land. In a kind of soliloquy, he thought, there's not a damned thing in the forest area. Are we wasting time? Is this the right spot? He brought his Zippo lighter to his wristwatch. "1:45," he said to Danny asleep in a sitting position, his head resting on his chest.

The hours passed in dreadful slowness. The early morning sea breeze chilled him as it penetrated his light clothing. The occasional squawking sea eagle served a warning against sleep. He lit another cigarette, inhaled deeply, then exhaled a long stream of smoke and shivered. His legs felt heavy and achy. The anticipatory excitement of discovering an enemy vessel had long faded, and the marine layer began to lessen visibility. He leaned over and shook Danny's shoulder. "Come on, kid, time to get up. It's 4:15 and nothing's happening. I'm cold, I'm out of cigarettes, and I could use a stiff belt. We'll come back this evening."

Danny turned his head and moaned, stretching his neck in slow circular movements. Squinting upward, he looked at Jack who scanned the forested area a final time.

Jack turned toward the sea again with little hope of discovery. Suddenly, he grasped Danny's shoulder. "Danny, quick! Get up. See the light out there? It's got to be a sub." He shoved the binoculars into Danny's chest. "Tell me what you see."

Danny grabbed the binoculars, struggled to a standing position, and for several minutes studied the intermittent beams of light. "Can't make out too much...gotta be freakin' German words... coded message...numbers for letters. Sh...sh...don't talk." Danny made silent calculations, then started to spell out letters slowly: "d-i-a-m-a-n-t."

"Bingo! How far are we from that light source at sea?" Jack asked.

"Dunno. Maybe one, one and a half miles, maybe more—can't say for sure."

"Can you see any light on shore?"

Danny turned toward the land. "No...nothing." Then excitedly, he said, "Yeah! I see a light, less than a mile from us!"

"Good. Grab your gear. Let's head out for it."

CHAPTER 39

Trudging up the path from the beach to the road with Danny's radio equipment, they stopped at the Opel and opened the trunk. Danny placed the radio equipment into the trunk. He opened his suitcase and pulled out his Luger and a "pineapple" grenade to put in his jacket pocket. He kissed the barrel of his gun, tucked it in his belt, squared his shoulders, and made the sign of the cross. "Okay, Ben Boy, let's get our pigeon."

"Not before we blacken our faces." Jack smeared lines of creamed lamp-black on his face and gave the tube to Danny who had been doing a nervous little jig while waiting.

"Jeezuz, Ben, you look like hell, maybe worse."

Crouching, they hurried towards the copse where they had seen the light. The fallen wet leaves made squishing sounds under their feet as they moved upward into the wooded area.

Following a crude path for about a half mile where leaves had been trampled, Danny halted and extended his arm backward to stop Jack. In a whisper over his shoulder, he said, "There's a light coming from a small hill up ahead." He handed the binoculars to Jack. "Take a look."

"Someone's beaming signals to that sub," Jack said. "I can see him." Through the lighted window of a shack he could make out a gray clad figure.

"Let's take the sonofabitch down." Danny straightened up and held the Luger in front of him with both hands.

Jack grabbed Danny's shoulder. "Hold your fire! Get down on your belly, dammit!" We need to get closer."

Danny hit the ground grumbling. "I coulda had him." They crawled on their bellies until they were close enough to see a shack camouflaged with branches and leaves. The faint light of dawn revealed a burlap curtain hanging over the upper half of an open window. A battleship signal lantern occupied the lower half, and the hum of a generator became louder as they crept closer.

A beamed message from the opening and closing of a slotted lantern came from that shack. Danny whispered, "How many are in there?"

Jack rose up on his knees to get a better look. "I see only one—could be more."

Danny stood up, ran forward and fired repeatedly at the figure in the window. The light in the shack went out. "Get back!" Jack yelled. Danny ignored him and kept rushing forward. Another gunshot pierced the air. Danny stopped, whirled around, fell backward; the Luger flew out of his hand.

Jack rolled behind a bush, his heart thumping, his sight and hearing keenly sensitive like cornered prey. He remained still, silent, hardly breathing, his gun positioned rigidly at his side. An interminable interval passed. His heart pounded fiercely. *Where is the bastard? What happened to Danny?* He squinted and blinked as a figure emerged from the shack and walked slowly toward him. Though he couldn't be sure, Jack thought the figure appeared to be a soldier in a gray uniform. *Does he see me? He's got a gun—he's raising it.*

BANG! Jack fired first and held his smoking pistol firmly as he watched the soldier's head tilt to one side, his knees buckle, as if in slow motion, then his body toppled over. With his gun aimed on the soldier, Jack crawled toward him. Nothing else moved. *Is there another sonofabitch in the shack?* Two minutes passed. Jack hugged the earth.

The eerie silence was not reassuring. *Not a sound from Danny or the enemy soldier—not even a moan.*

Crawling on his belly among the damp leaves, Jack moved to where Danny lay on his back, his legs and arms spread against the forest floor. Blood had covered his shirt like a grisly Rorschach. His glassy eyes stared upward. Jack felt for a pulse. There was none. A cramping chest pain gripped him as he knelt over the lifeless body—the earthly remains of a young man on the cusp of the greatest adventure of his life lay forever still. *Oh, God, this was not supposed to happen.*

Jack rose onto his knees and rocked back and forth over Danny's body, recalling an ancient ritual mourning for the dead. That profound stillness ended with the sound of approaching footsteps. Jack rolled quickly on his side catching a glimpse of high, polished boots glimmering in the dawn's light. A shot rang out. The debris next to Jack's ear kicked up stinging his face. He rolled farther away. A second bullet found its mark near the other side of his face. In reflexive movements, Jack fired two shots above the shiny boots; then he slid down the incline till he struck a tree trunk. He jumped up to stand behind it. Glancing around the tree, he watched as the Nazi officer fell to his knees, gripping his abdomen with one hand while trying to fire again with the other unsteady hand.

With little time to take aim, Jack moved out from behind the tree, spun around and fired two more rounds. One found its mark on the side of the officer's head knocking his hat askew; the other struck his chest. The Nazi fell forward, his bloody face buried in layers of sodden leaves.

Jack approached the fallen officer and turned him over. The dawn offered enough light for him to study his facial features. He gasped. *Betts, you sonofabitch. Did you know who you were firing at?* Jack got up slowly and thought: *What were the chances this could have happened? One in a million? Betts, you told me when we were on the ship sailing to Africa that you'd kill me if we ever met on the battle field...well, you bastard, you fired first.* Jack opened Betts's clenched fingers to remove his gun, then reached for papers in his inner tunic pocket and without examining them, shoved them in his own pocket.

He lifted Danny's limp body over his shoulder and carried it twenty yards, then laid him down. He pulled the hand grenade out of Danny's pocket, looked around before pulling the pin, then tossed it at the shack. He kneeled on the ground, his back toward the shack and his hands over his head. A blast ruptured the air and debris from the disintegrated shack rained down behind him. As the last bits of debris fell, with smoke in the air, he picked up Danny's corpse and carried it toward the car. The arduous trek became more treacherous from slippery dew-covered vegetation and his impaired vision from uncontrolled tearing.

After placing Danny's corpse on the rear seat of the sedan and covering it with his jacket, Jack sat in the driver's seat. *How was he going to tell Danny's parents? Oh God, he hated the thought of that.*

As he inserted the key into the ignition ring his thoughts were shattered by fierce rapping on the window beside him. He jerked his head to the side and met the piercing monocled eye of a Nazi officer shaking a riding crop.

"Lower the window. I want to talk to you," the officer commanded in clipped English with a Teutonic accent.

Ten feet in front of the vehicle another uniformed figure, a pot-bellied, bulldog-faced soldier in a brown shirt, jodhpurs and puttees confronted Jack. He removed a pistol from his belted holster, held the gun at his side and walked toward the vehicle.

Jack fingered the pistol on the seat beside him and revved the engine while the paunchy brown shirt with a swastika armband continued toward him. Jack glanced over at the man rapping on the window, the ubergruppenfuehrer, or whatever the hell he was, and thought something about this whole scene is whacko. *No uniformed Nazis parade around South Africa. These clowns would be arrested in town. General Smuts issued that order long ago. I might have disrupted a Bund meeting of the Boers around here.*

The officer rapped on the window again. Jack wound the window down and looked directly at the Iron Cross below the officer's collar, then up at the skull insignia on the hat. *This bastard means to intimidate me.*

"Your papers," he demanded.

Jack reached into his pocket and inadvertently pulled out the papers he had taken from Betts's corpse. He attempted to retrieve them when he realized what he had done. The expression on the officer changed abruptly when he looked at the papers. Stepping backward and clicking his heels, he gave the heil Hitler salute, and returned the papers, stammering apologies in German and English. He shouted to the brown shirt standing in front of Jack's vehicle. "Step away, you oaf!"

Jack put the Opel in gear, its tires screeching and spewing debris as it sped away. He never looked back.

The loss of Danny, for whom he had felt responsible and the experience of killing had a profound emotional and physical impact on Jack. However, the physiological changes could not have been based entirely on psychological disruption. He became listless and irritable. His symptoms included bloody stools, alternate episodes of diarrhea and constipation, aching joints as well as an alarming weight loss. As a healthy six-footer, he weighed between 195 and 200 pounds, but his weight had plummeted to 157. His complexion turned a yellowish-gray, his eyes sunken in dark hollows. He checked into the hospital.

The chief medical doctor of the Johannesburg General Hospital entered the private room followed by two associates, three interns and two nurses who quickly surrounded Jack's bed. A nurse handed Jack's chart to the chief doctor. He made a cursory review of the laboratory findings, studied Jack's face and pulled down his lower eyelid. With his stethoscope, he listened for heart and breath sounds. "Dr. Harris, you won't mind if our young doctors ask a few questions and examine you, that is palpate your abdomen, look in your mouth, eyes, ears; do a rectal..."

Jack put up his hand and surveyed the eager young interns. His facial muscles hardened as he stared at the chief doctor. "Listen, I've had two groups poke, prod and pull my private parts this morning, and I'm no damned better off for it; furthermore what is the reason for putting me in isolation? I'm stuck in this goddamned sterile cell with only the occasional fat-ass nurse wearing a mask and gloves coming in to take my pulse and blood pressure. She asks about my bowel movements and my appetite while I've got a thermometer stuck in my mouth."

The chief medical doctor, Dr. Baum, nodded and without apology said, "This is a teaching hospital. Young doctors must learn from patients. Secondly, isolation is just a safety precaution. We can't be sure you're not contagious."

"You've x-rayed me from my head to my anus, taken blood samples every hour; I've peed in a five-gallon jug for a week, and you've carved a chunk out of my breast plate and liver. Christ, you've got to have some notion of what's going on."

Dr. Baum cleared his throat. "Perhaps you would do well to return to the States and allow the tropical disease experts there to look into your situation. Quite frankly, we're at a loss here. I'll be happy to get in touch with Dr. Mansard at Walter Reed. " He left the room; his entourage followed.

Exasperated by the doctors' inability to diagnose and treat his condition, Jack, already depressed and irritated by a letter he had received from Martha earlier that day, became more edgy and resentful. She blamed him for his long absence and expressed little concern over his illness. Clearly, their relationship, already strained, had worsened. She seemed to feel that she alone had become the victim in this absentee marriage.

Her letter described in detail a dinner and dance she enjoyed with an office lawyer in an upscale Chicago hotel. The evening, she explained, had relieved her ennui and lonesomeness. It was the kind of affair she would happily attend if asked again.

What did she mean by an affair? Jack crumpled the letter and tossed it in the wastebasket. *Does she think I enjoy the misery of illness and loneliness? Where was their marriage headed? If I'm going to be gone for long periods of time, and she remains home alone...childless...*

A gentle knock at his door announced the appearance of the attractive young woman who had been working at his side for the past several weeks in the United Nations Office of Colonial Affairs in Johannesburg. Shirley Oates, charmingly English, in her mid-twenties, possessed of a warm and enchanting presence, asked, "May I come in?"

Like bursting rays of sunshine dispersing ominous clouds, her appearance shattered the gloom that had enveloped him. He was delighted and grateful. Shirley had been newly married, but shortly after she began working with Jack she received a telegram from British Military stating that her husband, Tank Commander Ronald Andrews, had been killed while bravely serving his country in the North African campaign. Jack had done his best to console her, and now she was raising his spirits. Thanks to Shirley, the rest of his stay in South Africa would be bearable.

233

CHAPTER 40

Walter Reed Hospital, Bethesda, Maryland, spring 1945

Jack, in a wheel chair receiving intravenous fluid in his right forearm, searched Dr. Kamatsu's eyes. Kamatsu, the head of the tropical-disease department, timed the drip rate in the tubing by his watch. Satisfied with the rate, he looked at Jack with a smile. "Dr. Harris, good news. I believe we've isolated the problem. It's the same one we found in several GIs returning from tours of duty in the Pacific. But it wasn't easy. We did a lot of testing and ruled out a number of parasites. We suspected invading colon bacteria, worm infestation...truth is, it was a type of infestation."

The doctor's search for proper wording made Jack impatient. "Doc, just tell me: what do I have?"

"Our findings made us suspect a tropical bacterial parasite, and upon further examination, and this truly elated us, we found a trematode, a fluke. Did you ever walk barefoot in African waters?"

"Yes, many times."

Kamatsu nodded. "Aha! I can tell you the parasite is a schistosome, a fluke. You have a condition of schistosomiasis—sometimes called, bilharziasis named after Doctor Theodor Maximilian Bilharz..."

"Fine, fine. Can you get rid of it?"

"Yes, of course, but the treatment may take a further toll on your health."

"This whole thing hasn't exactly been a stroll in the

park, Doc. Get me well, please. I've got a hell of a lot of work to do."

Over the next several weeks, Jack's health improved considerably. He gained weight as he developed a voracious appetite, and his doctors encouraged him to consume steaks, fresh fruits, vegetables and ice cream desserts. When Martha had phoned to ask about his condition, she made excuses for not being able to travel east to see him. He was not at all unhappy since the relationship had gone beyond reconciliation, and a new relationship, albeit by long distance, with Shirley in Africa, provided a new love interest.

Jack's health had returned after six weeks of hospitalization, but he fatigued easily.

Hostilities in Africa ended and Jack's O.S.S. appointment terminated. He reported to the newly expanded O.S.S. headquarters at Langley, Virginia, to muster out. An attractive female officer in her late twenties or early thirties sat at a desk and smiled pleasantly while Jack was signing and placing his initials on a number of printed pages.

"Dr. Harris, your service record is most impressive. While reviewing it, I thought it was quite unusual...read like a suspense novel." She continued her affable comments while Jack read and signed papers. He didn't respond to her engaging remarks, while he studied the pages he was signing. When he had finished, he handed the papers to her and realized that he might have appeared rude. "I'm sorry I didn't respond, captain. I was preoccupied with reading and signing. I wanted to be sure I wasn't re-upping for another term of duty." Both laughed.

"As you know," she said, "President Truman is re-organizing this office as a Central Intelligence Agency. There will be a strong need for men as well-qualified as you. You would probably earn as much as a colonel and..."

Jack cut her off. "No, my dear, not for all the money in the U.S. Treasury." He raised his brow. "However, a date with you might change my mind."

"Oh, Dr. Harris," she demurred, "you're putting me on."

"No, I'd like a date with you. I'm quite serious about that. As for remaining in this service? Never."

"May I ask why?"

"The story is a bit long..."

"Please tell me, I'd like to know more about you."

"Mind if I smoke?"

"Not at all. I'll get an ashtray." She rose and as she left the room, Jack noted appreciatively how her uniform clung to her gluteal symmetry. She returned shortly.

Jack lit a Pall Mall, pushed back in his chair, and took a long drag. "On an evening in Cape Town, South Africa, about a year ago while I was driving with my partner's corpse in the back seat, heading to the military airfield, I was stopped at a check point. The bodies of two Nazi soldiers had been discovered near a signal transmitting station. A description of me and the car was placed on an all points bulletin."

The captain, her elbows resting on the desk, cradled her chin on the back of her intertwined fingers. "For heaven's sake. Were you arrested?"

"I was. I was taken into custody by the local police. Danny's body, my O.S.S. partner and radioman, was removed from the car and placed in a room at that local police station. After I identified myself and told them my story, the police were completely sympathetic. They made arrangements to provide me with transportation to the airport and assured me that they would notify the U.S. military about Danny's body. They promised to return the rental car."

"This all sounds fascinating," she said. "I'm terribly sorry

237

about your partner's death, but obviously, you completed your assignment, and you're now home safely." She tilted her head, her eyebrows rose. "Was there a further problem?"

"Aside from Danny's death? Oh, yeah. The officer who volunteered to drive me to the airport in his own vehicle, was struck by a drunken SOB. It was a T-bone collision that killed him instantly and threw me out of the car. The vehicle was totaled."

"My God! What happened to you?"

"By some miracle I was thrown into roadside bushes. I escaped with only bruises and contusions and some unresolved lumps. If you care to see them, I can disrobe."

"No, no. I'll take your word for that. Please continue."

"I called O.S.S. headquarters, related the story and was told that the government would handle all expenses, provide the widow with money for funeral costs and would replace the vehicle. I was in contact with the widow until recently. She told me she had received nothing. Her children called this very office repeatedly and were told that the agency does not have a policy for reimbursement in such matters. My own intervention was unsuccessful, and in fact, I was told that I was not to question the decision of the agency." Jack stubbed his cigarette in the ashtray and looked into the officer's sorrowful eyes. She appeared clearly dismayed. "Now you've got to admit that's just about as shabby as it gets. So, pretty lady, don't ask me to re-join the O.S.S. or C.I.A. or whatever it's called now."

Chapter 41

Fall 1945, Ohio State University

Jack resumed his pre-war teaching post as an assistant professor at Ohio State. His status as a former O.S.S. agent had leaked out around the campus causing curiosity and giving him a measure of notoriety among the student body. Eager to see and hear him, students filled the ancient lecture hall with its dreary furnishings and musty smell. Incandescent fixtures hung from a tall ceiling and provided dim light largely absorbed by the darkened patina of wooden desks, oak flooring and wainscoting. At the front of the room a platform with a lectern for notes awaited Jack as he strode in wearing a blue serge suit, white shirt and dark narrow tie. His handsome, broad-shouldered appearance caused some women students to smile in approval as he started his lecture.

Recently returned veterans wore their GI khaki shirts, trousers, and field jackets. Their no-nonsense clothing reflected an uncommon degree of seriousness. Gone were the pre-war days of colorful collegiate clothing, freshman beanies and carefree life styles.

For the inquiring minds, Jack offered first-hand information on native tribal cultures that revealed intelligent and complex societies of so-called primitive peoples. His enthusiastic lectures provided seminal information and encouraged several students to continue with advanced studies in anthropology. After one year, he was promoted to an associate professorship with a modest increase in salary. The popularity of his class grew, and the dean asked that he teach additional classes for the following semester.

Martha's growing resentment of Jack's long hours of research, lecture preparation and grading of papers, led to further strains on their marriage. Bickering and hostility became more frequent and disruptive until both agreed upon a divorce. Martha left with her few belongings to be with her family in Chicago.

Following the divorce, he and Shirley maintained frequent phone communication while she worked as an assistant in the pathology laboratory at Bellevue Hospital in New York. She had received an acceptance for the fall semester, pre-medical curriculum at the University of Chicago. Knowing that, Jack had applied there for a teaching position but had small hopes of getting an assignment.

In a remarkable and unexpected turn of events, he did receive an invitation to be interviewed for the job at Chicago. Accepting a teaching position there would mean a lower academic standing and giving up tenure, but the trade-off was advantageous: Chicago offered greater prestige than Ohio State, and he would receive a larger salary. More importantly, he would be with Shirley and close to his family.

Upon learning of Jack's appointment, Shirley, ecstatic, flew to Columbus to be with him. At the airport she ran into his arms. He encompassed and caressed her. "Darling, this is simply marvelous, I couldn't have hoped for anything more wonderful," she murmured. They kissed again and again. She released him, took a deep breath and sighed. "I'm so happy." Just as suddenly, she registered concern. "Moving to Chicago might cause problems."

"Meaning?"

"Your parents will expect us to be properly married."

"I'm not opposed to the idea, although you may be right. We might face a bit of static."

"You mean because I'm not Jewish?"

"Pa has strong notions about marriage outside the faith."

"Would he accept me if I were a Jewish Negro?"

Jack's brow furrowed. A smile crossed his face slowly. He had been blind-sided by her incisiveness. "My dear, you pose a question that would cause Solomon the Wise to stumble. Quite frankly, I don't know, but I can tell you that he has enough temperament to throw one hell of a fit." He continued to embrace her. "Don't worry, Love, after he meets you, he'll be charmed."

"What about your mother?"

"We'll have to wait and see. Tomorrow we'll go to the county courthouse for a marriage license. We don't want anyone accusing us of adultery—not on this campus with its expectations of propriety and decorum."

Shirley smiled mischievously. "Perhaps we can arrange to sleep separately tonight."

"Right. Over my dead body."

Chapter 42

August 1946, Kostner Avenue, Chicago, Illinois

Pa was incensed. He tramped about the house mumbling. "Molly, he can't bring that woman into this house. I won't have it. I absolutely won't allow it." His face flushed and his lips pursed tightly; he was not about to brook any arguments. "I'm a Kahane, descended from a priest in Abraham's court. How would it look..."

"Max, stop this *mishigoss*, this nonsense. Your world has changed—it's gone forever. Stop living in the past. Think about your son. He went through so much tumult during the war. Did you forget how we prayed for him to be alive and well?" She didn't wait for Pa's response. "He's earned the right to make his own choices. Be grateful he still thinks enough of us to bring her home."

Pa was not mollified. "I don't want her here. It's that simple."

"Are you willing to throw your son away? Never to see him again?" Ma paused. "Think about that my *shoene gelibter.*"

Pa managed to contain his anger long enough to reflect. *"There's no arguing with her. She sees things differently and, okay, maybe more clearly than I do on some matters—and yet...* He did not acquiesce easily. "Tell me: what am I going to talk to her about? The price of pork chops? Maybe the crucifixion of Christ? At least Martha was Jewish."

Ma grew more impatient. "How about those *goyim* who saved Jews by hiding them from those Nazi murderers?"

"Molly, you have an answer for everything. For my

part, they can all ..."

"Max, please, enough! No more bitter talk." Ma spoke evenly. "She'll be like my Ruth, and I'll be like her Naomi."

Pa shrugged. "Since when are you such a biblical scholar?" He raised his hands, a sure sign of concession. "All right, let it be the way you say."

Ma greeted Shirley with a hug, while Pa, still wary, shook her hand politely. The dining room table, a virtual cornucopia consisted of Jack's favorite foods: roast beef, baked chicken, sautéed vegetables, noodle pudding, challah and apple pie fresh from the oven. Pleasant and innocuous chatter passed across the table. Ma smiled with the compliments given on the food and eagerly recited recipes to Shirley's questions about the preparation of ethnic dishes.

Pa's hostility ebbed in response to Shirley's warmth and friendliness; he became talkative and engaged his new daughter-in-law easily in conversation. She asked questions about family and religious traditions, endearing herself to him. In addition she joined Pa enthusiastically in several whiskey toasts to whatever celebratory topics arose.

After the meal Pa hurried to gather groceries from his store shelves to fill several shopping bags.

In mock despair, Shirley shook her head. "Pa, I appreciate all this, but I'm afraid we haven't enough room in our small apartment." Her protests were ignored.

"Push some things aside. You'll see, you'll have enough room."

Shirley kissed Pa on the cheek. He shied away from engaging in overt signs of affection. He never kissed anyone, not his wife, not publicly, nor his children or grandchildren. A kind of Victorian mindset acquired in his formative years inhibited any display of affection, and he habitually suppressed feelings of joy or happiness.

She hugged and kissed Ma who reciprocated affectionately.

Jack kissed Ma on the cheek and shook Pa's hand. "Thank you both for a wonderful evening, and thank you for welcoming my little *shiksie.*"

Pa helped Jack carry the bags of groceries out to the car, a shiny new Plymouth coupe. He handed the bags to Jack who placed them in the trunk. Pa stood back to admire the vehicle. "Nice car. Is it yours?"

"It's a gift from Shirley's dad. He's a Plymouth/Desoto dealer in Pretoria, South Africa. He arranged for the factory in Detroit to deliver it to us through a local dealer."

Pa nodded approval. "Drive carefully and come back soon. Don't be like strangers." He waved them off then watched as the car drove out of view. He returned to the room in back of the store where Ma was stacking dishes in the sink.

"Well, Max, what do you think of our new daughter-in-law?"

"She's a nice girl." He paused then smiled. "But I knew she would be."

CHAPTER 43

**February 1952. U.N. Secretariat Building,
Office of Dr. Ralph Bunche**

From a carafe in his office, Bunche poured coffee into
a paper cup and handed it to Jack, then poured a cup
for himself. He sat at his desk; Jack sat across from him.
"You've done a great job in some very tough areas, Jack.
We're damned proud of you." Jack shrugged while Bunche
continued, "I'm quite sincere. You've helped initiate health
programs, improved the distribution of food and more
importantly, gave impetus to better governance. The whole
of central and west Africa is much better served because of
your efforts."

"Thanks. My team deserves much of the credit." Jack
looked at his coffee and agitated it with a circular motion.
"I wonder if the General Assembly would be half as
gracious as you." Jack lit a cigarette, took a long drag, and
then spoke as in a reverie. "We've come a long way since
our student days at Northwestern. Who could have imagined that we'd end up in a place like this? Do you realize
it's been six years since you asked me to join you here at
the U.N.? I don't remember ever mentioning my qualms
about leaving the University of Chicago after you called.
I had been on the staff less than a year. When I joined the
university, I was practically isolated in a basement office
by the Social Sciences Division—like a contagious orphan.
But I was happy as an assistant prof. Being low man in that

hierarchy didn't matter. The U. of C. was prestigious, the faculty was excellent, and prospects for the department's growth were promising. Best of all, I was with my lovely wife in a cozy apartment off campus, and my parents and siblings lived in the city."

Bunche said, "As I recall, Shirley had started a pre-med curriculum there. Was she hesitant or remorseful about leaving?"

"No, no. The opportunity to live in New York City absolutely thrilled her. When I asked her to make a choice, that is, staying in Chicago or going to New York—she kissed me and said, 'Whither thou goest...' I was grateful for her decision, which encouraged me also. Of course, as you know, my work with the U.N. has been more than gratifying. I'm immodestly proud of what we've accomplished, even though so much more remains to be done. I'd like to see the British make concessions—less taxation and more self-rule in Tanganyika, and I'd like to see the Belgians in Rwanda-Urundi..."

Bunche interrupted. "What you're proposing will cause a firestorm of protest. The colonial powers will concede nothing. They'll squash you like a bug. If that isn't enough, there are sinister forces in Washington that are downright antagonistic to all of us here. Some senate committees are making toxic incursions into our U.N."

"Why?"

"Among some senators and congressmen, there exists the ugly impression that we're guided by wild-eyed liberals and Communists who are going to take over the U.S. government—making the U.S. second-rate and subservient."

"Jeezuz, that's almost too ridiculous to contemplate."

"Ridiculous, but all too true."

Jack's jaw muscles tightened, his eyes narrowed. "We have immunity against interference by member nations, don't we? The U.N. Charter provides safeguards..."

"Forgive me, Jack. You're correct, of course, but that's

an entirely naïve assumption."

"That may be, but I refuse to alter or conceal my findings. I'm not going to compromise my efforts or those of my colleagues. I've seen too much suffering, and we've worked too damned hard to buckle under. Let the world know about the shameful conditions in Africa. Those people are being treated as virtual slaves, and many are starving and dying from preventable diseases."

Bunche smiled wistfully. "You should be considered for the Nobel Peace Prize, but don't count on getting it. By the way, Trygve Lie, our exalted leader, approached me yesterday and made one of his priceless pronouncements. He said any U.N. employee who shows *disloyalty* to his own country, meaning the U.S., of course, would be in jeopardy of losing his position. He's caving in again under pressure from Joe McCarthy who accused him of hiring disloyal Americans. And Lie is harassed by the Soviets over Korea. The Russkies may make him step down as Secretary-General—which would be no great loss."

"What did McCarthy mean by disloyal Americans?"

"It's this over-blown talk about some of our own members having an association with the Communist Party—now or in the dim past. If you ever expressed sympathy for the proletariat when you were a rebellious college kid and someone remembers you doing that, that's cause enough for you to face a firing squad. You know Lie won't defend anyone on our staff. He's nothing but a damned puppet for those witch hunters."

Jack stubbed his cigarette in an ashtray. "I'm not worried. I have nothing to fear."

"Jack, you can't be complacent. These men: McCarthy, McCarran, Cohn—the whole lot of them, are rotten to the core. They have no ethical standards. They don't think as you or I do... fairness, understanding, compassion are not in their lexicon. They thrive on destroying reputations and careers. They're like mills grinding out lies, suspicion, and hatred. Look what they've done to Owen Lattimore, and their outrageous charges against Dean Acheson—two men of undisputed integrity and patriotism." Bunche shook his head. "Those sonsobitches make Torquemada look like the good fairy."

Jack walked toward the window and gazed absently at the various U.N. flags snapping in the wind. He sipped the last of his coffee, crunched the paper cup and tossed it in the wastebasket. "If those sonsobitches try to nail me under false pretenses, I'll quit and go back to teaching."

Bunche placed his hand on Jack's shoulder. "That might not be your option…"

Chapter 44

October, 1952

In a small senate chamber, members of the SISS met before the official hearing began. Senator Patrick McCarran, in charge of the group, sat with Attorney Robert Morris at his side. One of the members said, "Let's give this show more punch. Our crazy-ass compatriot down the hall, Joe McCarthy, is running away with most of the publicity."

Senator Westland spoke up, "McCarthy is going to implode. That jackass doesn't know when to keep his big mouth shut. The newspapers and magazines are beginning to expose his lies and tactics. It's downright embarrassing. This guy is going to bring the whole anti-communist movement to a screeching halt."

"If that happens, we'll have to close shop," McCarran said. "But before that happens, we're going to come down on those liberal, intellectual snobs with both heels and make John Q. Public shout, 'Hooray!' Most people still believe the commies are our biggest threat, and we gotta keep stokin' that furnace. We gotta keep the rubes believing in our mission."

Morris spoke up, "I can tear down that strong façade Harris presents. I spent hours researching his past in the F.B I. files."

"What did you find?" Senator Milbank asked.

"For one thing, he's a fraud."

The room fell silent. The committee members stared at

Morris waiting for him to elaborate.

Morris puffed up. "He's used at least three names that I uncovered. I asked myself, why did he change his name if he wasn't trying to cover-up something?" His eyes took in a consensus of approval among the members.

"That's a start," Westland said, "but not enough to hang him. If he takes that damned Fifth, we can do him in. Yes sir, as soon as he does that, I'm calling him a *traitor*. That'll get good press coverage. We've got our pigeons in the newspapers and radio. George Sokolsky and Westbrook Pegler will fall all over themselves trying to nail Harris in the Hearst papers; then there's Fulton Lewis Jr. on radio who'll slam him."

"This one will be a walk in the park after that Owen Lattimore case," McCarran said. "We dragged that lily-white expert on the Orient through the mud; it took twelve long days, but we did it. We interrupted that bastard so many times he couldn't get more than a half dozen sentences read out of his prepared fifty-page statement. I know those mewling liberals accuse us of bullying and tormenting witnesses—well, so be it. Our job is to rid this nation of subversives and communists, any and every way we can."

Westland said, "You mean intellectuals, east coast professors, Jews and rabble-rousing niggers."

The senator from Mississippi, Carlton Jensen, spoke up, "Westland, we know your family owned a passel of slaves on that Georgia plantation before the Civil War. I really do believe you've got a thorn up your keester worrying about how the darkies are gonna take over your property one day. Some of those lighter-skinned rebels might be your very own undocumented relatives—like a great uncle or two." His shoulders shook with laughter.

"You've got a big mouth, Carlton. Yeah, I want to get at this guy—this professor who tries to give those African jungle bunnies everything. Hell, they can't take care of themselves. How they gonna run a country? Best we remove this smart ass professor from doing any more harm."

"How do we *prove* he's a communist traitor?" the senator from Mississippi asked.

McCarran growled, "We don't have to prove a goddamned thing. If I say he goes, he damn-well goes."

CHAPTER 45

November 1952

Jack and his Attorney Leonard Boudin, sat in a taxi as it inched bumper-to-bumper over the Brooklyn Bridge heading towards the U.S. Courthouse on Foley Square. Initially, they made small talk to deflect thinking about the senate subcommittee hearing they were about to face. Jack studied the steel girders of the bridge and thought about his experiences as a seaman twenty years before. He remembered the flop house, one of the Lyons's so-called hotels on Fulton Street at the base of the bridge. The smell of the sea, the crashing of the waves against the wharf, and the screeching of the gulls recalled poignant memories.

The Federal government's program for unemployed seamen at the time allowed forty cents per day for meals. He remembered his belly growling from almost constant hunger as he waited and hoped for an assignment aboard a ship where he could eat regularly. At times, more than missing food, he yearned for a cigarette—even at ten cents a pack, he could not afford them.

Boudin removed a cigarette from a pack and tamped it against his wrist, then lit it and took a long drag. "It gripes me the way they grill you—you who've worked so damned hard putting your life on the line while most of them sat on their fat asses collecting big salaries and accepting graft during the war years." Boudin, usually circumspect and unemotional, grimaced as he recalled the hearings.

Jack looked at him. "Tell me what you know about McCarran."

"He's a contentious old mule—represents the worst in legal judgment and evil as hell. His views are an abomination and have no place in a democratic society. They contradict legal precedent and disregard constitutional guarantees... trample civil codes. His idea of lawful procedure is like pre-Civil War southern states judgments on slave infractions... maybe worse."

"How is he able to make judgments that disregard constitutional law?"

"Because those who are capable of stopping him are fearful that they too will be called before his committee. He and his cronies create a climate of apprehension aided by headline-seeking newsmen. Most people are generally fed-up with Congress. To them the government seems to do nothing, so when a member of the State Department or U.N. is accused of being a Communist they see that as a 'hurrah moment.' The public thinks someone ought to get after those rotten Communists who are responsible for their misfortunes."

"Basically, McCarran is like an old-fashioned western frontier judge, kind of an Isaac Parker with the power to hang people. He's a vigilante who's mainly after east coast liberal eggheads and wants their power removed from the government and the U.N. He won his spurs the hard way, no one denies that, but now that he's on top, he doesn't want anyone changing his landscape."

"What's his all-consuming obsession with anti-communism? Have any Communists been discovered in the government?"

"Not a damn one of any consequence. Sure, he's gone after some folks who toyed with the idea during the war or in their college days, but they hardly pose a danger today."

Jack asked, "What else has he done to make him so loveable?"

"He's despised for many reasons. If you recall, he

conjured up the law that effectively stopped immigration because of his paranoia about subversives sneaking into the country. In addition, he proposed a bill that sent billions to Nationalist China, Chiang Kai-shek's outfit. In fact, some of those funds boomeranged their way back to McCarran. There were other sweetheart deals: he got the State Department to offer aid to Fascist Spain, so you can imagine why General Franco regarded him highly. No doubt he and Franco had a deal in the works."

"There was always a deal to be had?" Jack asked.

"Precisely. Another deal comes to mind: the Dollar Steamship Lines bought large vessels owned by the U.S. government at an agreed price. The only problem was, Dollar never paid. The arrangements were brokered by McCarran. He and his wife enjoyed sailing on Dollar's ships, as guests of the company, of course.

"Then there's the very special relationship McCarran has with Las Vegas and Reno casino owners. He managed to deflect their taxes from the IRS. When he visits the casinos, he's treated like the grand Pooh-bah... enjoys presidential suites and first class entertainment without obligation, of course. These are only a few of his shenanigans, there are too many more to recount here.

"McCarran's main objective now is to get the U.S. out of the U.N. He's trying to persecute every U.S. citizen in that group if he thinks they are guilty of liberal thinking or supporting internationalism."

Boudin offered Jack a cigarette and said, "Sounds like a charmer, doesn't he?"

Jack remained quiet then turned to look at Boudin. "What are the chances I could leave this hearing with my hide intact?"

"We'll give them a good fight, but understand, we've been dealt a shitty hand."

"Leonard, if it weren't for the likes of you, I'd agree with one of Shakespeare's characters who said, 'The first thing we do, let's kill all the lawyers.'" Jack shrugged with resignation. "Funny thing, after the last hearing, three of those committee members approached me. We didn't talk about the hearings; we talked about the World Series like nothing else mattered. What a bunch of hypocrites, sitting up there spewing all that holier-than-thou crap for the benefit of the press and their constituents."

"No argument there. They've already caused the suicide of one poor soul, and they have yet to apologize. Hell, they never will. That one committee member said he wouldn't have committed suicide if he didn't have a guilty conscience. Jack, they mean to do you no good. Remember, their primary purpose is to keep this witch hunt alive and get as much publicity as they can. They've got to impress the folks back home into thinking they alone saved the country from the dirty Commies. Unfortunately, they have allies in the press to help spread their garbage.

"That young asshole, Roy Cohn, the one you faced at the Grand Jury, is one of the sleaziest characters you'll ever encounter—a self-promoting sonofabitch. Nothing about him or that bastard he works for, Joe McCarthy is legitimate. Cohn managed to get the Rosenbergs convicted and talked the judge into imposing the death penalty. That's how he became McCarthy's chief counsel. Hoover recommended him; he liked his style. Now Cohn gets witnesses who lie to protect themselves. It's the old game where one tries to save his own neck by offering up a sacrificial lamb—Judas for a few shekels." He shook his head. "Nothing has changed. Once Cohn gets a Communist suspect, he grills him or her in a so-called executive session away from public scrutiny. There he can bully the suspect with impunity. If the suspect is well known, McCarthy comes in for the kill. It's all play-acting. Theatre at its possible worst."

"Initially, I had no reason to believe I needed a lawyer to protect me."

"Now you know," Boudin said.

CHAPTER 46

Jack looked at the gloomy overcast sky. "Maybe this darkness is an omen." He turned to look at Boudin. "If any one of those bastards says anything I don't like, I'll tell him to go fuck himself, I swear."

"Oh, no you won't!" Boudin cut in. "That's just the kind of response they'd like—charge you with contempt of court; nail you for a few C notes and use any ruse to incarcerate you. You'll exercise decorum, act gentlemanly and give them no reason to suspect that you're anything but what you really are: a law-abiding citizen, respectful of the laws of the land."

"I always have been, but all this shit goes beyond the limits of rational thinking."

"If you're asked about anything that gives you pause, confer with me. When you're asked about certain people, don't hesitate to invoke the 5th. As soon as you give them a name, you involve yourself in a situation where you lose control and involve others who may be just as innocent."

"Yeah, I'm aware of all that." He smiled wearily. "Forgive me if I sound impatient or ungrateful. It's just that I don't understand where all this goddamned nonsense is coming from. What precisely in my background causes such a damned furor?" Before the attorney could respond, Jack continued, "Did someone remember that sixteen years ago I carried a sign on the New York docks for the seamen who were striking for better working conditions? I wasn't demonstrating because I had some crazy, far-fetched notion of the lousy working conditions on merchant vessels. I lived that life...eating grub at times no better than swill... sanitary conditions worse than prisons. I know, I've been there too. The pay wasn't commensurate with the hours. There was no union, no means of redress. Hell, I was a graduate student and I got everyone in the Anthropology Department at Columbia to contribute to that cause, including Dr. Boas. If that makes me a Communist, well then, these are damned sorry times."

"These *are* damned sorry times. I've asked you before, but tell me again, can you think of anyone who might have given a member of the House Un-American Activities Committee your name. Before the question was even completed, Jack shook his head, then reflected for a moment. "Wait a minute, wait one goddamned minute." He turned towards Boudin. "Those reports I made to the Secretariat on the non-self governed colonies in Africa must have put a burr up the asses of those British colonial delegates."

"Meaning?"

"They wanted me yanked. The reports indicated exploitation of the natives in western and southern regions of the British controlled colonies. Lord Llewellyn Chastain was after my hide. One evening at a U.N. banquet when he reeked of Scotch, Chastain cornered me and said my reports were unsubstantiated folly. Those were his exact words. Furthermore, he said, if I dared to have those reports presented before the General Assembly, he would do everything in his power to discredit and dishonor me. At the time I thought the old walrus was blowing off steam and thought no more about it. I felt compelled to indicate in my reports that those poor souls under the British yoke were working, or rather slaving, for mere shillings a day; children in rags sweating eight to twelve hours in deep holes, breathing dust while digging for tiny fragments of gold. Whole colonies were kept in a state of constant dependence, and the shameful part of all that, they're taxed on their pitiful earnings."

"Jack, that's been going on for years— actually, I suppose, for centuries."

"No argument there, Leonard, but these are different times. With the U.N. mandate censoring inhumane acts of labor on women and children, the British would face sanctions by member nations. They would be exposed and condemned. The Russians and their satellites would love that."

The attorney stubbed his cigarette in the ashtray and rubbed his chin. "Who acts on your report in the Secretariat? What exactly is the procedure?"

"The committee chairman, Ralph Bunche, reads it and confers with me, then he would bring it to the attention of the Secretary General who in turn would bring it to the attention..."

"Hold on. Are you thinking a deal might have been struck between the Brits and the U.N. Secretary General to squelch your report?"

"Now, I'm sure of that. Britain, being the closest ally of the U.S., can prevail upon the U.S. Ambassador to confront the U.N. Secretary General and ask him to delay or bury the report and remove the trouble-maker from the U.N."

"The trouble-maker would be you, right?"

"That's right. The picture doesn't get any rosier with Henry Cabot Lodge, the heir apparent U.S. Ambassador to the U.N. I know he sees himself as a super-patriot with a penchant for ferreting out U.S. citizens working in the U.N. who are *tainted*. He'll tell Trygve Lie, that the report on the British colonies is not to be discussed because the reports will need further clarification—or some such bullshit. Lie will do his bidding without question. With the U.S. paying about 40% of the U.N.'s tab, those anti-communist committee members believe they can dictate terms. Besides, Trygve Lie has the moral backbone of a slug."

Jack continued, "If Lie succumbs to those bastards, as I

suspect he will, my options are lost. No university is going to hire me. I'll be branded a Communist, a traitor." He became contemplative and murmured, "Are we heading toward a police state? I wonder when all this bullshit will end?"

"Not soon enough, I'm afraid."

"What the hell will bring it to an end?" Jack asked.

"I'm hoping it'll all spin out of control. People are beginning to tire of McCarthy's ranting and lying. In order to keep the public interest fired up, he'll be forced to bring people of greater stature before the panel and accuse them of being subversive. Eisenhower, by remaining quiet, gives tacit approval because the people being accused are liberals, mostly Democrats. When McCarthy starts accusing some of the GOP stalwarts or the top military brass, the shit will hit the fan and the army will take on the big-mouth senator. At that time even Eisenhower will come down on him. Ultimately, Tail-gunner Joe will catch one up his tail and explode. I hope this whole damn episode remains as one sorry footnote in American history."

Jack looked at the sky again as it turned darker with storm clouds. A crackle of thunder followed a zigzagging flash of lightening, reminding him of an ominous scene from Shakespeare's tragic tale of Julius Caesar.

The cab pulled up at 40 Center Street in lower Manhattan in front of the massive granite courthouse with its four stories high Corinthian columns. The ends of the entablature above the columns were embellished with roundels on which were carved four ancient lawgivers: Plato, Aristotle, Demosthenes and Moses. Jack pointed his thumb at the lawgivers and said, "These guys would have convulsed if they heard these hearings. People are pre-judged before the hearings start. Once you're in there, you're screwed."

"Remember to maintain your dignity."

"I'd like five minutes alone with any one of those bastards."

"What you will do is invoke the Fifth Amendment. It's your only protection against legal castration. It was designed to protect against a kangaroo court, much like the one we're facing. If you respond to the question of, 'Are you or have you ever been a member of the Communist Party, they can use your answer to incriminate you. For instance, if you say, 'No', some paid informant can say he saw you at a Communist meeting at sometime. Mind you, the informant's word is not questioned, and he doesn't have to prove a thing. You can be labeled a traitor, a perjurer and given jail time. If you say, 'Yes', they'll grill you for names, dates, activities and anything else they can think of. Of course, you'll be branded a traitor, but theoretically, if you repent openly and convincingly, you'll be able to go back to your position at the U.N. Meanwhile, the people you named will lose their jobs and be subjected to further crap by the committee.

"That's why you'll invoke the Fifth. " Boudin paused and with a sigh of resignation said, "There is no good way to address this dilemma. If we're fortunate, the Tribunal of the International Court of Justice at the Hague will see the miscarriage of justice and award you properly and handsomely."

Boudin looked up at the thirty-story tower that converged to a pitched pyramid with gold-leaf covering. "Maybe the architect purposely designed the building to look like a giant-sized phallus."

They were early for the 10:00 o'clock court appointment. Walking toward the tables and chairs for the defense, Jack took notice for the first time of the wood-paneled walls with arches and the Ionic-styled pilasters. The room, formal and cold, made him shudder. He brought his shoulders forward and back several times. "Damn, it's cold in here."

"Things will warm up when the army of news and cameramen arrive," Boudin said.

CHAPTER 47

Several somber committee members took their seats on an elevated platform. Boudin leaned toward Jack to whisper. "Looks as though the principal interrogator will be the guy in the middle, Robert Morris, an S.O.B. who's no stranger to the news media." Morris, an owlish, bespectacled man in heavy dark-rimmed glasses, bow tie and dark hair plastered and parted in the middle, looked about the room. Boudin continued, "Morris's raison d'etre consumes his every fiber— ridding Communism and the peril it poses to the United States and the entire free world. To him, Communism is a destructive giant seeking to enslave every democratic nation. By comparison, Joe McCarthy is a rank amateur who happens to have more notoriety. Neither possesses an ounce of human kindness, so don't expect any."

While they waited for the rest of the committee members to be seated, Boudin continued, "This security subcommittee has assumed the power to nab suspects in or out of the government. It has over-reached the House Committee on Un-American Activities. Its powers are absolute and limitless, even though they fly in the face of Constitutional guarantees. Its authority has even exceeded wartime measures. Picture this: a suspect attended a communist meeting fifteen or twenty years before and now holds a position as a scholar, diplomat, businessman or teacher. But someone remembered seeing him or her at a communist meeting and reports that to this committee. Immediately, that person becomes fodder for this committee's mill.

"I saw a television interview sponsored by Longines Wittnauer, where Morris described how he had burned the midnight oil in the FBI library stacks to get information to uncover the obscure, tenuous and questionable association of an individual charged with being a communist or having communist affiliations in the past. He then confronts that person with data to substantiate his charges."

The last committee member to enter the room, took his seat. It was the dreaded permanent head of the committee, Senator Patrick McCarran. Morris had surrendered his seat to him and moved to his right. Without the usual introductory protocol, McCarran leaned into the microphone and stared at Jack. "Mr. Harris, were you loyal to the United States when you were in the Office of Strategic Services?" Stillness gripped the room. A hundred pair of eyes bore into Jack.

He stiffened in his chair. "I resent that question. Of course, I was loyal! And I remain loyal."

McCarran, unfazed by the response, went on. "Were you a member of the Communist party at that time?"

Quick to respond, Jack said, "That's an invasion of my rights as an American citizen. I wish to invoke the 1st and 5th Amendments to the Constitution—the Amendments that guarantee freedom of speech and protection against self-incrimination.

McCarran responded, "The first Amendment cannot be invoked by those who are interrogated by this committee."

Jack regarded the interrogator skeptically, unable to believe him. He turned to his attorney with a quizzical expression, but Boudin didn't challenge McCarran. The committee's right to interrogate trumped a citizen's constitutional right to freedom of speech. *How did these maggots manage to subvert citizens' rights?*

"How did you get your appointment to the Office of Special Services?" McCarran asked.

"Shortly after Pearl Harbor I went to Washington to volunteer my services in any capacity. I met with Doctor Bunche whom I had known for some years. He asked me to work with him at the office of Coordinator of Information, the organization that preceded the formation of the Office of Strategic Services."

"What were your duties?"

"I was sent to Africa to report on military activities of the Axis Powers."

"How were you supposed to do that?"

Jack hesitated. "I don't believe I'm able to give you those details. I have been sworn to secrecy for an indefinite period."

"Nonsense! This committee takes precedent..."

Attorney Boudin objected. "Sir, Dr. Harris has been given explicit orders; he's under oath not to divulge orders he received from the O.S.S."

"We'll see about that." McCarran looked at his notes. "You refused a position with the C.I.A. after you left the O.S.S. Why was that?"

"Because of promises which the O.S.S. broke to certain of my contacts—people to whom I owed a debt of gratitude for helping me out of difficulties during the war."

McCarran turned to Morris. "You have questions for Mr. Harris?"

"Yes, thank you, senator." Morris shuffled papers. "Your birth certificate indicated that your name was Jacob Herscovitz, the son of Max and Molly Herscovitz. Is that right?"

"That's right."

"When did you change your name—legally?"

"I believe the year was 1938."

"You used another name, Russell Sumner. Why?"

"That was the name on a deceased seaman's certificate. I used it to get a job on an ocean freighter."

"Why didn't you use your own name?"

"I was too young to be issued a certificate."

Morris's skills as an interrogator were failing him. If he expected to impugn Jack's honesty, he was frustrated. He yielded the questioning to Senator Westland.

Westland adjusted his glasses then leaned forward. "Mr. Harris, why can't you tell this panel simply if you are or ever were a communist? Is that so difficult?"

"I refuse to answer on the grounds of self-incrimination."

Westland frowned and leaned further forward. He looked around the chamber and waited for complete silence. "I'll tell you why you can't tell us. You can't tell us because you *are* a traitor, a communist, an enemy of this country." Westland pushed back in his chair, folded his arms across his chest, his face awash with smugness.

Jack stood and straightened his shoulders. "You, Sir, are protected by a political shield that allows you to make accusations without fear of recrimination. How dare you call me an enemy of my country!" Jack's face darkened, his eyes narrowed; he was about to speak further when Boudin tugged at his sleeve. Jack stared at his accuser then sat down reluctantly. He continued to stare at the interrogator. The chairman banged the gavel. The hearing adjourned.

Chapter 48

November 5, 1952, a letter to Dr. Herskovits

Dear Mel,

You must have seen in the newspapers that I've been caught in a buzz saw. One heartening aspect of this miserable business has been the manner in which one's friends express support or at least, sympathy. It is also interesting to note how many scurry for cover. This latter effect is, of course, a major aim of the Committee: the spread of fear and the forced silence among America's liberals and intellectuals. Ironically and sadly, some have even joined the witch hunt to insure their own survival.

One is forced to note how successful has been the attempt to equate the invocation of the Fifth Amendment with an admission of guilt. Yet, since a stand on the First Amendment has been denied by the Courts, the liberal has no choice but to invoke the Fifth Amendment if he wishes neither to abandon his principles nor to degrade himself. It is a terrible choice with evil and swift consequences no matter which stand one takes. I have taken what appeared to me to be the one which preserved my honor and my dignity. My friends with knowledge of history, law or a tradition of liberty will recognize the moral as well as the legal propriety of asserting this particular constitutional right in the present period of political persecution.

Your comments and helpful words would be much appreciated.

Jack

Dr. Herskovits replied that he was aware of the committee's infamous proceedings, but that he was powerless to advise Jack other than to tell him to be forthright and honest. The whole of academia was under perilous scrutiny and in danger of imploding. Prominent faculty members at several universities had been falsely accused. One left the country and others were subjected to grueling interrogations and accusations of having sided with the Russians during wartime.

On December 1, 1952, a special delivery letter addressed to Dr. Jack S. Harris arrived at his home on Long Neck, N.Y. Jack opened it while Shirley looked anxiously over his shoulder. He scanned the official U.N. seal and the contents.

Trygve Lie, Secretary General of the United Nations, addressed the letter to Jack, asking him to answer all questions posed by the McCarran Committee without invoking the 5th Amendment. If he failed to do so by December 4th, three days hence, action would be taken against him in accordance with the recommendation of the Commission of Jurists appointed by him. Jack reread the letter and smacked it against his trouser leg. He turned to Shirley. "Can you imagine this sonofabitch threatening me with this? He's caving in to pressure from Joe McCarthy who accused him of hiring 'disloyal Americans.' He's acting as judge and jury and expects me to respond within three days. I'd like to tell him to kiss my ass."

"That will hardly settle matters." Shirley pulled him into the den. She sat down at the Remington. "Start dictating, we'll get this letter into Lie's hands by tomorrow, special delivery."

Jack ran his hand through his hair, paced the floor and dictated:

> Dear Mr. Lie,
> I have read your letter carefully of 1 December, 1952

in which you state that if I do not inform you by 12 noon on 4 December 1952 to withdraw my right to take the 5th Amendment you will be compelled to take action in accordance with the recommendation of the Commission of Jurists which you have appointed.

After careful consideration, Sir, and with all due respect, I am obliged to state that after searching my conscience and in full cognizance of my rights under the Constitution of the United States of America and of my basic human rights to maintain my personal dignity and integrity, I cannot find it acceptable to abandon my principles and to subject myself to what I consider to be an invasion of such personal and constitutional rights by replying to certain questions asked of me by the Internal Security Sub-Committee of the Senate Judiciary Committee.

I take the liberty, Sir, of recalling that the Supreme Court of the United States of America has not only recognized the right of an American citizen to refuse to reply to such questions by invoking his constitutional privilege but the Court has emphasized that the silence of a witness deserves respect; the Court, furthermore, has called attention to the nature of the setting in which such questions asked as sufficient reason for recourse to the constitutional privilege. The Supreme Court, Sir, has never equated the assertion of the privilege with an admission of guilt. On the contrary, in one of its famous decisions the Supreme Court has described the privilege as "...of great value, a protection to the innocent, though a shelter to the guilty, and a safeguard against heedless, unfounded or tyrannical prosecutions." Senator O'Coner himself, the temporary Chairman of the McCarran Committee, was quoted in the New York press as recently as 2 December 1952 as stating that the Committee would draw no inference of guilt from a recourse to the constitutional privilege.

Therefore I trust that you will understand, Sir, that I cannot return to the Committee to pursue a course of action which I firmly believe would force me to abdicate or to violate my rights under a Constitution designed to safeguard and to protect me and my basic human rights and freedoms as a citizen of the United States of America.

I have stated to the McCarran Committee that I am and always have been a loyal citizen of my country and that I resent and reject any implication that I have been otherwise. I would welcome the opportunity, Sir, to face any charges in a court of law where due process applies. No one would dare accuse me under such circumstances.

I state to you, Sir, that I am and always have been loyal to my country and to the United Nations and that I firmly believe that it can offer the possibility of peace to the world. It is with great regret therefore that I find that I cannot for the first time follow a course of action you have suggested to me.

Sincerely yours,

Jack Sargent Harris

Jack looked at Shirley; his shrug indicated resignation.

"I'm really not expecting him to do anything heroic for me. He's going to toady to the committee, and he may never even read this letter. I think we have to be realistic and start planning a future without the U.N. or any university appointments. While you're at the typewriter, let's get a letter off to Dr. Herskovits."

December 1, 1952

Dear Mel,

I expect to be axed within three days. I enclose a copy of my reply to Lie's ultimatum. Shirley and I have come to accept the fact that my participation in formal aspects of intellectual life in America is now ended, perhaps forever.

I have retained legal help to fight the termination through all the appeal machinery available at the U.N. I shall request reinstatement but only as a form of vindication. It would be intolerable working again at the U.N.

I feel that my decision is a just and principled one. I think that the news each day in the papers tends to show that it is a wise one also.

Jack

Attorney Leonard Boudin approved of the letter to Trygve Lie as Jack read it over the phone. Boudin restated the necessity of claiming privilege under the Fifth Amendment. Non-Communists, he assured Jack, were not immune to indictments under the Smith act or of prosecution for perjury based on "memory contests" regarding events of a decade or more ago. He continued, "The historical trinity of political persecutions and witch hunts are: one, *circumstantial evidence,* two, *paid informers,* and three, *perjury charges.*

"Unfortunately, these trials can effectively blacklist you for asserting your rights guaranteed under the Constitution. This panel of super-patriots wants to discredit you, and even more importantly, they want to feed the flames of hatred against the U.N."

CHAPTER 49

April, 1953

More than three months had passed since the last hearing. Jack's disquietude was partially eased when his lawyer called to advise him of an appointment with a noted constitutional lawyer.

The mid-morning rain created a minor traffic crisis on Pennsylvania Avenue delaying Jack and Attorney Boudin's appointment with Tom Mc Inerny, the old sachem among constitutional lawyers in D.C. Both men stepped out of a Capitol Cab in front of a gray stone, three-story building. Boudin said, "This old building houses some of the most influential lobbyists and lawyers in the country: reps for Saudi Oil interests, U.S. and German armament manufacturers, contractors for federal highway construction... you get the picture."

Boudin closed his umbrella and shook off the rain before entering the revolving doors. "I've got a lot of respect for Tom McInerny. He's a crotchety old goat who's been close to the Washington scene for over forty years—a Harvard-trained attorney, a former law professor who knows what the capitol bureaucrats are thinking before they do. I've phoned him about your case and sent him copies of your portfolio and my notes."

"Leonard, do you really believe he can be helpful?"

Boudin put his finger to his lips as they stepped into the elevator with several others. When the elevator door opened and they stepped out, Boudin looked around before speaking. "Quite frankly, I don't know, but I do know he can advise us. He pulls no punches. Diplomatic talk and sweetly worded phrases are not his style. Years ago, he wouldn't permit students to use recording devices when he lectured—he used too many cuss words and named too many living personalities.

"Let's face facts. You're up against an unscrupulous gang of self-serving bastards who'd think nothing of..." He stopped talking as a man walked by.

"Someone you know?" Jack asked.

"Yeah, a political hack reporter probably looking for inside dirt."

Boudin opened a door with frosted glass and lettering in gold leaf outlined in black that read, *Thomas James Mc Inerny, Esq.* In the anteroom a matronly woman sitting behind a desk typing on an IBM electric looked up and smiled. "Hello, Leonard."

"Hi, Maggie, sorry to be late." He introduced Jack.

She looked at her watch and pointed to it. "You're ten minutes late. Mac will charge you extra for that." She stood up and walked towards Boudin for a mutual embrace.

Boudin said, "He would have ordered me out of the lecture hall if I came two minutes late. In twenty-five years, he's mellowed, I'm sure."

"Don't bet on it. He's still the same miserable, horny old codger. The only difference is, now I make him pay in advance for it." With that she laughed and Boudin laughed with her... a moment of levity shared by old friends.

"Is it thirty years of marriage, Maggie?" Boudin asked.

"Thirty-two and two boys who are the spitting image of their father. Lord help them; Harvard-trained lawyers also, scrupulously honest and into Civil and Constitutional Law. Have you ever heard of such a thing? I mean honest lawyers—there's an oxymoron for you."

"There was Abe Lincoln," Leonard said.

"Uh-huh, and look what happened to him." She walked to the closed door, opened it partially to peer inside, and then turned to face Jack and Leonard. "Gentlemen, behold Mr. Charm and Grace...God's gift to the legally deprived."

Mc Inerny sat at his desk in a room of shelves lined with law books and smelling of Lysol disinfectant that failed to mask the underlying cigar odor. Pictures of Thomas Jefferson and Theodore Roosevelt along with documents attesting to Mc Inerny's qualifications, awards and accomplishments hung on the wall behind his desk.

Tom Mc Inerny looked at Leonard Boudin and Jack. "Well, well, Lenny, you've gained some belly girth, and you've lost some hair from your pate. But I see you brought a good-looking young fellah, so I won't complain further about your appearance." He extended his hand to shake Jack's, then Boudin's. He pushed papers on his desk aside then reached down for a pad of yellow legal paper from a desk drawer.

With pen in hand he said, "All right, Leonard, present me with the important facts."

"Mac, I've sent you everything: Jack's history and my office notes. We need your advice. You've read his dossier including minutes from the first hearing of the Senate Internal Sub Committee on Security. You know he's being skewered along with eighteen others for allegations of un-American activities, and we'd..."

Mc Inerny put up his hand to interrupt. "I know all that, and I know what that cretin McCarthy and that bastard McCarran are up to. I have my informants, and I read the congressional reports." After loosening his tie and throwing his pen on the pad of paper, he reached down into a drawer to lift out a pinch bottle of Haig and Haig Scotch. With a second reach he produced three tumblers and started filling them when Boudin said, "Not for me. Thanks Mac."

Mc Inerny smiled when Jack nodded and indicated about one inch with his thumb and forefinger. "This confirms my impression of your client, Lennie; he's a man with an educated palate and strong character. I like that." He raised his glass to click with Jack's. "Here's to liberty, freedom and the castration of those donkeys sitting on their asses up on the Hill." He reached for his reading glasses and scanned the pages, then tossed the brief on his desk.

With fingers entwined behind his head and leaning back into his tall chair, Mc Inerny said, "All right, how can I advise you?" Before either could reply, he said, "Let me tell you at the outset: if you think I or anyone else can extricate you from this tub of shit they've thrown you into—well, unfortunately, you're wrong. Those bastards have taken away your constitutional rights and all manner of civil liberties to deny you justice." He opened a desk-top humidor to offer cigars to Jack and Boudin. Both declined.

Mc Inerny clipped the tip of a cigar, lit it and puffed once then removed it from his puckered lips and studied the lit end. "From what I understand, you are accused of being a Communist..."

Jack squared his shoulders. "I'm *not* a Communist! I've never been a Communist."

Mc Inerny looked over his reading glasses, nodded and said, "That's fine. Let me go on." He brought his head back, blew out two smoke rings and watched as they floated and disappeared. "Those malignant sonsobitches mean to torment you to the point where you'll give them information and name names just to get them off your back. Don't fall for that game. Invoke the Fifth Amendment every time they begin to badger you. Of course, if they're not satisfied with your responses, they can always throw you into prison on trumped up charges."

Jack's brow knitted. "What do you mean, 'trumped-up charges'?"

"Simple. It'll be your word against some lying witness.

Some paid informant who will say he or she saw you at a Communist meeting at a specified time and place." His eyes narrowed. "You can shake your head son, but I'm telling you, they've done it. Hell, they've condemned bigger fish than you. I, for one, will never be convinced of the so-called findings in the Whittaker Chambers and Alger Hiss case with all that mumbo-jumbo crap about a hollowed-out pumpkin in a field and thirty-five millimeter film that showed nothing but scratches and indistinct marks." With the cigar clamped in the corner of his mouth, he continued, "And what about Tricky Dick Nixon, that nasty little pimple on the arse of progress, who nailed Hiss and burned Helen Gahagen Douglas at the stake?" He shook his head. "These are amoral sonsofbitches you're up against. Make no mistake about that."

Attorney Boudin interrupted to add. "And those ten Hollywood black-listed writers and directors they sent to prison?"

Jack looked at Boudin then at Mc Inerny. "You men aren't giving me much to hope for."

Mc Inerny sipped his Scotch. "Son, I'd like to tell you that you have nothing to worry about. In a court with honorable men you wouldn't have to." Mc Inerny reached into a desk drawer and withdrew a folded edition of the *Washington Post*. He flattened the paper on his desk, pointed to a column on the right side of the first page and turned the paper toward Jack and Boudin. The column indicated that Abraham Feller, attorney for Trygve Lie, U.N. General Secretary, jumped to his death from his Manhattan apartment. His distraught wife told investigators that her husband had become inconsolably depressed when he was ordered to issue dismissals to U.N. workers accused of being Communists."

"I knew Abe Feller," Jack said. "He was a quiet guy; he shouldn't have been swimming with those sharks."

Boudin added, "What about those thirty New York and

New Jersey public school teachers who took the Fifth when questioned about their affiliations with the Communist Party and were then fired?"

In a conspiratorial tone, Mc Inerny said, "Of course, if you want to play footsies with these charlatans, you can go back to your U.N. job. Yes sir, all you have to do is give that prick McCarran five names of suspected communists..."

Jack leaned forward on the edge of his chair. "I'd have to lie. Even if I knew five..."

Mc Inerny cut him off. "Makes no difference, son, the truth doesn't matter in this charade. If you can live as a hyena feeding off the carcasses of innocent lambs, you might survive a while longer." He paused to flick the ash off his cigar. "But if you went back to the U.N., your tenure would be mighty short, I can promise you that. You've made powerful enemies." Jack became less sanguine as Mc Inerny continued. "The Brits want *you* out of the U.N.— you and your honest reporting that exposes their exploitation of colonized people. No, sir, you'll be given the old heave-ho by Trygve Lie or any successor of his ilk. Lie's nothing but a puppet for the U.S. and its allies. And he's afraid of Joe McCarthy. McCarthy accused him of hiring disloyal Americans at the U.N."

Jack glanced downward and shook his head. "I'd be happy to leave all this and return to a teaching post."

Mc Inerny grimaced. "As for returning to the academic life here in the States, forget it. No American university relying on federal or private funding is going to hire you. They won't want to be tainted by your alleged Communist affiliation."

Jack's jaw muscles alternately tightened and relaxed as he listened to Mc Inerny.

"You won't face any more hearings from Tail Gunner Joe, that fraudulent, stupid, dumb-ass Irishman, who'd rather guzzle whiskey than read a law brief... or that side-kick of his—that sniveling, self-promoting faggot,

Jew-bastard, Roy Cohn, his chief counsel.

Mc Inerny leaned back in his chair. "There's a worthy twosome of venomous snakes, rotten to the core, incriminating decent people and feeding fucking lies to a gullible public through reporters who serve up their shit with pious righteousness." Mc Inerny leaned forward on his desk. His ring and little fingers rubbed small circles on the side of his forehead. "I could puke just thinking of those bastards."

He took a deep breath. "Thank God there are a few honest reporters, like Murrey Marder, with the balls to challenge McCarthy. Then there's Drew Pearson. He's a lying, slandering sonofabitch himself, but he's right about McCarthy."

Mc Inerny smiled sardonically. "McCarthy literally kneed him in the balls and attacked him in the Senate."

Jack asked, "How did McCarthy get so damned powerful? How is he permitted to ignore constitutional law and civil freedoms? How did...?"

Mc Inerny held up his finger to denote time out. He pushed the intercom button. "Maggie, cancel my appointment with that union attorney. Better yet, have one of the boys talk with him and don't allow anyone to interrupt us for the next hour."

Mc Inerny pushed back in his chair, held his Scotch in one hand and a cigar in the other. "I've known Joe since he came to the Senate from Wisconsin in 1946. Initially, he got by, seemed to blend into the background. He rode in on anti-communist slogans popular with other Republicans who blamed Democrats for being soft on commies. It was the same old tiresome tirade, well received by the brain-dead."

"Was there ever a real Communist threat?" Jack asked.

"There's been trumped-up Communist threats since WWI. It makes for good propaganda—a cause célèbre whenever things get quiet. Politicians must have an enemy to engage, real or imaginary. But to get back to Joe, he worked hard but only for his own self-aggrandizement.

He passed himself off as a WWII hero. Called himself *Tail Gunner Joe*. Hell, he never flew a combat mission but posed for the camera with a machine gun in a plane for public relations... wore a grin like a pig eating shit, knowing all the while he was conning everyone.

"He got into the Senate by beating young Bob LaFollette who thought the vulgar upstart was no competition. LaFollette was wrong. McCarthy waged a really filthy campaign against him, accused him of ducking military service among other things. 'Just call me Joe,' was his slogan; he knocked on doors, smiled and shook everyone's hands. He gave those Wisconsin farmers a real song and dance.

"He wasn't in Washington long before he was seen by his colleagues as a boorish, unrefined, chronic alcoholic. No hostess wanted him around. His popularity tanked. At the end of his first term, and with a reelection coming up, he needed money."

Mc Inerny sipped his Scotch and dabbed the corners of his mouth with his finger. "Joe never met a bribe he didn't covet."

"Was he ever nailed for taking bribes?" Jack asked.

"Bribes are difficult to define because they masquerade under different names, like campaign donations, advertising expenses, charitable funding, things like that. Since many politicians are guilty of the same thing, none of them wanted to prosecute. Did you know his fellow Senators called him the 'Pepsi-Cola Kid?'"

"Why?" Jack asked.

"War time price controls on sugar hampered the profitability of the Pepsi soda manufacturer who wanted the controls lifted. It was a complicated matter but Joe managed to get a $20,000 loan from the company unsecured and without documentation. He handled the debate on sugar pricing by telling lies and compounding them with more lies. His fellow senators could see through him and marked him as an unbridled cheat and low-life. But he didn't give a damn what they thought. He wanted money.

"In another caper he got chummy with the real-estate lobby and opposed public housing. He took ten grand from a manufacturer of prefabricated homes who opposed public housing. The money was given supposedly for the distribution of a pamphlet that Joe had written opposing public housing. Of course, Joe pocketed it."

"Those examples of cheating don't make him any more unscrupulous than some politicians I know," Boudin said.

"Is that so? Well, let's try this." Mc Inerny brought his chair forward, placed his cigar in an ashtray and leaned on the desk. "Do either of you recall the 'Malmedy Massacre?'"

"Vaguely," Jack said.

"I don't recall the details," Boudin said.

"Let me refresh your memories. Every time I think about this caper I get heartburn. Near the end of WWII, the German army ambushed several hundred American GIs near the Belgian village of Malmedy. After disarming the Americans, the Nazis machine-gunned down more than seventy. Following the surrender of Germany, seventy-three of Hilter's crack SS troops were convicted of the crime in an American war-crimes trial and forty-three were to be hanged for the massacre." Mc Inererny picked up his cigar, puffed then paused, waiting for a response.

"How does McCarthy figure in this?" Jack asked.

"I'm coming to that. Of course, the condemned men said that their confessions had been beaten out of them by vicious American prosecutors. I know that was unadulterated bullshit since I was one of the prosecutors. Action was delayed and the sub-committee of the Senate Armed Services got hold of the matter. McCarthy got right into the hearing. The sonofabitch wasn't even a member of the committee, but he barreled his way in." Mc Inerny's voice rose with exasperation.

"He was acting as a super patriot?" Boudin asked.

"Yeah, sure. He came in on the defense of the SS

troops *against* the U.S. Army. In typical McCarthy style, he badgered witnesses, yelled at the army attorneys and the senators on the hearing committee. He lied shamelessly and stormed out of the chamber shouting that the committee was giving the army a *whitewash.*"

"You've got to be kidding," Boudin said.

Mc Inerny shook his head. "I'm damned serious."

"But why?" Jack asked. "That's like an act of treason."

"Not quite, but he became even more unpopular around the senate. That didn't faze him. Joe never did anything that wasn't profitable for him even if that meant being totally obnoxious. Ironically, his ranting carried some weight. None of the prisoners was hanged, not a goddamned one, and interest in the case died. After a year or so, all the Germans were released."

"But why did he speak on behalf of the Germans?" Jack asked.

"We can only speculate, but some facts we know. Joe wasn't interested in the rights of the accused; he never showed that kind of humanitarian concern. Again, there was the profit motive. McCarthy was urged to disrupt the Malmedy hearings at the behest of some wealthy German families in Wisconsin who were Nazi sympathizers or who thought the hearings would incite more anti-German prejudice."

"Was McCarthy a Nazi sympathizer?" Jack asked.

Mc Inerny paused. "No, I don't think so. Nothing in his background suggested that. Racial and religious bias didn't enter into his way of thinking, ostensibly, and besides, he had experienced anti-Catholic sentiment himself in Wisconsin.

"His quirky behavior and attitude toward his own party caused the senators to brand him, a 'loser'. The real-estate fiasco, the Malmedy affair, the Pepsi-Cola Kid label began to take a toll and his popularity back home hit bottom. He figured he'd lose the next election and was desperate for help. He asked one of his cronies for advice. He was given an improbable issue, but one that would have a remarkable political impact."

"Which was?" Boudin asked, but it was a rhetorical question.

"Communism in our government and particularly in the State Department. The rest is history—flawed, devastating, corrosive history based on lies, innuendos, supposition, all planned by a besotted sonofabitch whose only purpose was to seek notoriety and contributions for reelection. In his reckless wake a number of people lost their jobs, homes, families; some went to prison and at least one poor soul committed suicide." Mc Inerny sipped his Scotch before continuing. "This is the sonofabitch you faced."

Boudin said, "Slandering Jack won't give McCarthy the kind of publicity he needs. I think we'll be relegated to McCarran's internal security committee for grilling."

Mc Inerny smiled sardonically. "Believe me, McCarran is no altar boy, and I can tell you stories about that prick also." Mc Inerny walked to the window and absently watched the traffic below, then turned around. "You want my advice? Of course you do, that's why you're here." He didn't wait for Jack to respond. "You're young, you're smart, you've given, what is it? Eight precious years to your country and the U.N. trying to make this shitty world a better place? And what do you have for your trouble? I'll tell you: humiliation and rejection. According to these reports," he pointed to Jack's medical history, "you almost died from those goddamned tropical diseases. And those shitheads on the hill would think nothing of putting you in the slammer for a few years."

Mc Inerny banged his empty whisky glass on the desk. "Well, if I were you, I'd tell all of them to go fuck themselves—diplomatically, of course. They've already prevented you from holding a teaching job in this country. Those fat asses spewing hatred sat out the war while you were in life-threatening assignments for the O.S.S. Then, if that weren't enough, you came back and tried to make the world a better place through the U.N." He nodded. "Noble deeds, son, noble deeds." He glanced at Jack who looked away. "Yes sir, noble deeds," he repeated. "But those super-patriots can't stand the fact that you're telling them that half the world is enslaved and exploited. No sir, they can't stand that, and what's more, they're doing their damndest to get rid of the likes of you and the U.N."

"My reports to the U.N. were factual. I reported what I knew to be true. I did not slant my reports to disfavor governing nations."

"Son, I believe you, Leonard believes you, your wife believes you, but you're bucking rotten policies that were put in place by colonialists hundreds of years ago. You didn't mince words about condemning Great Britain for the poverty in Tanganyika. And that might have been your undoing."

Jack remained silent.

"Your suggestion for a diamond export tax to keep some of that money in Tanganyika didn't make you popular at Ten Downing Street." Mc Inerny smiled. "The crowning insult will come when Lennie here initiates a lawsuit on your behalf against U.N. headquarters at The Hague for their illegal firing of you. Lennie will probably get you a settlement that will be larger than several years' salary for those assholes. I'd like to see their faces when they're told about your award. Since the U.S. pays about 40% of U.N. expenses, that'll really burn their asses. Those archconservatives in Washington worry about the U.N. Department of Trusteeship and certain Secretariat officials like you. And you know they'll contest that settlement of yours. You just wait and see. I know those sonsobitches too well."

Mc Inerny continued, "This McCarthy bastard, this lying, besotted sonofabitch, the darling of all those whoring newspaper reporters, one day will splatter like a bag of shit thrown off the top of the New York County Courthouse." He placed his cigar on the ashtray then leaned forward. "When that happens, you watch those newspaper whores scramble to write about that stinking sonofabitch. They'll wish they'd joined forces with the newspaper guys who saw through McCarthy from the outset—Murrey Marder, Ed Murrow, Fred Friendly. Marder did all the legwork for the *Post*. Murrow and Friendly are following his lead."

Mc Inerny's face flushed. "Pundits will name this era after McCarthy and then shout with righteous indignation about how he trampled our liberties and damned the innocent." He shook his head. "A shameful period in American history. Yes, son, a goddamned shameful period in our history."

Chapter 50

October 1953, N.Y. City

Several days prior to his next appearance at the Senate Internal Subcommittee on Security, Jack phoned Dr. Ralph Bunche at the United Nations and asked if he had time for lunch. Bunche said he would be delighted and suggested a Chinese restaurant on a side street where they could have greater privacy.

Both arrived by separate taxis within minutes of each other. They embraced like old warriors grateful to have survived many well-fought battles. In the dimly lit restaurant amid fragrances of ginger, garlic and incense, they requested a table in a secluded corner. Bunche rubbed his cold hands and with a frisson sat and poured tea for both.

The background sounds of dissonant, tinkling Chinese music did not disturb their conversation.

They spoke of family and friends for a proper interval, then Bunche said, "Jack, old friend, it's been one long harried odyssey, and I know what you're feeling—misery from those bastards at the county court house. If this is any solace, I appeared before them earlier this week, and I'll be going before them again. They requested my files as well as those of a number of U.N. members in the Trusteeship."

"You responded, of course."

"What choice did I have? It was a summons. Trygve Lie insisted that I answer all their questions without invoking the 5th. I've lost what little respect I had for him. He's a real puppet, jumps at all their demands and expects me and everyone else to do the same. That committee would like nothing more than to accuse me of being a communist sympathizer. Those so-called southern gentleman senators would just as soon lynch me as a renegade nigger as to talk with me. They know damn well how I feel about self-rule and the abuses of Africans in the colonies," he paused to sip his tea, "and for the abuses of Blacks in the States.

"If they were to dig into my past, they'd find my early life filled with demands for political, social and economic equality for all, but especially the Blacks. Like so many youthful stalwarts, I was full of optimism and hope; I carried placards and marched with my brothers and sisters. Some of the organizations I belonged to would be classified now as downright *pinko,* if not flaming *red* by those old fogies. Hell, I was young and imbued with the cause of freedom for all—especially my own people."

He breathed deeply then sighed. "Actually, my principles haven't changed, but my means have taken a more diplomatic route." Both men smiled.

The waiter arrived with their orders. Jack waited until he left, then leaned across the table. "Ralph, they're not going to crucify you. They won't ask you anything about your past affiliations, except perhaps about your friendship with me."

"Really? What makes you so sure?"

"For starters, you're regarded as a highly successful black man. Eisenhower says you're the most important diplomat in the country. Praise can't get much higher. Condemning you would be seen as prejudicial, bullying, a cowardly act by vindictive old white men. Secondly, you're the recipient of the Nobel Peace Prize. You're an international hero. You're the most important nabob in the whole U.N. next to the Secretary General, although he certainly doesn't command the respect you do. Those old farts in Washington wouldn't dare discredit you. If they did, they'd expose their own stupidity and culpability. You have nothing to fear from them. Your only obligation is to answer their asinine questions and maintain a civil attitude. That, of course, could be difficult."

Bunche ate slowly and listened but hesitated before responding. "I hope you're right. What you're saying makes me feel even guiltier about you."

"Why should you feel guilty about me?"

"What I did in my war effort, I did sitting on my butt with a little so-called shuttle diplomacy: writing well-worn phrases on a contract that two war-weary parties, the Israelis and Palestinians, were eager to sign. You, on the other hand, were a field soldier—no, a field general dodging real bullets as well as the slings and arrows of diplomacy."

"Ralph, you're going poetic on me."

"It's all true. If I hadn't lured you away from your teaching post at Chicago, you'd probably be a full professor now with tenure, free from all this humiliation."

"Nonsense. After my initial qualms about leaving Chicago, I was eager to get into the United Nations. Besides, Dean Redfield assured me that my position at the university would be available whenever I returned."

Bunche shook his head. "But I, more than anyone, got you into this kettle of stinking fish. I begged you to join me at the U.N. five years ago." Before Jack could respond, Bunche continued, "As soon as Trygve Lie asked me to come to the U.N.'s temporary quarters at Hunter College, I had to put a staff together to organize the Trusteeship for Non-Self-Governing Territories. You were at the top of my list. Only five Americans in 1946 had field experience in Africa; you were the most qualified. Frankly, our position without you at the U.N. would have been feeble."

With a note of resignation, he continued, "For all our ass-busting efforts in Africa … I hope it wasn't like pissing in the ocean trying to raise the tide."

"What did they ask you about me? Did they blame you

for bringing me into the U.N.?"

Bunche paused and seemed to have difficulty formulating an answer. Jack studied his face, waiting for a reply.

"They asked me if I knew why the State Department had not accepted your application. I told them I didn't know. I was overseas at the time when I received a bulletin from the home office telling me there was a glitch in your resumé. I didn't know what that meant. I didn't think too much about it at the time. Shortly afterward it occurred to me that the State Department might have had reservations because of your religion.

"I thought about that. There were no Jews or Negroes in State then. I had the distinction of being the first Black to join that august body of white knights. It took the personal intervention of the Secretary of State, Cordell Hull, to get me that post.

"When I was asked by Morris if I ever suspected your loyalty, I told him absolutely not. You had gone through a thorough investigation by the O.S.S., you handled sensitive material and were exposed to life-threatening dangers that few men were asked to make. I told him while you were waiting to hear from the State Department you were offered a teaching position at the University of Chicago. I thought no more about it then."

The server left the bill and two fortune cookies. Bunche took one, broke it open and pulled out the slip of paper. He smiled and nodded as he read the message to himself, then read it aloud. "This is a declarative message, not a foretelling one. It reads, *It is sometimes better to be diplomatic than completely truthful.* "That little truism might have been written by someone in the State Department." He looked at Jack. "What does yours say?"

Jack unfolded the slip of paper and read: *Success will come after a long journey.*

"I hope that's prescient."

Bunche leaned forward, and in a subdued voice

sounding both pleading and apologetic he said, "Jack, I've been thinking: maybe you'd do well to answer frankly all further questions and avoid invoking constitutional immunity."

Jack pulled back and regarded Bunche warily. He paused before answering. "If you were asked whether you knew anyone who struck for better working conditions—anyone who carried a picket sign along with you, would you give them the names of those people?"

Bunche shrugged and pursed his lips. "I would prefer not to. I'd finesse that response if I could. However, I'd answer all questions as best I could and politely since I don't have your temerity or audacity."

Jack wiped his hands and mouth with a warm, moist towelette. "Thanks for the advice, old friend, I—I'll think it over."

Outside, the men shook hands and regarded each other with a twinge of unspoken sadness as though they knew they might never meet again. A cold drizzle added to the aura of gloom and despondency. Waiting to hail a cab, Jack stood next to a newspaper stand and glanced at the front page of the *New York Times*. Side-by-side photos of him and Senator Herbert R. O'Conor of Maryland appeared in the left hand column. In an interview, the senator called Harris a Communist and a traitor to his country.

Jack turned up his coat collar and stepped quickly into a waiting cab.

Epilogue

Shortly after the U.N. was formed, several Costa Rican members sought Jack's counsel and were grateful for his friendliness and advice.

When Jack was forced to leave the U.N. after five years, these men remembered his kindnesses and prevailed upon him to immigrate to their country. In 1953, Costa Rica, largely agrarian, needed enterprising men to aid in the country's transformation to one of industrial and commercial competitiveness.

Jack's qualifications were those of a fearless, honest, analytical person capable of solving problems in a persuasive and congenial manner. He accepted the offer and flew to San Jose, Costa Rica; his wife and infant son flew to South Africa to be with her family. He intended to call for them as soon as he made suitable arrangements for housing and work.

His first business venture involved a miniscule taxicab operation consisting of four well-worn Renault cars whose drivers had been eking out minimal wages. Having triumphed over language difficulties but forever sounding like a gringo, Jack initiated growth plans for the cab company. He created greater efficiency and increased availability. His analysis of traffic patterns and passenger usage aided in building the company into a fleet numbering over two hundred fifty taxis within several years. Then he did the unimaginable.

After the drivers had been with the company a number of years, he gave them the cabs free of charge. This was an unprecedented act of benevolence. For the first time those men had become proud and independent businessmen.

His entrepreneurial successes led to partnerships with the emerging captains of industry. They entered into the manufacture of basic products: cement, asbestos and paper. Plants were erected for diverse products, including food processing, brewing beer and manufacturing toothpaste. Other projects included banking with lending capabilities, an airline office and real estate management.

With much pride he and his partners built over five thousand well-constructed homes for middle income families. The homes were erected with utilities, parking spaces and recreational areas for children.

His wife, Shirley, had become an active member of the community and initiated a popular newspaper for the English-speaking residents. A second son was born six years after their arrival. Both sons, Michael and Jonathan, became successful geologists with international reputations.

In an afternoon tea interview in Costa Rica by an American anthropologist several years ago, Jack was asked if he harbored any bitterness toward the events of almost fifty years earlier during the inquisition-type trials in the U.S. Senate. He replied, "I really had no time for recriminations. Initially, I was mad as hell. It was as though I had been tossed into an inferno. Nothing made sense, and I was relieved to get away. There was so much promise and work here in Costa Rica that I became too busy to engage in self-pity. Everything was new, exciting and challenging. If I felt any uneasiness in the beginning it didn't last long."

When asked if he missed the academic life, he said, "I thought about that a number of times but never dwelled on it. The American Anthropology Association or some influential friends, I thought, could have exerted pressure or at least registered a protest on my behalf. But they did nothing. In all fairness to them, they were simply fearful of raising dissenting voices against the madness that prevailed in Washington. There was simply no way to reason with the type of insanity that existed.

"In spite of all that, I consider myself to be one of the luckiest people alive. I could have lost my life in Africa during the war. I could have succumbed to a dreadful tropical disease. God knows I was near death more than once.

"I've had two major careers: both magnificent—the first lasted until those horrible times, and the second...," he lingered a moment, "was exceedingly fulfilling. When I think of what we've accomplished here, even I'm in awe."

"Did you ever think about returning permanently to the States?"

"Some years ago while I was visiting in New York, a member of the State Department approached and asked if I would like to restore my citizenship. I thanked him but told him my world and my friends were in Costa Rica. My children, who were raised here but now live in England and in the States, visit us regularly, and we visit them. If I were to leave Costa Rica permanently I would worry about the futures of our domestics. We're obligated for funding their retirement. The government does not. Besides, who would hire the older, loyal ones who are like members of our family?"

"Do you believe your work in the U.N. had any effect on the conditions in Africa today?"

"I'm not that presumptuous. Africa is quite different now. Unfortunately, there is rebellion and destructive insurrection. Britain, France and Belgium have their hands full—that was inevitable." He paused to sip his tea. "Foreign governments might be completely ousted by rebels one day. I suppose I might have contributed in some measure to the natives' unrest in certain areas, although I never wanted those murderous wars. I had hoped to create a greater awareness of the poverty and inequitable living conditions of the exploited and especially their children." His voice trailed off... "Perhaps one day in another lifetime or two... perhaps in a gentler, kinder world."

Dr. Jack S. Harris died of natural causes on August 2, 2008 in Escazu, Costa Rica, Central America. He was ninety-six. A great many mourned his passing.

About the Author

After serving in the Pacific Theatre during WWII as a field and hospital medic in the U.S. Army, Alvin J. Harris, M.D.F.A.C.S. graduated from the University of Illinois, College of Medicine. He completed an internship and residency in Orthopedic Surgery at the Cook County Hospital in Chicago, Illinois. There he instructed physicians as well as medical and nursing students in post-graduate courses.

In Los Angeles, California, he served on the staff of the Children's Hospital, guiding residents in clinical and surgical techniques. While tending to his private practice, he served as chief of the orthopedic section at the Presbyterian Hospital in Van Nuys and the Holy Cross Hospital.

He practiced for twenty years in Washington State and founded the Sequim Orthopedic Center. As an expert witness, he has testified in cases of vehicular and industrial accidents, as well as physical abuse, and trauma.

When he isn't writing, Al attends lectures at the university or researches information for his novels. He occasionally squeezes in a game of golf or attends a concert with his wife Yetta.

Other Novels

Did you enjoy Farewell My Country? Be sure to pick up more A. J. Harris novels at amazon.com.

Here's the direct link to all of the A. J. Harris novels: amazon.com/author/ajharris

Paperback and ebook formats are available.

A. J. is currently working on his sixth book.

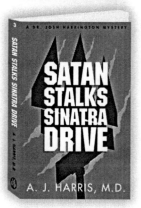
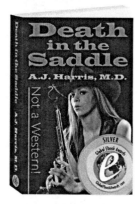

CPSIA information can be obtained at www.ICGtesting.com
Printed in the USA
LVOW10*0257221013

357971LV00001BA/1/P